ALSO BY LEON ROOKE

NOVELS

Fat Woman

Shakespeare's Dog

SHORT-STORY COLLECTIONS

Last One Home Sleeps in the Yellow Bed

Vault

The Love Parlor

The Broad Back of the Angel

Cry Evil

The Magician in Love

Death Suite

The Birth Control King of the Upper Volta

Sing Me No Love Songs I'll Say You No Prayers

A Bolt of White Cloth

How I Saved the Province

PLAYS

Sword/Play

Krokodile

A

GOOD

BABY

A GOOD BABY

LEON
ROOKE

ALFRED A. KNOPF

NEW YORK · 1990

Copyright © 1989 by Leon Rooke
Illustrations copyright © 1990 by Miriam Schaer

All rights reserved under International and Pan-American Copyright
Conventions. Published in the United States by Alfred A. Knopf, Inc.,
New York. Distributed by Random House, Inc., New York. Originally
published in Canada by McClelland & Stewart, Inc.,
Toronto, in 1989.

Portions of this work were originally published in *Brick* and
Columbia: A Magazine of Poetry & Prose.

Library of Congress Cataloging-in-Publication Data
Rooke, Leon.
A good baby / by Leon Rooke. —1st ed.
p. cm.
ISBN 0-394-58541-0
I. Title.
PS3568.06G6   1990
813'.54—dc20   89-71667 CIP

Manufactured in the United States of America
First American Edition

For John and Rosie, for Maria, for Ellen S.
and, as always, for Constance

Whereon do you lead me, bright rider?

A

GOOD

BABY

One evening in the autumn nub of the year a girl appeared out of a clump of trees by the side of a gravelly mountain road and steered along the wet mud bank toward the black car that was waiting. The driver removed the cigarette from his lips and spat out of the window, then turned to see would she jump the ditch, to see would she skitter and fall and cry out.

He won't going to come, but here he was, and he wondered about that.

He wondered what would he do with her tonight and whether tonight won't going to be the last night.

It was hell's own darkness out there, but here it was November, an alien month anyhow.

The car rocked like an enchanted frog in the highland folds, a blue mist beginning at the tail pipe and gradually forming full around the car.

She was calling his name.

Truman Truman. Now don't ye leave me, Truman.

The man wiped a finger along his teeth.

It won't so much life, he thought at this moment, had let

him down, so much as it was these teeth had, with their some-times loathsome ache, though thank God not now, and this slickness on them almost like a pus.

He slumped back, squinting from his smoke, his head cocked by his right armpit, as the girl scrambled over the ditch, her feet sliding, her hands high and daubing the air.

She was a shade balloony, he decided. Yes, maybe morn a shade, though not so far-gone his goose couldn't be saved for another day.

He stayed bent so, idly scratching under one sock, as she tugged at the passenger door and got clumsily into the wide seat beside him, now taking a minute or two to arrange her-self. She was breathing heavily.

The man grinned, his teeth a spangle of yellow and black in the darken light.

Brrr, the girl said, shaking herself.

How you? the man said.

They made no move yet to touch each other.

Give me a drag on that, she said. She took the cigarette from the man's lips and snung in its smoke deeply.

Better now, she said, for the first time looking at him, that look tempered with caution, as though searching the face of a stranger. She reached down and removed one shoe, holding it up to him. Ick, she said. I won't never git this clean.

It was a cloth shoe and not a shoe he would have bought in the first place.

She pitched the shoe over into his backseat.

Here now, he said. My car ain't no rubbish bin.

She shot him a stern look.

Since when? she said. She reached down to pull up her stockings on splayed legs.

He watched her stretch and twist and knot and roll the

stockings, then flip back her hem to hide a snaggly hole big as a half-dollar.

She smiled him a crimped smile. I won't sure you'd be here.

When did I ever disappoint you?

Never yit, the girl replied, but I know it's comin.

The man snickered.

You a mind reader, then? he said.

The girl screwed her eyes over his way.

The lashes over the eye nearest him were entirely absent. They'd somehow been burnt or scalded off when she was a baby. He dimly recalled her telling him this.

I can read yourn, she said.

He slid quickly over. His hand darted under her dress.

You didn't even shave, she said, her voice sorrowful, softened by disappointment and the futility of expecting anything better.

I bin busy as a black man in Hades, he told her. Give Truman a hug now.

She flung her arms around his neck, moaning as though in pain, and for some few minutes, half-prone on the wide seat, they explored each other with hand and mouth.

Don't bite, she said. I wishen you wouldn't bite.

I wishen you would kiss me, she said again a few seconds later. And not bite. I wishen you wouldn't tug and yank.

I wishen I could trust you to do right, she said.

You tear my stockins you gone buy me another pair? she next said. Or do you mean even to buy me a Co-Cola? I'd have ice cream, I was ast, and we saw us a place we could git one. They's got strawberry cups over to Oven's Place.

Now and again her hand would flit down to his crotch, as much as to smack him, then quickly to fly away.

He was having difficulty. Her stomach was coiled bandana tight. She had cloth of some kind wrapped over her stomach and over her buttocks and furled between her legs and he could not slide even a single finger through.

He tugged to unleash one of her breasts, shoving the worn, wiry brassiere up around her neck.

I've known'um would stand on their heads, he said. Praying for a minute more of my time.

He laughed, and after a second of cautious indecision, her laughter joined his.

His hand maneuvered along her thighs.

Now I jist oil the gate, he said.

The girl whimpered, pushing herself down against his hand.

You ready, I can see that, he said.

I'm ready for anything, she replied.

They both laughed.

What's this here you got on?

It's a curtain.

What?

An old kitchen curtain. It's elastic-like, not much morn gauze, and I done swathe it around myself to keep the kitten in. I can't hardly breathe.

What?

So's it don't show. My folks see it showin I'd be good as ruint.

Unhuh.

My name be mud.

Well, it do do the job. Ain't nobody know?

The girl nodded.

Lessern my sister does. You don't sneeze she's not up in your mouth studyin your tonsil-works. But she won't say nothin.

I bet she's a pretty little thing, same as you. I ever saw her, I bet you're scared she'd steal me away.

Somethin got holt of my sister when she was little and she never growed up much.

My my. Well I be dog.

The girl tapped the side of her head. Up here, she said.

Mercy me. What a shame.

Anyway, I'm not pretty.

He stayed silent. He was propped up over her, studying the skewed brassiere, rolling and unrolling and snapping a stocking, halting this now and again to cut little nail paths in her thighs.

When's it comin?

It what?

You know.

She smacked the top of his head. I done tole you and tole you, she said. There ain't no doctor up here I could go to, and I don't know. But if we give it the seed that time in the rain with you wearin the hat, which I reckon we did, then it's gittin close. I'm right smack-up by the gatepost.

He lifted her dress up over her hips and ran a hand over the tight circles of cloth encasing her from waist to belly to thigh. The other hand scratched at his ankle bone.

Do the hucklebuck, he said.

For the next little while she bucked and groaned, calling his name.

Truman Truman Truman.

He squinted open his eyes and saw that she was wide-eyed herself, staring through the windshield with a pained, pouty, disconsolate expression even as she continued to moan and press and writhe urgently against him.

He moaned too, watching her, shuddering and thrusting his

hips and driving one stiff leg repeatedly against the floor-board.

Hot dog! he said. Oh lawdy me!

He watched to see did his words affect her.

Truman Truman Truman, she moaned.

He saw her wet a finger in her mouth and squirm to find her face in the rearview mirror as she shaped one eyebrow with spit.

He thrust his hips more violently.

I'm comin, he said. I've got come could float away this highway. You gone think the universe done flipped over.

Oh honey, she said. It's so good I can't hardly stand it.

He saw her wet that other eyebrow.

He uttered a throaty, convulsive cry. She grimaced and clung to him, then went rigid in her limbs and her own throes echoed his.

He slumped off her, snagged his cigarette from the ashtray, and sucked hard upon it.

Woo! he said. Now that there was good as a bucket lunch.

He rolled down his window and spat out into the dark.

The girl slid back to her seat and wedged her body against the door, tucking one leg up beneath her, rearranging her dress-top the while she stared gloomily through the wind-shield on which swaying trees danced visibly.

You don't give a person a half-chance to think, she said petulantly. The first time you done it, you never even taken off your hat.

Won't it rainin? he said.

He watched the twitch in her lashless eye.

Let's go, she said. I'm hearin somethin in them woods each breath I take.

He uprighted himself and took a last pull on his cigarette and spun the butt out through the window. He stared out into the darkness where nothing moved except fog, the earth's ghostly, footless tenants, the road swirly, that swirl disappearing into a span of unkempt and stubborn trees and then the black sky taking hold of that.

He wondered that he'd been patient with her this long.

She fell off the face of the earth this very night there won't one person would grieve a single heartbeat.

Divine agency, he thought, done dropped down the noose around this'un's neck eons ago.

He swerved his car out onto the road clabbered with mist, doubled-clutched the machine through the gears, and steered on along this remote, highland route, humming the tuneless hum that was his trademark in the amorphous depths from which he hailed.

I love a drive, she said softly. I could drive and drive till I didn't know even my name. Ridin like this, I can see God right up afore my face.

Shoot, the man said. Shoot. I bet you had a fool in your mouth, was a fool there the first word you ever spoke.

She heaved herself up to face him.

You don't mean to do right by me, do ye? she said. You don't mean to marry me or hep me out or do nothin a decent man would.

You're right in that one regard, though, the man said. They's two things good on this sorry earth, and it ain't but they both happen when your both feet are off the ground.

Then they both done already happen to me, she replied. I got nothin else to live for.

The man stole a look at her, long and hard. In his rearview mirror one baleful eye, shorn of its lashes and enigmatic in its meaning, was staring intently back at him.

Where you takin me?

Do it matter?

It would to some.

The eye didn't veer.

The car whooshed on through the night.

On the road behind them stood the traveler's sister, watching the red taillights appear and disappear down the steep grade, ultimately to fade away.

I see you, the girl said to the dark and to them.

Ye can't hide, she said.

Ye can't nothin hide.

Whereupon, to the crunch of wet gravel, against utter darkness and into a swirl of fog, she started down the long road after them.

They drove through a patch of thick rain on the other side of the mountain and for some time along the snake-turns of a valley road cloaked with mist. Where this road ended they turned into a weedy dirt lane and rumbled down that, alongside a warped derelict fence, until they came to a locked gate blocking their path. Truman turned off the lights and sat smoking in silence for a good many minutes, looking up at his mirror to the expanse stretching rearward from them or angling his neck to study some indeterminate fixture beyond the gate.

She came out of a light doze to see him picking his teeth and nodding his secret smile, his body so low and crumpled behind the wheel her first thought was that a midget person had moved inside his body and thrown the other out.

What you studyin? she asked.

She heard him suck on the cigarette, his face tinged blue-black under the glow.

He pointed into the darkness.

They's a house, he said.

Where?

Mystified, she looked to where he was pointing.

It was a two-story house she finally saw, black square against a blacker sky, and over to the side maybe a barn.

What do we care about some old rotted house? she said. You born there?

The man snickered.

Now that's precious, he said. I was born in these parts, you'd have to douse me with oil and brand me with fire afore ever I'd admit it.

Well, why we lookin then? Can't that heater go no higher? You're not seein after my comfort one little token.

They sat in silence, the darkness seeming to stretch and hover menacingly about them, as darkness will.

No, he said at last, his voice timbral with a mirth that made her own flesh shiver. They's a man up by the door lookin at us.

She squirreled up to shade her eyes and study the space.

Lawdy, how can you see that? she asked. Are you a cat can see in the dark?

He laughed.

She plopped back down, stabbing a finger at him. You're makin that up, she said. You can't see doodly-squat, same as me.

In another minute, he comes sneakin up to this car, a shot-gun pointed at your guts, you see him then.

You jist foolin me, she said.

His hand brushed her jaw. Then his finger shoved violently into her open mouth. She gasped, instinctively biting down. His finger was in up to the shaft, gagging her, though still he held it there, his other hand locked in a painful grip around her neck.

That how you goin to feel, he said, whispering at her ear. Like you done bit off somethin you never seen, big as a hefty log. And that somethin gone git bigger and bigger till you think it have you in the jaws and mean to gobble you whole. All gone be left of you is the sweaty footprint where once you stood.

You hurt me, she said. Why do you always have to hurt me so? she whimpered, rubbing her neck where bruise now would be. You ought not to, she said.

Then, overcome with the fatigue of issues surpassing her comprehension, made nervous by the closing in of night and sensing her own inability to alter the course upon which she was set, she spun to him with a soft cry of shame, covering his face with kisses and burrowing into his neck. His flesh was rough and broken, smelling of cigarettes, of salt and grease and some undefinable aroma, and in his sweatlines her tongue could distinguish tight wads of dirt. She could feel on her tongue the grit.

Yo! called a voice from outside. That you, Dawson?

Truman cranked down his window.

Naw, he said. Dawson's done swallowed the cat and won't be showin tonight.

Huh? the voice said.

A face bore up out of the darkness and peered inside their car, peered a long time, looking across Truman in a witless regard of his companion. He had a bloated face and eyes watery with incomprehension.

Do I know you? he asked Truman, though still weighing the girl.

Truman got out of his car and the two men disappeared into the dark.

A light came on inside the house, a child's face smeared up against the glass, with shielded brow and flattened nose.

Then the light went off again.

The girl opened her purse and for a brief time wept into a handkerchief yellow with age, but creased so sharply with her own and others' ironing that she did not dare unfold it.

Truman returned and slid in, and a second later she heard the rattle of paper, and smelt the alcohol. She watched him snort and shake his head, and tilt the bottle back again.

Here, he said. A snag of this'll git your pump primed.

How come you to know where to find licker? she asked. I thought you won't from round here.

He didn't answer.

I ought to pour this out, she said. But she wiped the bottle opening and brought it up to her lips and wet them, wet them only, the lips closed, a small trickle of beverage sliding down over her chin, which excess she wiped away with the back of a hand. Then she licked her lips clean, making a face.

I don't know what prompts you, she said. I don't know why a man can't be content with what I give him and not need this here licker both.

How many you given it to? he asked.

That ain't what I meant, she said. You know you're the first.

Seems to me you didn't so much give it, as I tooken it.

That's right, the girl said. That first time with the hat. Then I realize it was a hopeless cause.

But you liken it, didn't you? You liken it and can't hep yourself.

Nome, she said, after a time. I can't hep myself now and I never was able.

He took another drink, then slid the bottle into its paper sack beneath his seat.

I ain't never known nobody was, she said.

Was what?

Able to hep hisself. Or herself either.

Shoot, the man said. I've hepped myself ever minute.

The slow pitter-patter of black rain came down.

I've seen dogs would move from a pocket of sun into a pocket of shade, she said. But that's the nearest to heppin yourself I've ever seen.

Probably not nobody cares what you think anyhow, he said. I'd say you done dropped your whole brain down a well.

She gave a quick startled cry as his hand shot over and squeezed a breast.

They's science and exactitude in all events, he said. From small to large. They ain't nothin executed ain't executed in accordance to laws known and writ, or yit to come down.

That there's all you need to think about, he said.

He went on squeezing.

It took so little to ruin them, he thought. You had to have one hand up to take away, for that every second your other hand was up givin. You had to tie your hands behind your back, and hobble your feet with chains and walk your back facin China, or they'd wind up ruint anyhow, they were that fragile in their wantin. They were that hungerin in their need to have you do it.

Oh, he thought, they's so much dereliction in the need of things.

You strained them thue a cloth, what would rise to the top of the bucket you trapped them in would always be that part of them hungry to be ruint. It was they whole essence, you boiled them down, and you couldn't hardly hep it, that boilin.

𝓨

They motored along a country road she didn't know, high along a treeless rim, a vast abundance of boulder and craggy knoll, a thin streak of darkest blue in the black sky, a rumble of thunder adrift in the distance though not a ripple in that universe to reveal its promptings or from which direction such disorder came.

Don't go fast, she said. You know it scaredifies me. I wishen I never had to look back. Was only starry road ahead.

You safe with Allstate, he told her. You safe in the arms of Truman.

I bet Truman's not even your real name.

It ain't but the one word, he said. It's real as I can make it. You gone find that out, you live long enough.

They lapped onto hardtop and went for a spell along that, him burrowed low, his head hardly higher than window now. The road dribbled down, down, their time measured by the squeal of his foot pumping the brake, by the whine of third gear, by her inhalations of breath and the clutch of her hands upon door and dash. Thence they sojourned through swampland to either side, the somber odd ragged stobs of elkhorn trees, their ghostly formations illuminated by brief stabs of light that made her blink and shudder within, now and then the sweep to either side of quick pools of black, gloating water—and not human being nor four-footed beast anywhere along their path. Beyond this place they commenced their climb again, the motor withery and pinging its complaint, the sky rumbling once more, and once more, too, that liquefied drift of fog.

Here, near the road's apex, they came upon a leaning mud-splattered sign announcing the new county line. The surface dipped, all but hurtling them off the road, and for the next while the road was cratered and pockmarked, open-shouldered, with packed mud tracks to guide their wheels, here and there a rubble of piled trees, a wrecked and rusting car, the odd heap of gravel trucked in but never laid. Their machine traversed this terrain like a thing hobbled, lame front and rear, a haggard, sputtering dome of steel. And at one point, slowing for a curve that loomed and reared up and never seemed to want an end, the brakes smelling, the car clanging against sapling bush and rock, sideswiping this and that, he yanked up the emergency lever and found it dangling loose in his hand.

I never bin up to this county, she said. Folks my way says they's backwards up here, though fierce, and loyal to the dog.

Unhuh, he said. Well, they's two kettles, both black.

Later, they crossed a series of wooden bridges near fallen down, and idled through other creeks and rivers and branches of the same, where bridges never had been laid or thought about, the water sloshing up over the axles, weighted bushes slooshing against window and door. They mounted a road hollow with echoes, as though endlessly vacant beneath, the road surface barooming and thumping against the car's underpinning until the driver was made to slow whatever journey his mind was intent upon, him halting the car by one leering vein of trees, there to stand windblown in the corrival wilderness stomping his shoes, the red nub of his cigarette in bloodscript scrawl against the night, as now, and then again, he strode and studied roady manifestation unique to him—at last plunging back into the car's confines to state his rebuke of things, saying: That there is what's left of a plank road. Now why in the name of God would a fool think to build hisself a plank road, and him to know it's goin to rot with each tread his boot plops down?

He sat a while in deep cogitation of what he perceived to be the manifold disorder of man's habitat and his own bleak patrol within it.

Sometimes, he said, you can't find no plumb line a-tall to mortal man's flimsy script. Now can ye?

No, she said. Nor in woman's either. I've spent my whole life, retribution starin me in the face. Retribution, she said, or God's fist. It there from the cradle.

Go ahead, she said. Hit me. Ain't a woman I've ever seen was sposed to utter nary a word.

He wondered this land he'd ventured into was so switch-backed, so witchified to its cones and to its depths.

He wondered what numerous and untold transgressions it was he'd hear about up here, him to stay on that long.

He wondered this woman won't right, baby's rattle and God's fist being part and parcel of your every infant's cradle.

But here was a new mark to his line of credit. He hadn't yit until this go-round dropped his seed, if seed is what she had. Though he won't entirely surprised, and his doubts few, because when she'd looked up at him that time they'd talked about, that time with the hat, he'd seen some special light in her face he'd never seen in no female's face before, hat or otherwise, and it was some kind of radiance afloat there.

It tickled him, that radiance.

In a spring cornfield this was, the rain pouring.

He wondered what had come of that hat.

She was now up, snoogled against his neck, her face was, her lips grazing his neck, that hand in his lap where he'd put it. She won't asleep, she said, but restin. Wore out, she said, with worry.

He wondered she wouldn't git plenty of rest, that place she was going.

She had it now, that radiance, he might could excuse her.

Umm, she said. And he felt her give a little squeeze to where her hand lay. One heavy leg intertwined with his, giving out just short of his floor pedals, her other leg hooked out at prop against the window vent, that stocking long-since cropped down to thickened swirls over her ankle. Her mummy wrappings had loosened in the night, her hip up hot against his, and it seemed to him she'd ballooned. It seemed to him she was naught but wall-to-wall belly.

He wondered she was still breathing, and it tickled him, this prolonging of his caretaker's mercy.

Oh tremble ye, he thought, at the caretaker's mercy.

Between his lips, glued there and now down to nub, was near the last of his cigarettes.

First item on the agenda, then, was to git hisself smokes. Some smokes, and gas.

The night sky echoed a distant, rumbling thunder and he could see, achurn in his headlights, the abiding haze of fog which marked their passage.

Yes, gas. His gauge long-since straining on toward empty. My congregation awaits me, he thought. I got bizness up the loops and divides of every hawk-daughter's road.

There was so much to put aright, so much to put asunder. And so little the time. The pilgrim's way, he thought. It does go at a crawl.

I git me my gas, my gas and smokes. Then I git down to my appointed task.

She wiggled herself up, and a moment later he felt her fingers lightly stroke his cheek.

Truman? she said.

He all but laughed, her that sheepish in her appeals.

Truman what?

You don't love me, do ye?

I've done count the ways.

She squirmed away from him. Oh God, she said. I've got to go take my leak agin. You best weasel-down the car.

He'd seen a bird come by him once, him a boy, a bird with broken wing, that bird high at first, but dropping with each single flap. It was that bird's wing the girl's one good eye put him in mind of now.

Truman? I mean it, you don't want a flood. You best halt this buggy.

He did so, by the pull-in of a closed country store called Cal's Place, and sat hatched up under the steering wheel, watching the drift of fog in his headlights and the road he'd traveled by in his side mirror. That road a picture postcard of aimless dark. By his speedometer he'd covered a fair handful of jackknife miles.

He wondered she didn't have the dignity to waddle off into bush, or leastwise to kick up dirt on her leavings the way would a cat.

The man kept dogs, whichever Cal it was owned this sludge-hole.

He could hear their barks away yonder, likely off in some fenced-in place out back, because they hadn't yet come running to nip at the squatter's heels or leap up scratching at his door.

He rolled his window down and hollered at her. You goin to rouse the kingdom, you don't hurry, he said.

He inclined his head away from her meek reply, staring off thoughtfully into the dark at what would be a gas pump.

He needed gas and he needed his weeds.

Them dogs won't howling, he could git both right here.

He emptied his ashtray in his lap and eyed the pile, picking out the few bent stubs he might smoke again. He could

unpeel these butts and tamp out a nice tobacco heap, he had
wrappers to roll them in. But he hadn't no wrappers and no
patience for that.

He was running out of patience, he thought, and that won't
no pretty sight. She'd see it won't, she held on to breath long
enough.

He brushed ashes onto the floor.

He reached over the seat into the back and retrieved from
among his belongings the shoe she'd tossed there. The mud
had caked. The shoe won't hardly no longer than his hand.
He tapped the toe and a chunk of mud fell off. It was a cloth
shoe of dirty white, the thick lace still tied in its bow. She'd
look better, he thought, that bow was in her hair. He liked a
woman could dress herself up, in bows and frills, a nice sash
around the waist. A little flaring skirt you could see her
bloomers in. He liked she would have puffy sleeves, and long
skimpy legs, and maybe a little play pocketbook. She
wouldn't have no chest to speak of, though you could see one
day where chest would be. She'd run and hide, that one
would, and you'd spend your whole life chasing her from bush
to bush, chasing her and bringing her to ground.

But he won't going to stew his brains again over that ancient
history.

He thunked the heel of the shoe against his dash, then
rubbed the rubber sole against his beard. He picked up the
mud chink and tasted it with his tongue. Then took more of it
into his mouth. He worked it with his tongue and when it had
dissolved he swallowed it.

Dust to dust, he said.

He wondered what the time was, and whether they knew
sunrise in these parts.

Him and that little girl he used to spy on, her with the

skimpy legs and play pocketbook, had sat together in a tire swing until she'd pushed him off. Then he'd chased her round and round.

He wondered this one won't worried more. Could be she didn't have the sense.

He wondered he'd given so little time to thinking of his flock.

Idle hands, he thought, next the checkmate.

She whooped at the door, scratching to get in.

Brrr, she said. I've froze my skin off.

She fumbled her way down, shaking with cold.

My irrigation's plugged, she said. Them barkin dogs done skeered me end-to-end. Pass the ammunition.

He lifted up the whiskey bottle to her.

It was near empty, and he watched she didn't drink over-much.

You don't have no gum, do ye? she said, snuggling up to him. My mouth is somethin else.

A few hundred yards down from that stretch of road his head-lights picked out a lane off to the left, and he stopped again. An aged sign nailed to a tree named it the Old Wheeler Road. Someone had slashed through this and inscribed above it a second name. Taper, it seemed to say. The lane looked un-used, gullied and washed out and mostly overgrown. Likely no one lived up that road.

He could take her up that lane—his car could make it— and the world never see her again.

She was holding her belly, bent over, rocking herself. Her breath had a vomity tinge.

I wishen—But she didn't say what she wishened.

I'm feelin so poorly, she said. I'm feelin pinkish to my gizzard-bone.

She was a whiner, he noted, and a whiner grated his nerves.

It come to whining, he might mention his toothache, for that tooth was acting up again. But would she hear a word from him?

They drove on, and a minute later crossed a wooden bridge over a stream called Low Creek, so said the leaning stob, and just beyond that they came to a divide. A dirt road veered to the right and he backed up for a second look.

Ziggerdy-dog, he said. Looky there. Civilization starin us in the face.

A rusted, bullet-riddled tin billboard off in the woods said Frog Eye's Fish Camp & Guest Home, with a faded black arrow pointing the way.

Her head popped up.

Goody, she said. Oh goody. Can't we spend the night there?

He spun off down the dirt road.

Maybe at the fish place, he thought, I can git me my smokes. Maybe siphon me some gas. Shed this lump.

An animal's black form, opossum by the stride, shot out onto the road and he swerved to run it down. Then forlornly wondered he hadn't heard no whump.

Once or twice over the next minutes the girl bolted up, yowling, hit by what she said was her stabbing cramps.

She was sweaty of brow, cringing under the spasms, her face strained white.

I need hep, she said, whimpering, clutching at him.

Hep's on the horizon, he said. It always is, jist out of reach of poor mortal's uplifted, entreatin arms.

He lit up one of his cigarette nubs.

He stroked his jaw, wondering how soon it was his toothache would gallop in.

I git her in a boat at that frog place, he thought. Knocked
up and knocked out, and I float her corpse downstream.

They entered the Fish Camp lane in a deliberate crawl, the
trail hacked in years past though dense forest now largely re-
claimed by woodland growth, the car bucking and wheezing,
icy puddles cracking like windowpanes beneath the slow roll
and crunch of tires, the bushes here ice-covered and spar-
kling under his beams, the headlights angling weirdly as their
vehicle made gain over uneven ground, the terrain floor slick
and whirling with mist, while beyond and around them
stretched an unencumbered black.

It's way colder thue here, she said. Why's that?

The fires of hell rage, he said, but they's shut the door to
save on the heat bill.

I'm skeered, she said. I'm goose-bumpy all over.

You heathen in your outlook, he told her. Little lovin soon
warm you up.

My baby comes I'm up here, she said, I be good as dead.
Me up here at this North Pole.

They crept on another few hundred yards, him now with his
head out the window, watching for ruts, their path all but dribbled out.

There, he said. There it is.

She could see nothing, just the fog-swirl in his beams, and
the black night.

He inched the car on another dozen yards.

There, he said, his voice low, halting the car.

There what?

But he flicked off his lights and the blackness closed around them, and she didn't know which way to look.

He drank the last of his whiskey, and tossed the bottle into the dark.

This here inn is shut up and all gone to hell, he said. And you a woman out of luck.

He heard her suck in her breath, and shift away from him, but she didn't say anything.

He sat composed at the wheel, in the dark, not looking at her.

He reamed a finger into his mouth and felt along his swollen gums.

Way yonder, he said, me not as old as you are, I seen his light before me and his finger beckonin. I seen the Lordgod's very thumbnail. Come, God said. But I won't ready. He'd come once, I figured, he'd come twice, and I won't in no hurry.

You mean to hurt me, she said. I can tell it in your voice.

He heard her scratching at the door and reached over and grasped her arms.

Oh, he'll come, he said. That's known, and it's known too we are rarely ready. Oh yes. Me, now, the years went by and still I tarried. One day I seen a team of oxen lift up out of a field into the very air. Oh yes. Another time I seen a tree split wide open and a swarm of insects sweep up out of that tree and turn into a thousand butterflies before my very eyes. Oh, I've seen a multitude of wonders, marvels would lay slabs on your tongue or bring hot flames to your bowels. The air is full of these wonders, it is happenin each second we breathe. I seen it on your face that time with the hat. I seen you'd seen it yourself then. But your one eyelash fluttered and all was gone. Was a little girl one time would hide so good you never could finder, but I learnt how. I've learnt, I reckon I have, all there is to know, and not many can say that. Oh yes.

Don't hurt me, she said. Let me first have my baby. Then you can—

Oh, I can anyhow, he said.

He let go of her arms, lighting up another of his butts. He studied her face in the match flare, nodding to the fear he saw there.

Was one time I put a pebble in my shoe, down against the heel, Truman said. And I walked with that pebble grindin my heel for three days, and never that pebble to work a hole in my sock, or to bleed me or cripple me with ache. Oh yes. God says, Come, and you're not ready, it's pebble in your shoe thue many the mile. But that day with the pebble I was ready. Come, he said, I show you the way. And I went along with him. I looked up the road and there he was up ahead, seated on a forked log, smokin and waitin. Take out that pebble, boy, he said to me. Remove you your impediment. So I took out the pebble and put it in the open palm of his hand and he blew on it and out of that pebble, shootin straight up, was the ugliest thorny vine you ever saw. But way at the top was these pretty blooms and thue the blooms was a shiny kingdom you could see plain as the eyes in his face. And God said to me, he said, A man knows thorns could climb up there. Yes, he could climb thorny vine and reach shiny kingdom, he was a person wanted to and knew how.

I've knowed thorns, Truman said. I reckon we both have. Say, I do.

The girl grappled with the door latch, and he laughed.

Say, I do, he said again.

She didn't reply.

She opened that door, he wondered where she thought she could be going. He wondered how far she thought she would git.

I can marry us, he said, bein an ordained minister of the word, ordained from the very minute I lifted that pebble from my shoe.

She cringed and keened, and he could smell her sweat.

I do, he said.

She uttered a feeble sound that could have been yes or no.

That fixes that, he said.

The next second she gave a startled cry as something seemed to flutter about in her hair.

It's a bow, he said. A pretty little butterfly bow I bin carryin in my pocket lo these years.

He pinned the bow to her hair.

They's a cabin off that way yonder, he said. And a river. Let's us walk down by the water.

You oughten to be more careful with your next life, he said. You oughten to.

He got out of the car. She did too, a second earlier.

She was running.

Hey now! he said.

He could hear her scrambling about, a harried, shadowy creature in the dark.

Hey! You see if you can find that thorny vine.

He won't in no hurry. It won't befitting a caretaker, he should rush.

He locked his fingers together and twisted his arms over until the knuckles popped.

Here I come, he called. Ready or not.

I bin everywhere, Toker said, and I can't git no one to take it.

You bin to the wrong place then, the woman said. You bin to the right place, you'd of got somebody.

She scratched at her hip, looking back over her shoulder at something or someone inside the house. One bare foot was on the porch proper, the other down on the top step with her toes hooked over the edge. Rooted below her on the parched ground, Toker was mindful of the sling this put in her hips and how that porch knee was bent to put a wrinkle in the green houserobe, with a little air to come thue where he was of a mind to go hisself.

Maybe some bright day.

She was a whale more blossomy than he remembered.

Folks are not hogs, she said. Folks would do right by that load you're carryin, you did right by it your own self.

She was slim in the ankles, he saw, for that was where he next looked.

Right smart feet too, with an instep high enough you could crawl under.

He heisted the bundle up higher in his arms and jostled it

about, a frown on his face, as though he meant to tell her it won't his aim to carry this parcel much longer and wished now he hadn't never got started.

I bin up and down and all over, he said, and most wouldn't look at it. They figured I was up to somethin.

Knowin you, the woman said.

Toker squinted up at her. They hadn't never bin the best of friends, him and this woman, and he knew he hadn't never tried nothin on her or hardly passed a word with her afore this minute.

She had a devil-may-care look would crack fence posts.

She put a hand up to her hair and scratched. Then she looked at her curled fingers and softly blew on them.

That hip was still poked out there.

That robe still doing its bizness.

He figured she didn't have a stitch on beneath it—and him here without his X-ray eyes.

Is it a he or a she? the woman asked. That load you're totin.

It don't hardly matter, the age this'un is, Toker said.

No, she said, what matters is have you got the breastworks to feed it. All I see is slim pickins in that regard.

Toker grinned. She had the full works herself, that he could see, and not a care to who knew it.

It's a her, he said.

She accepted this grimly, half-lidding her eyes as though she couldn't bear to look upon a world brimming over with fools.

That'd explain it, she said. You try a sex-change operation on that bundle, you'd git shut of it in a minute.

She peered again through the screen door inside the house, studying the silence or the darkness in there, he didn't know which. He wondered what she had inside that house that so stirred up her interest.

Word was she'd bin livin by her lonesome nearly a year.
No man yit had stomped out to run him off.
Maybe no more than some part of herself in there she was bound soon to get back to.
Maybe a pot on the stove.
Right slim-hipped in the rearview department.
Little raw spot on one heel made you want to drop down and kiss it.
Little briar scratch runnin up the one leg. Had she been runnin naked thue fields?

Black hair piled up one side of her head, the other side fallen, all so billowy Toker doubted a yard rake could make a dent in the thickness. The robe she had on was a silky green one that had not a spot on it. It looked to him lick-spankin-new and not like she'd made it her own self and he wondered what man had boughten it for her and what distance that man had to drive to find it.

Though she might had mail-ordered it. Mail did git thue once ever blue moon.

That robe fitted her right loose and made him wonder which way that robe might look better, whether off or on.

If you're done lookin, she said now, with a throaty, smoky laugh that let him know this won't the first time men's eyes had lingered on her and seen something they wanted to have a go at.

He backed up a few steps, which she did herself, and they both looked at the sky, looked at the same place in the sky, where dark and voluminous clouds were forming.

A black mist swooning over the mountains.

She had one hand smacked up behind her neck, with the other hand cupping that elbow, her breasts, under fold of cloth, squashed up, Toker thought, like two heads on a single pillow.

I've not got all day, she told him. I've got my own bizness to be lookin after.

But she made no motion to leave.

It's goin to rain, he said, toeing the ground. I give it one hour.

Her face squinched up as she lifted one leg and scratched at the other with the bottom of her foot. He glimpsed a thin run of dark hairs along the raised thigh and felt a wooziness sweep over him.

It don't matter to me, she said. It can pour slops out of a bucket and I won't be one tick carin. It's not as though I'm goin anywhere.

She gazed down at him, some sort of lazy fix in her eyes. A lazy smoldering, or dare. Something there swimming anyhow, in how she looked at him. He wondered if that look meant he might think about coming back later, after he'd got shed of this bundle.

He knew she was single. Single and said to be willin. He knew morn one had said they'd hadder.

Not that you could credit what issued from the mouths of no-accounts round here.

Toker cleared space above the baby's face and took another hard look at it. He was conveying the infant in an old sack picked up from a field during one of his many sojourns and meanderings. His hands itched and smelled faintly of the fertilizer the sack once had contained. The baby's skin would be chafed, rubbed raw most likely, but was he its mama? Was he?

Whyn't you take this child? he said, lifting it toward her. You can see she won't be no trouble.

I don't want it. I don't have me a solitary need for it.

I know that.

So why you askin?

Because you're a woman.

I am that.

And it ought to be a woman has it.

I know that too, but here's one not available.

Damn! he said. It's by me what the world's comin to.

He backed up a step, and then another one, and stared off again at the mountains, stared off for some little while, computing the number of miles he'd walked that day, all to no avail, and the number he'd yet have to journey.

Is she ugly? the woman asked. Is she got a blue head or missin her limbs?

Naw, he said. She's normal as you and me.

That'd be the day, the woman said softly.

Toker darted looks at the woman's naked feet and ankles and raised his eyes to follow the split in her houserobe. Oh, that robe was open and she knew it. She had this one toenail fresh-painted, painted bright red, the rest chipped. She had this here what looked like a purple bruise on the inside of her leg, jist a hand's length above the knee. Maybe a birthmark. And maybe where some lucky so-and-so's lips had plowed. Oh, she had that robe open and them hips slung, first one then the other, and it unnerved him and she knew that too. But she hadn't yet troubled herself to glance down at this baby, and that vexed him.

Goddamn baby, you thought it weighed not an ounce till you'd carried it long as he had.

I wishen you'd stop oglin me, the woman said. She said this smiling, throaty-like, smoothing both hands slowly over her hips where not a stitch of cloth was rumpled and his own hands had a yearning to travel.

With her there won't but one route you could take, and that the scenic one.

But she knew that. She knew that or she wouldn't have that

tongue licking at the corner of her mouth or that leg up again taking daylight. That flouncy hair. Them eyes.

I wishen you would, she said.

Toker smiled. She'd let that robe ride near free on one shoulder.

I wishen I was able, he said.

She laughed at that, laughed and threw back her head. She moved forward from the screen door, moved and kept on coming, coming all the way down the three steps to take up a split-leg stance directly in front of him, her eyes holding his, a hand raised as though she might decide to stroke him. Might even decide to kiss him. Might slide her body up skintight against his, uncurl her tongue in his ear, and say, Toker, my devil man, show me what you're made of.

One of these days.

That shoulder was still uncovered.

Even down here on level ground, in her naked feet, she was taller than he was. She was every inch flesh and you could feel the heat that flesh put out. She had a scent which he could smell now, and the scent won't one from around here. It sure won't honeysuckle or vanilla flavoring, and it was a far cry from Lily-of-the-Valley; it was a scent cost you five dollars each ounce, and went along with the creamy skin under that fine bathrobe.

Cost you an arm and a leg, this one would.

She was a wizard-woman shot in from the planet Venus to bewitch and bedazzle.

What's your name anyhow? she asked, her head tilted, her eyes probing. Ain't your name LeRoy?

She had eyes deep as tea leaves in a tea jug.

No mam. LeRoy's my brother, the one that took off. My name's Raymond.

I thought so. One of them flea-bitten Tokers.

Yes'm.

Had a sister?

Yes'm.

Was burnt out?

Yes'm.

Now said to be livin in a hole in the ground?

Yes'm. Near enough to it.

Well, Raymond Toker, burnt-out, had-a-sister, livin-in-a-hole-in-the-ground, listen to this: I've not had nary youngan of my own, I bin hatin them that much. So I'm not likely to be takin yourn.

It ain't mine, he said. I tole you up front I done founder.

You ought to of left her then. Now if I found myself a baby in the woods it wouldn't break my stride one fathom.

Yes, Toker said. Well, unlike some, my heart ain't yet been harden.

Unhuh, she said.

She stalked over to the side of the house and looked vehemently at something there, maybe at no more than a weed in its wild bloom, then came back and mounted the porch steps and sat down on the porch, sat down promptly and as though in full indifference to his opinions or even presence. She sat down with a wide split in her legs, scowling, withdrawing a small bottle from her pocket.

I think I'll paint me my toenails, she said.

She immediately twisted off the cap, crossed a foot up into her lap, and started in painting.

She started in on the one big toe that Toker already had seen was bright red as a tow truck.

She had this tongue out between her lips, her face scrunched up as though enduring diabolical pain, though this wasn't where Toker next leveled his gaze.

The one shoulder of that gown had slipped down to her elbow. The two heads on what he'd called the single pillow won't squished the least bit now.

I rightly couldn't of left it, he said. Some hawk would of gobbled this baby whole, I followed your advice.

Hawkinfuckinspitshit! she said. Babies, I can't stand'um! The anger spun up out of nowhere, darkening her face, seeming to startle her much as it did him.

Don't mind me, she said gloomily. Some days I got scum in my mouth sunrise to sunset.

Me and you both, Toker said. I reckon we come from the same egg.

He could see the egg, a nice green egg, and him inside it with her slipping and sliding.

She fluttered a hand over the fresh paint, leaned forward and blew air over her foot, then started in on another toe.

What color's its eyes? she said. It's got eyes, I hope.

They's mostly shut right now, he replied. It's sleepin, thank God.

You been feedin it?

Now and then. I ain't hadder that long. I giver tobacky juice off the tip of my finger and you ought to seen the face she made.

The woman giggled.

I giver an old shoe-tongue to suck on.

She laughed heartily.

She gets antsy, I blow inner ear.

If it's blowin you want doin, the woman said, you could hang a breeze over these toes.

She extended her leg out toward him, smiling naughtily, wriggling the foot.

Toker blinked. That long leg was naked most up to her bloomers.

If she was wearing bloomers.

Hold on, Toker said. You jist hold on one sweet minute.

He put the sack down on the ground beside him, the baby waking and squirming. A little pink arm worked its way free, then another one.

The woman wiggled that foot impatiently. She wasn't looking at him.

He squared himself about, took hold of the woman's foot by the heel, and blew.

I spose you bin washin it too, she said drowsily. I spose you bin changin its drawers.

No, he said. When it gits right ripe in the nose I hightail off to creekwater and let the current take the worst out.

The woman tucked the gown between her legs, and lay back flat on the porch, flopping an arm over her face.

Her tucks slid up and open a bit.

He wondered she could be so calm, him holding her raised heel. He kept blowing.

The five toes in his hand looked to him like five little red tugboats all ready to dock.

He heard her stifle a giggle.

Whyn't you paint that other foot? she said dreamily. You bein a man with such steady hands.

The baby made offended noises, thrashing on its back, flaying its limbs, doing its best to break its head free of that sack.

Whose you reckon it is? the woman asked.

I ain't carin whose it is, he said. All I want is to git its hinges off me.

She wriggled her toes in his hand.

He lifted her other leg straight and leaned his weight against her two feet, reaching for the nail polish. He could feel the heat of her feet against his stomach and cool sweat on his brow.

He thanked heaven he'd journeyed up this road.

He dabbed the paint on.

Oh, luxury, the woman said, her voice soft. Like she was ladling up honey. I've never known luxury till this minute.

That arm was still thrown up over her eyes. She looked like a woman a breath away from sleeping.

The robe kept riding up her leg. Kept opening.

That briar scratch he'd seen was one of a number climbing her thighs.

That one bruise up there looked like a thing requiring his best physician's attention.

She groaned.

She had fine, hefty feet somewhat out of keeping with her trim ankles. By the ankle bone was a sweep of darkish hairs she'd overlooked in the shaving.

Here was smooth skin, he thought, could give that baby a run for the money.

He finished one toe, went on to the next.

I got me a foot fetish, he thought. I got me a foot fetish I never realized till this minute. My pants goin to walk away with me, I don't watch it.

One shoulder of that gown was all but clear of a nipple.

She won't making no extra effort to keep them knees together.

I got me a foot fetish, he thought, that don't stop with feet. More like it climbs on up to include the whole of this woman's body.

If he gave the wee-smallest tug to that bathrobe both them nipples would spring loose.

If he edged a foot up on the next step, he might could claim a more pristine angle.

He polished up the last toe. And blew.

She laughed mildly, rousing herself. Wriggling that big toe.

He was sweating. He wanted to take that toe in his mouth and suck it thue to nighttime.

He wondered what a gentleman would do.

The baby, down on the ground, was thrashing and gurgling. Fighting that sack. It had both arms and one leg free, and its head most out. It was plonking itself each which way.

I'm done, Toker said.

He lifted her heels and placed them back down on the step. She sat up, smiling, though not so much at him as at some wayward thought.

I do declare, she said, admiring his work. That's right smart. Maybe you done found yourself a new career.

I could use one, he said.

They both glanced about as the baby's head burst clear of the sack. The face was lit up. The baby seemed to be reaching her arms out at them.

The woman stood up.

Where is it exactly you got that thing?

In the woods by my house, Toker said. Bright early this mornin. Under a laurel bush. I've not had me a lick of fun since I founder.

The woman arched her back, stretching and inhaling.

Toker watched, hoping she'd pop right out of that gown.

Yes, she said. Fun around here is in short supply. Fun is the original lost article around here. You can ask me about that. I'm an expert on that question.

Maybe it was good company you're needin, Toker said. He managed to keep his gaze level.

Her expression clouded.

Maybe, she said.

He watched her pat her foot, eyeballing him.

And maybe this good company would go shootin off his mouth the way others I've heard of have.

Toker wiped a quick hand across his mouth. You seein here the original zipped lip, he said.

They weighed each other in silence.

You don't have the sense God gave a bedpan, she said after a minute. She whirled up to the door, there shading her eyes and sighting through the screen at the darkness inside.

I've not made up my mind about you, she said, her voice gritty. You sound half-decent, but they all do, till they get they head in. Is that what you're plannin? To get your head under my gown?

Nome.

But you wouldn't mind tryin, I bet.

Toker looked over at the baby. He wondered should she talk this way in front of a baby.

Maybe partway in, he said. One part or another. He smiled. That there green houserobe sure is fetchin.

She held his stare, her look dubious.

I believe I got me a Don Wan, she said. I do believe I have.

Toker looked at his feet.

You do it then, she said. You do it, if you've a mind to. I wouldn't fault you none for wantin to git your head in wherever you could git it. Bettern you have, or have tried.

He stobbed his toe about in the dirt.

When would you come?

This evenin? He blurted that out without thinking, without saying what next came to his mind: If I can. If I'm able. If I don't have this baby to keep me home like a mole in the cellar. And if later I still got the courage.

Because he had an inkling this one here in the silky bathrobe and her painty toenails spelt dark trouble. She spelt full disaster, you rubbed up her wrong side.

Don't bring that youngan, she said. I've vowed never to let

no infant step foot inside my portals. The minute one does I'm burnin the house down.

She strode forward again in a growl, some kind of new anger flaring. She was shaking a pointy finger first at him, then at the side yard.

You see that stump out there, she said. That yard stump?

Toker looked. She had see-saw moods would make your head spin.

I see it, he said.

Well, she said. Used to be that was a tree. It was on that tree our family used to would hang'um.

Toker looked on, astonished. Her face had gone snow white and she was steaming mad. What did she mean?

You ask ol' Hindmarch, she said. He'll tell you. He lives right there yonder over that ridge. He saw it.

Saw *what*? Toker asked, getting steamed himself. Hanged *who*?

She hurled herself inside, slamming the door.

Toker stalked over and examined the stump. He didn't know why, them gittin on so well, she'd now went and got so mad.

Or, he said, is one of us crazy.

He went to retrieve the baby. But the baby had rolled or squirmed its way out of the sack and now was taking the sun. Its head was up high, erect and riding the small valley of its shoulders, the arms fully extended from its body. Like wings, Toker thought. Only a smidgen of its belly was touching grass, the chest lifted, the legs elevated too, and shooting straight out from the apple-roundness of the buttocks. Feet pointed, the heels up like high rudders. It was some kind of ballet-type baby, or winged sculpture—an airplane. It looked ready to fly.

A jay bird was singing blue blazes off somewhere.

Toker jumped the woman's steps, calling.

Come look! he said. This baby can fly!

He heard a string of curses inside the house.

The baby lifted its head higher, smiling at him.

It's a goddamn wonder, he thought. A newborn baby hardly got bones.

The baby went on with its flying.

But when the woman appeared, rubbing cream between her hands and looking faintly composed, looking for all the world as though she had imagined herself done with him no less than with yard stumps, the baby had gone limp and puddly. Its face was screwed up an ugly, bloated red, as if on the verge of a howl. The flesh was blemished all over where ants and mites, bugs, no doubt even wood ticks had taken their plugs out of its hide. The skin looked raw. It looked twisty. It smelt of fertilizer.

Git that thing off my property, the woman said.

Toker scooped up the baby and placed it over the mouth of the sack and dropped the baby in. Its grubby fingers pawed at his chin. He pulled the sack over the baby's head, and slung the weight over his shoulder.

He heard a sound behind him and turned. The woman was sliding through her screen door. He saw a hand fly up and latch the hook. In that same second her bathrobe flowed open and he had a clear view through the screen of the woman in her full nakedness.

He had a dry taste come to his mouth.

You seein somethin you like? she asked. She spoke with a torchified voice that could melt ice or icehouse.

He was rooted to his spot.

Yes'm.

She pressed her nipples up against the wire.

You come then, she said.

Toker chugged on down the woman's path, crossed her road, and headed on up toward the woods. Here was cleared field, it still furrowed, though nothing planted of late, splashed through with wizened stalk, with weed clumps and spreading clover, hardened cowpats, though no cows now grazing, the soil given over to the maze-like tunneling of mole, to burrowing rabbit and licey field mouse, the cornstalks mossy, a fungusy rot would crumble in your hand—the land rising at a graceful slope up to tree line of poplars till it reached the ridge. It was a pretty country, he thought, though lame in the siring, right royally poor, and pickish in its blessings. He trod on, the grass folding under his tread and springing back up out of stubborn refusal to be smitten by the likes of him. Thue these poplars, yes, about here, baby. Why not we strike off this way? Then pure rock for a while, lengthy curvature through the mountainside, curvature of old, one heaved up by ancient cataclysmic eruption, he supposed, here and there decorated by the odd pool of trapped growth, this mostly denuded now. Then mica chips beneath his boots, a swatch of leafless saplings and thorny bush or wild hedge, each bent to the single slant driving wind season after season impressed upon them.

Now the woods proper. Why not we go that way? Let's you and me plunge right in.

He came to a blackberry patch grown tangly on a hillside, the berries moldy, shriveled like raisins, a puff and they'd blow away. But you could poke down in earth and find a runner, you could upend dead leaf and move aside stubble—mind you don't prick your hand now—and maybe find a few late-ripening and somehow hardy in the survival. He poked so and found them, some five or six, and crushed these and fed them to the baby off his fingers. Then he trudged on.

Sweaty, he thought. I'm sweaty all over, that's what that vixenish woman has done to me.

But a berry a day keep the heebie-jeebies away.

I bin a long time between women, he told the baby. I bin an eternity. Yes, I'm loath to confess it, and won't abide your repeatin the news, but me and women had come to a standstill up to the time of that little episode.

Otherwise, I'd of shown more spirit.

She was smart, won't she, puttin that latch on her door?

She don't want you either, he said. Won't not a soul have you. And you are sure as tarnation puttin a wrench in my day.

But she a brazen number, won't she? If a thousand done hadder, I wouldn't mind bein a thousand and one.

They's snakes thue here, baby, they not hibernatin. You best keep your eyes open. Bears, too, you so much as cleared your thoat.

He came to a barbed wire fence and followed that, the wire growing deep into the walnut tree line that secured the fence.

He scooted under the strands to take a plumb line across pas-
tureland, a half-dozen steers looking at him from the far side,
the log cabin with white sheets flapping from a clothesline his
destination.

He knocked at the back door and waited down on the
ground and back a ways from the door so that when the woman
answered there would be space between them and faint need
for her alarm.

The woman who came he'd not seen before, neither her nor
the two young children who clung to her legs and batted their
eyes as they examined him. He set himself to explain what it
was he wanted, which was to find a home for this baby, but the
woman was talking a mile a minute before she reached the
door. And came on down, near running him over.

Well goodness gracious and how nice it is a man would
think to call on me, and me lookin such an ungodly mess this
day. My name is Mrs. McElroy, what is yourn? This is little
Mac here clingin to my left leg and that is Mary McElroy, my
oldest, hidin under my skirt and suckin her thumb. Oh I wish
I could make her stop that thumbsuckin, though short of cut-
tin it off I don't know what I can do. Oh don't whimper Mary
McElroy, you know I wouldn't—why what a pretty baby! I
don't know I've ever seen prettier lessern it was my own. My
husband is in the barn, poor thing, he's always in the barn this
time of year, was it my husband you were lookin for? Are you
a McElroy yourself? Though I must say you don't resemble
one, no it's the hair that stamps you and if I studied you a
spell I bet I could name the very crossroads you come from.
Still, it is mostly McElroys we get round here, on their usual
road from wrack to ruin, some spellin their name with two *l*s,
and some with one, and some without the *c*, though they's still
McElroys to hear them tell it, and God knows God has higher

bizness, I reckon, than to concern hisself with the antics of McElroys. Oh do look at that baby's scalp, jist soft and precious as flower by springwater, but do you know there are McElroys who claim soothsayers there are, or McElroys who are themselves soothsayers, who can read a child's future in the scalp? The same as they can with the palm of your hand, though how they can do either of the two is a mystery to me.

She went off to the side yard then, testing her sheets for dampness and looking at the sky, then to claim it never rained but that she'd jist got her wash strung, and did he think it would? Rain? Before the next hour?

Yes'm, Toker said, backing up, getting set to run, because he could see this woman would talk the baby to death and, yes, it would rain soon, and he'd better hurry.

So he did that, backed away with her hardly even slowing down her word-roll and saying:

But you haven't yit tole me what you wanted? Ain't you goin to look up Muriel, in the barn? Well, I never! And us hardly even yit had chance to say hello!

He was crossing the pasture again, the steers with their swivel-necked sighting of him, when he heard the woman calling:

Say! What's that child's name? You never even tole us her name!

On another hillside his footsteps frightened up a covey of late-season quail from among tall weeds, then a second flurry, then silence until he clapped his hands and a third covey a dozen yards away fluttered up on urgent wing and likewise dispatched themselves into the loaming sky. He stomped out a flat space in the dry weeds and settled the baby on its stomach within the clearing.

Now let's see you do that flyin number again, he said. I'm waitin.

But the baby only whimpered, chilled some little bit, it seemed, its limbs folded up the way would a bug, so Toker returned the baby to its sack, flung the sack over his shoulder, and pressed on.

Look about you, he said. Here in these trees you'll find crow and hawk alike roostin on the same limbs. Once thue here, me still in my knicker-pants, I seen a hawk swoop down and snatch away three nestlins while the mama-bird swooped and squawked, her objections to no more avail than smoke from a chimney.

Soon he came to another dirt road and this one he followed downhill until he reached a few outcroppings of weathered barns and a leaning slathouse which had a mailbox out front, it secured in the double boughs of a dusty tree by the side of the road. The name I. E. Priddy had been carved into the tree bark and lightened with whitewash.

Toker looked for some minutes at the tree, the dented tin box, and at the Priddy house where nothing and no one stirred.

Them Priddys ain't known for their vinegar, he told the baby. I could stuff you inside the box, and never a soul know the difference. I be shed of you and march on, my stride broke not one fathom.

An old dog came up out of the yard, dragging a dead hind leg, and there by the tree it paused, regarding Toker out of its own melancholy disfigurement. The eyes were droopy, a shortened tail aswerve under its legs. It whined lowly, and Toker said a greeting to the dog. It was not a dog he had seen before, though to his mind it clearly was a Priddy dog. As if in a sorrowful sleep, the dog hobbled over to lick his ankles and sniff at the babysack, then it moaned its low apology and ambled loose-legged on back to its quarters under the house.

No, Toker said, I ain't givin you up to these dirt-lappin Priddys. I stuff you in that box, afore mornin they'd have you out earnin they's keep. Out trappin and shootin, your nose behind a plow.

Come along now.

He retraced his steps up the road, and at a certain point to his liking again veered off into thick woods.

Once in a while he felt a kick in his backside, or heard the odd, nonsensical complaint, though for the most part the baby seemed content with her ride.

The odd soaring bird up in the sky accompanied them.

Them birds got it all over you and me, he told the baby. You be a bird you could eat nice insects and drink at brooks and vacation in the tropics come each winter. You wouldn't be livin in no hole in the ground like me. Now would ye?

Fasten your eyes on them yeastin clouds, baby.

The fermenting clouds of a while ago were hanging lower now, pushing over from the next county and coming their way with a renewed boil, blackening, distant treetops already asway, leaf and limb jittery, and the air damp on his face. He quickened his stride.

Not that we got a crawdad's chance of outrunnin that rain anyhow, he told the baby. But maybe we can make it to Cal's.

Some bit on Toker left the path altogether and swung off to follow a gully laced to its furthermost depths by a stream so weak and trickly this time of the year that he could follow it most the way down to the highway and Cal's Place, or near enough to road and Cal's Place that taking it, that route, was worthwhile, so long as Cal's Place, or road, was where a body was going.

We wet our whistles when we git back there, he told the baby. I buy you a Dr Pepper. You smile for all the nice people, show them you bright as a monkey.

Here, brush, briar, broom hedge, and swampland took over. He had to forsake gully and climb some, climb maybe more than he wanted to with an orphan baby in his keeping.

Though once or twice in a blue moon he'd come through here with worse. A gored dog once, that time when he kept dogs, and not your lowly Priddy mongrels either. Them days when he was full of beans and vinegar and thought dogs were the end-all and be-all and would see him through into gizmo-heaven.

I hadn't hardly yit learnt how to wipe, he told the baby. The same as you, though you deny it.

Another time I come thue here my daddy was chasin me, chasin me with a bullwhip, and me not knowin what I'd done, only that I deserved it.

Now how'd Bathroby know about my sister Princessanne perishin in that fire?

How come she to hate youngans with God's own wrath and what's that she was so hepped up about with that stump and hangin poor folks from tree limbs?

It sure is growed up a lot thue here since I last come. Nothin but vine and thicket.

This here bog will suck your boot off.

Land not worth a crawdad in hell.

But an hour more will do it.

We git back to Cal's I'll treat you to a popsicle. Have myself a right smart snack of saltine crackers and potted meat.

That there you are hearin is called a whippoorwill.

Hold up now, let's see you know how to sit down.

Toker dropped down to his haunches, picked cockleburrs from his ankles, and swung the sack under his legs. That there you're blinkin at is called skylight, he told the baby. Though for the minute it's gone right ruddy. See that beetle? That beetle has a hundred legs and can walk till you're blue in the face, with never an oil change. You can pour brains six days into a bucket and you still won't never have one-half the brains that beetle has.

Now that's your Grade One education. Grade Two, you're in somebody else's hands.

He picked a black tick away from the baby's ear, saw blood swell up in the pocket, and dabbed his spit on.

Ticks got to live too, baby, he said.

That circlin your face is called gnats. It's gnats shall inherit the earth.

In you go, he said. Time we peg-legged on.

He swung the baby up again over his shoulder, and once more they went on.

Not long now. But we don't beat the rain yourn and my tail both gone be soaked and soppin.

The woods were hunkered down, subdued and humbled. A massive congregation, all bowing. Bowing and scraping. Saying, Toker thought, Do with me what you will, Lord, for I am as nothin. I am as barley dust in the wind. I came as nothin and will leave as nothin and in between I am worse than nothin. So which will it be this time, Lord? Avalanche, hailstorm, hurricane, or Armageddon's grinnin plague?

What sky didn't tell him the stilled forest did. You could stand and hear your own heart beat, and that a fluttery thing that come up thue your shoes.

Nature, he said, it does give you pause. It does remind you your woeful size in the scheme of the universe.

slug on its march into paradise . . . But I do wonder why she done it. I do wonder why I was the one set up to find you. What it means, my findin you, is my string of bad luck has some distance yit to go in the unravelin. My pit ain't yit hit the pendulum.

Tell you the truth, I'm still diggin out from the last load dumped on me.

Throw me a little rope, darlin.

Bathroby's right. I'd of left you where found, I had good horse sense.

The land here rippled and heaved. From a high bluff he saw the wind and rain coming, saw it a good mile off—Over there, baby, jist sweepin over that ol' Fish Camp—solid gray shroud of rain and wind shoving down all beneath it. Tree and bush, vine and grass, they were all bending and bowing. Rain and wind folded them over, wave after wave, snaky undulations green and misty, and the folds kept spreading and coming, the sky deepening by the second, almost to full black now. The air ripe with it now.

I know me a cave here somewhere, he said, running, the baby locked in tight under his arm—if I can find the sonofabitch.

The rain came down like switches against his face, a good part of it ice, drumming against his clothing as he ran stooped over, his shoulders rounded to protect the child. An arm across his brow. Scrabbling on, reversing directions, cut off this way, only steep cliff the other. The earth roily. The wind swirling. His boots weighty.

It's my fault, baby. You got to stroke God's chin, speak nice to his face, or this is what happens.

In minutes the creek was gushing, no way to cross that. Lessern I wade it, he said. Sweet singing Jesus, now which way?

You'd think he had been dropped down into these parts only yesterday.

Lightning cracked. He could feel the earth shake.

No shelter, no cave, nothing to do but brake in. Ride out the bastard.

He hove up next to a thickish tree trunk, awaiting his bearings.

Hush now, he told the baby.

A sodden downpour. Black thundering drench of rain, rain already purging the tree, rain driving down as though neither tree limb nor leaf existed, rain splattering up from the ground, coursing down his neck, pouring off his face. The ice rat-a-tatting.

Ain't we the fine lynx in butter?

The air chopping cold now, cold as a witch's tit.

Two by two, he said. Ye got your ark handy?

Up in heaven they's throwed out all the dishwater.

Down on his haunches, his body bent over the wet bundle quivering in his arms.

You a tough lil runt, I hope.

If the baby took sick there won't gone ever be anyone to taker.

First thing I know you be callin me Grandaddy.

Of course if you croak then it's all over.

The rain drumbled on.

Now it could wash away sins we'd have somethin.

Toker rocked on his heels, eyes closed, moaning out a remembered song or dirge, now cuddling the silent, squenchy-eyed baby.

Sweet li'l baby
don't you cry

find you a mama
by and by

The wind blows and all is erased. The rain comes and all is erased.

They's erasin us, baby. That's old slack-jawed Jupiter up there sayin we are less than spit in the stream.

That morning up Hunt Road long before full daylight an elderly farmer named Moss had been returning to his kitchen from the barn, a milk pail knocking at his side, when he heard a scratching by his fence, looked up, and there in the darkness was a smallish, stringy girl with wet hair and no coat, wet all over, looking back at him.

She'd seen his lantern in the barn, he guessed, and had come up off the road to unload her mind.

Ye ain't seen no man and woman come by here in no old car, did ye? she asked him.

Nome. Not recently.

Did ye? There'd be the two of them, in that old car, and him right mean-lookin.

She could be no more than ten or eleven, he at first guessed, though when he took closer gauge he wasn't sure.

He felt his skin ripple, under siege of some kind of fear or foreboding. He knew something was wrong, either with the girl or with him—or maybe just because he sensed this was the way the day was going to hang. There came days like that now and then, days in which you knew you should just throw in your hat.

Where do this road go? she asked him.

You're up early, he said. What is it gets you up with the chickens? You look like a soul that has been trampin one road or another all night or maybe even a spate of nights. Maybe even since the dawn of creation.

She didn't argue with any of that. She examined him with her scooped eyes and asked again where the road went.

He told her it went up and down.

But where do it lead?

It leads down, he said. Like any road, if such is how you are pointed. What are you doin on my road this hour, the day not yit drawn hardly a wee breath?

Is it your road?

He told her the part she was standing on was, and naturally enough that was the part of the whole that meant most to him.

She seemed to think he had a peculiar way of talking, or that it wasn't worth her time talking to him any longer, and for a moment said nothing. She stood scratching her legs, in fact, scratching all over. She was biting her lips from the cold, her flesh densely freckled and pinkish, smudged and streaked with dirt or bruise from top to bottom. She had hair he guessed had never seen a comb, and skin no doubt she'd claim was allergic to soap and water. She came about up to his waist, a wastrel lean as the fence post her hands kept wrapping around.

Again, he sensed a deformity in the morning, and felt his flesh prickle in acknowledgment of some vague anticipation of fear, or something not right, of matters soon to go wrong or that already had, that sense either borne up by her presence and thus attached to her and not to him, or it a dread or gloom his own flesh imparted, and her, the girl, innocent to the misfortune.

But his skin prickled and he felt uneasy, whatever the cause, taking a moment to look over at his dark house in surmise of whether it was there that the trouble was roosting.

She was tired and had come a long way, he could see that.

You done left your lantern burnin in the barn, she said.

He looked back, considering a minute the orange streaks of light in his barn wall, that orangey hue in which the whole of the structure was cast, then agreed with her that indeed he had. His cow liked the color that lantern cast, he said, and it put the cow in a mood to let her bountiful goodness flow. Now maybe you would do the same, he said, and tell an ol' no-account fellow like me what you are doin out on my road before daybreak and dressed, a weatherman might say, in a manner too skimpy for travel.

How come you livin here but you don't sound like no one who do? she asked. How come that?

I don't know, the old man said. I guess it is that I jist naturally come to this world from a different egg. But you probably know about that, I'd say, about eggs, because I'd conclude you were a shade different yourself.

The girl scratched a scab loose from her knee, her lips pouty, gazing off again at the lit streaks in his barn and further wrinkling shoulder and face out of disagreement with the foul night cold.

That's so pretty, she said. That is so pretty, that barn. I've never seen prettier.

He saw now that she was somewhat older than he had first assumed, that age being told somehow in the weary slack of her face while being denied in her voice, which was certainly

youthful, and in her body, which had all the impulsive movements of a very young person not overmuch accustomed to
these early-morning discussions.

Why don't you come on up to the house? he said. Warm
yourself up good and proper.

She told him she couldn't. She had to git on down the road.

Lookin for somethin? he asked.

My sister.

She's gone missin, has she?

Unhuh.

Run away?

Unhuh.

Skipped loose of the reins, he said. You will yourself one
day. But if she's of age and gone on her own free will, then I
reckon it's out of our hands. But this is Hunt Road and it could
be that you will finder.

The girl gave him a shrewd glance. She stood up on one
foot, her head angled.

What you mean, of age?

Oh? he said. I meant, if she's of age, sixteen, then she's a
free spirit, to go and come as she pleases. Is she sixteen?

The girl reflected a bit, her face set in earnest puzzlement.

I've never knowed how old she is, she said finally, as
though undecided. She keeps growin.

Well, now, said the old man. I was goin to say that lookin at
her, lookin at a person, ought to tell you somethin. But jist
lookin at you, lookin in this dark, the shape you're in, the
shape my old eyes have got to, I might guess you were
seventy-five. So lookin's not got either of us anywhere.

The girl scrunched up her face.

You've got goose brains, then, she said. I was seventy-five
I'd be dust in a coffin.

She executed little jumps by his fence, their faces at times almost touching.

I look all the time, she said. I got eyes in the back of my head. Ain't no one pull the wool on me.

He touched her shoulder to stop her jumping.

This here milk's warm, he said. You want a taste? You want to come inside and git cozy? The wife's not too spiry, she's bedridden, but she'd be proud of the company.

The girl stared at his milk pail.

It's good Jersey, he said.

Jersey what?

My gracious. Jersey milk, don't you know?

I got to go now.

She was backing off.

You don't have seen no car come down this road, did you? she asked.

There was one a week ago Sunday. Might of bin one last night too, I think the wife said. But I was noddin.

It's black, she said. Black as this night. She done got herself in deep trouble.

Your sister?

Unhuh. She's biggern me.

But not smarter, I bet.

She's goin to learn her lesson this time, the girl said. But there won't be nothin left.

Oh sure there will be, the old man said. Sure there will be somethin.

Only if dead is, the girl said.

The old man watched her go. After a bit she turned and looked back at him, looked off at the lit barn. Then she kicked up her heels and was running.

He watched the empty, lightening road some little while,

watched the sky awash with slate, then shuffled into his house, thinking how he might most arrestingly compose this fence adventure with the shorn creature who had passed by, and how best to consult his chairbound mate on these forebodings that so made him sag.

Toker and the baby emerged dripping wet out of dense growth at the side of the road a short distance from Cal's Place. He slogged along the gravel shoulder, water sloshing in his boots, the boots weighted with mud—making out Calvin down at his store with his nose poked out the screen door, no doubt saying, Well, I believe it has let up, I believe that humdinger has passed.

Hidy, Cal!

Toker threw up a hand in greeting, but the door pinged, slammed back to its derelict hang, and Calvin wasn't there any more.

Don't think he didn't see us, Toker told the baby.

Ain't they the fine drown rats, that's what he's sayin.

He could hear, though not see, Calvin's two dogs, George and Martha, in their pen behind the store, yipping and yowling.

They's a proper string quartet, they are, he said. It does lighten my heart, to hear them dogs.

Smoke was rising from the chimney of the square-boxed house behind the store.

The air was moist, the trees drippy and shiny, boughs dragging the ground. A pinkish mist churned in soft disarray over the valley, and above the mist white clouds hugged the mountain range like a strung clothesline.

It was pretty up here after a storm.

He saw three old men, Cal's perpetual clientele, Hindmarch among them, totter up to the windows and door, nod their acknowledgment of the abysmal world, and disappear again into the store's environs.

You got your bearins yit, kid? Toker said. He gave a small shake to the bag.

Now that he'd got here he won't any too happy about entering. They'd josh him, them inside would. They'd rake him each which way, and have their fun. But if ever he was to git shuck of this child he'd have to taken it. One wantin you, he said, soonern later will cross that threshold.

Look fresh now. Put on your best Sunday manners and you'll be breast-cradled by mornin.

The entire parking space, normally riddled with hollows and dips and mud holes, was under a puddle of dank, oily water. They'd have to slosh thue it, over to them boards. Two planks had been laid down, reaching from the doorway to the gas pump, the dull orange glass jug up high atop the red cylinder, half filled with Cal's smoky fuel. Three empty drink crates with broken ribs leaned against the flaked white front, along with a straight-back chair boasting a cracked board seat. The faded sign above the door hung at precarious slant, secured by a single twist of fence wire. Flattened tin cans, your Spam, your baked beans, your Vienna sausage, and your sardines, floated in the muck at the door. Over to the far side were strewn a half-dozen automobile tires, some bobbing in water, inner tubes, gaskets, ropes, tail pipes, radiators, mangled fenders, bumpers, and grilles hanging from nails at Cal's little workshed there. A wood water trough to find where your tire punctures were, it brimming now. Cracked windshields, axles, twists of iron, slats, tubing, cages and traps of all sorts. A rusted car engine near hidden away by crabgrass. A wheelless tricycle some child had abandoned or Cal had plucked up along the highway. Oil drums. Wire sprockets, spools, tangles of wire, a few busted plows. Sofa chairs, bed springs, gutted iceboxes, wringer washers, buckets, rusted road signs.

My livin, Cal would say, back when I had one. Back when I had two nickels to rub together. Now it's bone scrapes bone.

At the opposite side stood the square, red kerosene tank, and behind it, stacked in formless abandon, hundreds of soft drink empties—Grapette, Orange Crush, and Diamond Lil— in their weathered wooden crates.

He gone lose those, Tucker told the baby, one these dark nights. Or my name ain't Elmer Fudd.

Behind him the door pinged, then thudded. Toker halted at the entrance, taking in the three old men slung up on log, lard can, and wood crate around the lid stove. Civilization's harried keepers. Their flapping tongues could make you want to hang'um. He'd bin trying all his life to rid hisself of the notion that these three aged barons, as with the whole of the world's walking elderly—whatever their faults and however decrepit their station—knew a good deal more about the ways of the universe than he did. And all bound together by a single purpose, the keeping to themselves of that grave knowledge.

Light inside the store was a deep rain-shroud color. Cold, though.

Hidy boys, he called now, for he knew the old men would not speak until he first had acknowledged them. How you boys doin?

The three, their hands aloft to the dead fire, lifted rancid eyes his way.

I'm on my last leg, the one answered—and it totterin. Wallace that would be, stretching to pull up his trousers on the leg in question, so that all might be witness that his every word was truth.

It's hog-killin time, the second old man said. And we'se layin low. This was Ol' Trout, there on his lard can, creaking his rheumatism.

Toker looked to Hindmarch, oldest of the three, patiently waiting his turn.

Yessir, Hindmarch said. We'se hidin out. He paused while he racked up a cough from his sunken chest, and flayed spent hands there, before stooping to kerflooey his waste into the Louisianne coffee tin at his feet. Last year was a passel come to gut us, confusin our split hoofs with that of the swine.

The other two erupted in cackles and poked frail hands at each other's shoe-work.

They were all three near-rounded and creaky as a cart wheel.

Drag youens up a throne, Wallace croaked out.

The store still carried the chill of last night. Normally a fire would have been going but today Cal hadn't yet got round to it. There was much Cal never got round to, though to hear him talk he had finger to bone every minute.

He was up now with a rag behind his showcase counter.

Was that you I saw on the road? he asked. I thought it was, but my eyes is retchid.

The storekeeper had sties over one eye, that lid mostly shut.

Toker hung in the doorway, extracting the baby from wet burlap, his hand cupping the baby's icy bottom, tugging the infant forth. Now settling that baby at low ride on his hip, since that seemed the more manly way to show her.

She was trembly, close to a weepy mood.

Swooshes of mud streaked her kneecap to chin bone.

Her flesh bites ziggerdy-zagged each which way.

The skin was blue.

A regular bob-wire baby, from the look of her.

The blue flesh smelt of moldy fertilizer. And something else too in that sack, gauging by the odor. Dead cats, it smelt like.

It needed a wash, the baby did, else its skin would crinkle and slide right off.

But was he its mama? Was he?

I see you still got it, Wallace called. I see we can still call you Aint Jemimah.

The two seated around him cackled their merriment.

You give birth to it yourself or you have hep?

Cackle, cackle.

Air your nipples sore?

Cackle, cackle.

Toker sat the baby up naked on the counter where for a second its head slumped and sagged; it became rounded ball and made to tumble over.

I give a dime for a cup of coffee, Toker said to Calvin. I give twenty cent if it come without no bottom.

He sat the baby down on the rippled, dusty floor, propping her backside up against the counter and holding her there with the sole of his boot.

I brewed up a fresh pot only this mornin, the storekeeper said. It's cooked good and tender by now. Walk on hind legs straight down to your belly.

Toker waited for the coffee to be poured, then drank the cup empty without lifting it from his mouth. Ahhhh, he said, wiping his lips with a sleeve. Grow fur on a eel, that Nescafé will.

The baby plopped over on its side, letting out a surprised squall.

Ain't that jackrabbit havin none? asked Cal. Looks to me like, goin out on a limb, you two got caught in a gusher.

We did that.

You ain't seen rain lessern you was here in the spring of twenty-nine, one of the old men said.

You call that rain? said another. I call that no morn a widow-woman's spit.

Hindmarch and Wallace hove up out of their languor and poked their way over to the counter.

Let's look at that whippersnapper, the one said.

Their bones popped like muffled gunshots as they bent over, probing swollen, knobby hands over the baby's body. Hindmarch, with two trembly fingers, tucked back the baby's eyelids.

I see she ain't no Dowdy, he said.

He peered from face to face, nodding to each, and having deposited this spare news, shuffled his way back to the stove, Wallace trailing.

Dougherty, he means, said Calvin. No, she ain't no Dougherty.

Yessir, the Dowdys, ruminated the old man. Now they was a handful. Ye never had the pleasure of havin yourself a Dowdy, now had ye? He clasped arms over the shoulders of his two ancient companions and with laborious glee began telling them all he knew or could dream up about the Dowdys. I ain't proud to claim it, he said, but in my day I had me a Dowdy girl, every one afore they'd hardly got out of cradle or could tie shoelace.

He means the Doughertys, Calvin said to Toker. A worthless bunch had the Stiggs place down Frog Road past that fish camp about a million years ago.

With me it was the Dewswops, Trout was saying. I had me

a Dewswop even up in a tree one time. Big oak, it was. The
limb cracked and I durn near broke three legs.

Bin broke ever since, said Wallace. Ol' Trout there's got to
shake it straight each time he unlimbers it to pee.

Now mine won't never broke, said Hindmarch. Though I
had it in plaster cast morn a year. That's what them Dowdys
will do to a man.

They talked on, more quietly now, huddled together like
medieval scholars pondering a text, or ragged mendicants
panning for gold, arguing the merits of the Dewswops and the
Dowdys and trying to beat one another on what queer spot
they'd had it best.

Betcha never had it in no flour mill, now did ye, the one
said. Now where else I've had it is on a mule plow, on a tree
stump, on a cedar-rail fence, on a bicycle, in a feed shed
in hot August, in a frog pond, in a midnight bog with a wild
hog chewin my left foot, on a front-porch swing in a snowy
blizzard, and ridin the back of a three-legged donkey down
number five road durin a cyclone. You done it them ways,
Trout?

Cackle, cackle.

Calvin's wife, Sarah, appeared in the rear doorway, coming
in from her and Cal's abode out back, sweeping a rank look
over the interior and all the refuse she found hanging about.
The old men fell silent, gazing out at her with glutinous, ran-
cified eyes. She worked a foot out of one worn slipper and
stood there pondering, it seemed, the upheavals of her life
and all the spoils within it to which she had minute by minute
to administer.

I see the dead can still walk, she said after a bit. Myself
among them. Brrr. Whyn't no one built a fire yit?

White chicken trails crisscrossed her scalp, her hair bound
in tight rollers fashioned years before out of the wooden spools

of house thread. Over this, inches up from the browline, she had tied a flimsy scarf, it a runny, see-through color. Stockings thick as gauze, muddish of hue, climbed to her knees, there to be twisted, knotted, and rolled.

She was swarthed in a houserobe too, Toker noted, it at a high and skewered angle above her knees. All the women in the county stayin abed this day.

What's that smell? she said, holding her nose.

Toker lifted one of the baby's arms and flapped the appendage her way.

I ain't surprised to see you again, Sarah said to him. Air it perished yit?

Nome. Not yit.

Come here.

Toker strode over and Sarah lifted the hem of her robe, wiping spittle from the baby's mouth. She lifted the baby's face by its jaw and gave it a shake. I'm glad I can say it's not no kin of mine, she said. A big pin secured the gown up high at her throat. One of her hands went to that.

I've seen uglier, she said. She worked her toes back into the limp slipper. Though I can't say when.

They's all ugly, if I'm any judge, said Calvin.

The woman shot him a scalding look. Was anybody talkin to you? she asked.

The three old men punched each other, delighting in the rigorous soldiering of married life.

You best warmer up to the fire, Sarah told Toker. Lessern you wanter to come down with croup and die in your arms. No, I ain't holdin it.

Toker went past her through the rear door, returning a few minutes later with kindling slithers and a load of split logs from the shed out back.

They could hear the dogs yowdling terribly.

Your wood-haul trip done stirred them up, mused Cal. They bin nervous as bedbugs since last night.

Yes, said Sarah. But you so lazy you didn't even roll over.

Oh, replied Cal soothingly. Jist somebody pullin in to have a drink. Not a mornin comes I don't find a dozen bottles thowed out.

The trio assembled around the stove spoke up about how many jugs they'd gone through and how a good drop now would sweeten the tummy.

They watched Toker build the fire, withholding opinion as to the right and wrong of how he went about it, though nudging each other.

When the fire was blazing they embraced the stove with open thighs and palsied hands, crooning their delight and throwing up the odd insult of Calvin who would refuse to light a match even if they were freezing. Then to debate which wood burnt best and how many miles each had chopped in his day, and whether coal won't an invention of Lucifer.

Toker placed the baby down on its stomach on the floor beside the stove. He took off his boots and lay them up next to the fire, along with his wet socks with their blackened heels. He held the baby's wet sack up to the heat, flapping it from time to time, until it began steaming, emitting heavy fumes, and he looked about for a place he could hang it. He pulled up a straight-back chair and sat rocking on the hind legs, embracing the warmth, until his own clothes were steaming. His boots were smoky, giving off a big stink.

That there baby looks nigh to shriveled raspberry, Wallace said. You dipper in the pickle brine?

All three slung themselves over and sighted down at the baby which lay naked and amberish, though relaxed and snoozing.

Did chiggers git at it?

Ticks, maybe. Say you come cross that rascal under laurel bush?

Be a lump of pus, come tomorry. I'd say the cat done hadder.

Roller over, let's see she's hinged.

Sarah pressed up out of her own dour hibernation or vigil and stared at the form for a time in disabled wonder, then said to Toker, It can't git no heat down on that floor, now can it? Heister up a smidgen. She waved an arm toward Cal. Git me that buckboard seat from back there. No, no, bring me that fold-up tray, that'll holder up real fine.

They rigged up the shaky tray before the fire, placing the baby up on it, rolled to the side. The baby squiggled, but didn't wake.

She's worn out, old Hindmarch said. Ye won't git no work out of her today.

Feeler, the woman said. She's icy cold.

Nicest crease ever I saw, Wallace said. Thatern between her legs.

Reckon itterd melt in your mouth, said Trout.

Yessir, she'll break morn one heart, that there one will, Hindmarch added.

The three cackled, going on with it in renewed vigor as the woman rebuked them with a furious shake of her finger.

Cal drifted up. Not morn a day old, he observed. Else she would have hair.

He and the woman found themselves in argument over this.

She's got hair, Toker put in. Little peach fuzz you can see in good light.

Peach fuzz ain't hair, Calvin said.

Toker pitched in more wood. He was feeling back to normal now that he had others to look after the baby.

I must of covered near thirty miles this day, he said. Not

one single durn party got the faintest innerist in adoptin that baby.

Sarah was rummaging back behind the counter, a-chooing from the dust she raised up. She emerged with a glass baby bottle colored swirly blue.

Don't we have no nipples the rats ain't chewed on? she asked Cal.

By me, he said, I see me one nipple in a year I'm happy. I see me two I'd faint dead to the floor.

She went on looking, grumbling to herself as the three old men cackled.

Then they fell silent and went on with their usual timekeeping, their heads sometimes together and sometimes not together, nodding off to crackle the air with their hang-jawed snoring, or mutely staring at the floor, examining hand or kneecap or fly speck upon a wall, occasionally rousing themselves to make inane comment on this or that improprietous calamity, or to issue this or that lame blessing. In Toker's memory so they had always been: ever aged, ever in doleful assembly around Cal's stove, a walled triumvirate of woebegone insignificance—refugees to whom time showed only the most ragged mercy. When he was a boy, their cackles had frightened him, their silences too. Their leathery faces, the soft, wizened skin of their hands, their wrinkled, bland, liquidy eyes into which he could not peer without trembling, without despairing, without feeling that in those eyes was foretold his own grim fate. The earth's inaccessible sorcerers. Custodians of the universe's uneasy future. Each of their faces bearing the same weary stamp. Fatigue in which impunity did not weigh, wrath did not weigh, contriteness did not weigh— only time and its betrayals did. They unnerved him, these old men did, and he felt the same irritations he'd known as a boy, felt them now, as Hindmarch kerflooed his spit into the Louisianne tin—dead-on, despite the meager opening—and tugged his drink crate over, sagged his rear end upon it, and settled a weightless hand on Toker's knee.

A word, son?

Toker's eyes floated away as Hindmarch tightened grip on his knee and for a prolonged minute studied his features.

Did ye give any thought to how thatern hove up? the old man asked. To who it is have birthed her? To where the woman is now and why she done it?

Nawsir, said Toker. Nawsir. I don't know as that aspect of the case is any of my bizness.

Well, I have, said Hindmarch. And I've the feelin we've not heard the last of it. It may be you'll find it's bin made your bizness.

Shoot, said Toker. Shootfire. All I am is the innocent finder.

Hindmarch slipped his crate closer. He leaned in.

All I'm sayin is ye best be wary. It's a hard road, you the good Samaritan who would trek it.

Toker laughed. These old men with their biblical scholarship could always give him a chuckle.

Now don't ye be wrankled, the old man said. The Samaritan on the road, he gits lumps in the journey. That's all I'm sayin. Be wary.

The old man raised his bottom and jiggled his seat back. He lowered himself down and once again huddled the stove.

Sarah, behind the counter, was shoving boxes and bags one way and another, threatening to pitch out all she found into the yard.

This here mess is the way my own life is, she complained. It's my whole future back here, dusty and cobwebbed and mostly rubbish. I once drew a pleasurable breath, but now for my life I can't remember when that was.

Trout piped up.

Ye better watch out, Cal. There's nothin more fearsome than a wronged woman turned vengeful.

Unhuh, amended Wallace. Wronged women, they stalks this planet like a starvin coyote.

Cackle, cackle.

Toker watched the sleeping baby. It had been born dead, he thought, they wouldn't no one of missed her.

He wondered had she been dead would he of got his spade and buried her. The way you would a sparrow tumbled from the nest. You'd heel out a spot, you'd smooth that spot over with earth. You'd hide it away with leaf and twig.

He won't going to think yet about this baby's mama. He won't going to argue the pros and cons. Could be she had good reason.

But, well now. A thief come in the night to slit your throat—you asked him, that thief would say he had good reason.

Trout and Wallace left their seats and spent a minute eyeing the provisions on a dry-goods shelf. Then they started jawing at each other.

Name me the name of one free soul on this earth, the one said.

Judith Iscaret, the other replied. Judith Iscaret done her evil deed, seen by all, the deed of the scapegoat selected for her evil deed by powers on high without her agreement or connivance.

He means Judas, Calvin put in.

Yessir, the one said. Judith Eloise Iscaret selected for her evil deed by powers on high without her agreement or connivance, and therefore innocent as a three-footed messenger. Judith Iscaret, yessir. Hereafter and evermore free to roam this earth in endless and perpetual misery, and all for the one piddly mischief.

What's that? the other said.

Being in the wrong place at the wrong time, said Wallace.

Yip, said Trout. They's truth there.

The two drifted back to the stove, there staring at the flames as if in communion with Judith Iscaret's bedraggled specter.

It ain't the Devil roamin this earth and pilin up her mischief, said Wallace. But Judith Iscaret.

Unhuh, said Hindmarch. Now name us another.

The three cackled.

Toker approached Calvin, asking if he had a spare washcloth he could use to cleanse this baby.

They's this'un I'm holdin, said Cal. He flapped dust from it and passed it over to Toker.

The three old men were now debating the Iscaret issue proper, Hindmarch now the one most vocal.

They's not one free soul on the face of this earth, he said, includin your Judith. We'se all driven to the road taken as woman is to sunbonnet or the bird is to worm. We'se all selected for that road without our agreement or connivance, and there you have it. All our sinful livin sets full at the door of God Almighty, and you and me are blameless as that there smokin baby.

Yip, they all agreed. That's it in the nutshell.

Cackle, cackle.

They bin at it for hours, Calvin told Toker. Like buckshot in a windstorm. My ears have done growed a beard from all the lies I've heard them buzzards tell today.

The baby rolled over to its backside on the skitterish tray, and Toker ran to catch it.

Where you goin? he asked it.

The baby's eyes opened, cloudy with pleasure; she reached her arms up to him.

Then the fingers of both hands shot into her mouth.

The three old men gaggled in and crowded about.

A one-arm man I once knowed, said one, got that way from suckin on his thumb when a infant. Over time, he gnawed that arm right down to stump. Then, fully growed, he started gnawin the othern.

His two cronies wheezed their laughter.

The baby's breathing, so it seemed to Toker, was shallow and raspy. She was ribbed like the chest of a chicken. You would swear each breath was going to be her last.

Could be the little nose needed reaming. But he won't its mama. A nose that little, how could you ream it?

Was the one leg twisty?

The head looked way bigger than the body.

The belly button looked afloat there. Like a fishing cork in water.

It didn't have no eyebrows. The top of the head was a pinkish swirl of blue veins.

Yet the skin was amazing soft up there. No more bone to it than raw egg.

You kept wanting to rub it, hardly believing the perishable nature of that crown. The palm of your hand won't hardly satisfying; you wanted to nudge your cheek up against it. You wanted to nuzzle it, to let your lips graze. To ask yourself how, in this world, a thing come to be so soft. You rubbed it and the softness spilled all inside you, made your own bones crumble.

It was like that Bathroby made him feel; he wanted to scamper inside her, to get down with her where the feeling was all cushiony. To get down there and claim some of that softness for his own self.

That was women for you in general, and Bathroby, now, she held the patent on giving you that feeling.

One look, and you stood like a flagpole.

Toker wondered what it was he felt about this baby. He

hadn't hardly felt nothing this mornin, finding her in the woods. Except surprise, he'd felt that. Consternation, he'd felt that. Okay, he'd gone into a headspin, so he had, but anyone would. But he'd carried it all day and felt nothing, othern how to move it over into another person's keeping. A baby won't a thing you could like or dislike, the way you would for instance a dog. A dog would gnaw on your hand and growl and tug your sleeve and root its nose inside your shoe, or it could hunt, but a baby now, all a baby was was worthless. Worthless and helpless. He could look at her now and feel nothing. Sorrow for her plight, shivers for her future, some little morsel of grief for the waste and folly, but that was all.

Sarah, beside him, nudged his arm.

Landsakes, Toker. You look like you've plummeted down a well. You look plain lovesick.

Calvin threw his two cents in.

That baby won't smile afore it's a week old, he said. And that near the last time, in these parts, they ever will.

Toker, smiling himself now, watched the baby's smile.

That's right, replied Sarah. Run down everthing walkin on two legs.

She sighed deeply, scratching at her throat. She had a mean rash up there, the fingers ever digging.

I never wanted me a child of my own, she said. Lookin at that one now, all white as albino toad, I can see my wisdom.

That's right, called Cal. The human race come to a screechin halt, she had her way about it.

Sarah sighed again. Scratch, scratch. You tied her hands behind her, Calvin often said, and she'd go crazy in a minute. Toker noticed her eyes now roaming dejectedly from shelf to shelf, past the old men, and back down again to the baby. He saw them moisten.

That man, she said, gritting her teeth. I've struck him dead a million times in my sleep. I've used pistols, knives, poisons, horsewhips, and once I run over him nine times in a car. I'd whump him once, then shift to reverse, rev up, and my tires whump him again.

She halted, glancing over at Calvin who had a pencil between his teeth, his brow scowly, pretending he wasn't listening.

It was an old car we used to have, she said. Hadn't run in a coon's age. You can still see it hiked up on its axles up behind our shed. I used to go out and sit in that car when I was young and still could dream. Sit there for hours.

She paused, looking at Toker in a strange, hurt way, then settled a full milk bottle onto the tray.

Was another woman round here I could talk to, she said, I might could endure it better. But there's nothin save riffraff men on my horizon and you can sooner try talkin to a tree stump than a man. How you can stand bein men and go to sleep at night content with yourself is beyond me.

She pressed a scarred plastic baby rattle into Toker's hand, explaining that she'd found it in a box back there.

I dropped a bale of hay on Cal once from a barn loft, she said. For days afterwards I ran around scratchin in my mind, tryin to remember whose barn it was. Then I come to remember it was where I'd growed up. It was my daddy's barn.

She placed a dirty yellow rubber bone down in the baby's hands.

In my next night's dream it was my daddy I dropped the hay bale on.

The baby can play with that, she said. But I'd wash it first. It was some dog's bone Calvin got from somewhere.

She started on out, heading for the back door.

I'd feed that baby, I was you, she said. I'd wash it and that smelly toesack too, and I wouldn't spare either elbow grease or ammonia. You can come back do it in my house, you want to. No, throw away that toesack. I'll see I can't find you somethin decent you can carry that baby in.

She stood in the open doorway, hand smacking her brow, not yet done with him. Toker hadn't never known her to be so talkative before. He hadn't never known her to invite anybody into the house neither.

Calvin was staring at her with open mouth.

If I live long enough, she said, I reckon, I'll kill half the men on this earth. Or my dreams will. She smiled a ragged smile at Toker. Includin you, she said, if for no other reason than you were a perverse child, obnoxious and pouty as a dread scumrat.

She took a quick step out, then whirled back.

I reckon even now it's my dreams keeps me goin. It's my dreams give me faith. Last time, she said, how I did it was a noose round Calvin's neck. I draped that rope over his head my own self, without a thought for how I'd rot in hell. Then I shoved the chair out from beneath him. As the chair toppled over I thought to myself, I ought at least to of give'm a haircut first. His hair all goaty like that, people will talk.

She went on out, slamming the door.

You could hear her for a minute or two, outside rattling on to herself.

Don't ast me, Calvin said, though no one had, and waiting until she was out of earshot. I don't know what gits into her.

They listened in silence to the drone of his drink box cooler.

They's all forlorn, old Trout ventured, his voice sorrowful. They's forlorn as breadcrust in the bread pan. It's a rough furrow to cut, bein a woman.

Hindmarch lay a hand upon the speaker's shoulder, then mildly thumped Trout's back, raising a small wheel of dust.

He then crossed from the stove and went to stand by the front door for several minutes, in abject scrutiny of the terrain before him.

They's opened hell's door this day, he said mournfully.

No one inquired of his meaning.

A while later he pushed open the door and hobbled on through, splashing heedless through the puddled water and heading south down the highway in his stooped and shabby dignity.

There he goes, observed Cal. Another solitary migrant trudgin this earth, for lack of any spot will claim him.

Unhuh, Toker said. They's truth there.

Trout soon followed Hindmarch's exit, steering in the opposite direction, his hands deep in his pockets, his head low on his chest, adroop from his shoulders with invisible burden.

The last old one was dozing on tilted log, arms astretch over his knees, head at deep arch between his legs. Through a slit in the toe of his formless shoes you could see one knobby toe protruding, the nail tea-colored and swoopy, curled over the edge. You could see the shredded cardboard the old man had folded there.

Toker bathed the baby in Sarah's kitchen, in a shallow pan of rusty water on the stove, in light the color of a creek bottom.

The baby watched him do it.

It watched with wide open eyes, turning its face to wherever Toker sailed the cloth, smiling as Toker held the cloth over her belly and squeezed the water drip-by-drip over the rippling flesh.

The cloth soured and the sourness seeped into Toker's hands.

What's your name, baby? he said to the baby. Where'd you come from?

The baby thrashed and looped its back and kicked water into puddles over stove and floor.

It wriggled about and made a face as Toker with wrapped finger tried reaming its nose and ears and cleaning its eyes.

It grabbed at the cloth and tried pulling the cloth and Toker's hand into its pumping mouth.

Strong as a rodent.

Little stub of a nose small as the tip of a finger.

Feet a thimble would fit over.

It giggled and gooed as Toker lifted the two legs in one hand and soaped its bottom. As he spread its legs and tentatively, bashfully, opened its crevice and washed there.

Oops now, let me clear them leafy twigs out.

The baby liked it.

You could maybe see some personality in a baby, you let your mind bend that way.

Wait now, don't want to leave no soap up that trench.

The baby spread its legs, fully agreeable, it seemed, to Toker's probing.

A whimsical bit of a thing was a baby, mostly just belly and head and thrashing limbs.

Seemed it could change color quick as a lizard. You run the cloth here, you run it there, and the skin changed like light thue a prism.

He'd washed Princessanne once or twice when she was little, though not so weensy as this. Washed her out of a galvanized pail with lye soap and a scouring brush.

They'd picked lice out of each other's hair, him and his sister had.

The baby's bites were puckered now, though none festering. Reddish bumps toe to heel.

That head all catty-cornered from the birthing, he guessed. We'll grow you a real head, he said, your luck holds out.

It had a trick it kept doing with its stomach. The stomach would puff up, then deflate, and the baby goo and giggle and fling its arms.

No more showin off, he said. I'm done with you now.

Sarah had left out a pink towel on a wall peg by the stove.

He lifted up the baby, rolled the baby within the towel, slung the bound baby up across his shoulder. The round bottom seemed molded for the fit of a hand. He paced with it for a spell.

You're warm and clean, he said. Your own mama wouldn't recognize you.

Sarah had put out a can of talcum by the stove.

He sprinkled powder over the baby's flesh, and saw the baby jiggle its arms and make as to capture handfuls of whirling dust.

The baby laughed. It whooped out great volleys of mirth, and all the time it seemed to Toker that the baby was maintaining a steady watch on him. It seemed to Toker that the baby's big I-don't-want-to-miss-nothing eyes never once left his face.

It watched him the way you'd watch something magical; the way you'd watch something so extraordinary you mightn't couldn't believe it was happening, or imagine what next might transpire.

Your first bath, he said. It ain't that special, let me tell you.

Sarah stayed locked away, or near locked away, in the next room. She stayed silent. The door was cankered, wouldn't entirely close. Through the crack he could see the foot of a bed, and see her feet, still clad in her ragged mules, up on that bed. She had a box wedged up under her legs, a pillow up on that box, and her legs elevated up over that. For the circulation, he guessed. She had swollen ankles, he'd long ago noticed that.

But she won't sickly, in the normal run. Maybe today was her special day: worn out, maybe, by all the killing she'd done.

The light in there was the same creekwater color the kitchen was. He could see a knickknack nailed to the wall beside the bed. A weavy, black object not immediately identifiable, and he looked closer. Some homemade thing. A phonograph record, looked like. Heated, and while heated, fluted about to the shape of a bowl. What folks wouldn't dream up next. She had herself dried flowers, or straw, taped up where label would be.

He moved and saw white lacy cloth spread over a sewing machine upright on metal legs. He'd always liked those. He wondered she didn't sew up the hem, sew up the pocket, on that tatty robe she had on.

A pitcher sat in a bowl on the sewing machine. The long face of a horse, stamped onto the pitcher, looked back at him. A colorful wreath of flowers encircled the horse's neck, and he could see a word printed beneath the wreath in horseshoe lettering, with a horseshoe's shape, though not make out what that word was.

Some souvenir of a place they'd been, most likely, though if Sarah and Calvin had ever stepped two feet away from this valley it was news to him.

He turned to leave. If Sarah was sleeping, as she might be, if she was having them dreams, as she might be, he didn't want to wake her.

I ought to clean up my mess, he thought, but I've got an itch to git out of here.

So gloomy it was. Bad in its own way as his own pit in the earth.

But she'd left out something else. On the same peg where the washcloth and the towel had been. A white clothy thing. A pillowcase.

Well, he wondered, am I to wrap the baby up in this, or use it to hauler the way I did in that toesack?

He planted the baby's feet down and pulled up the pillowcase over her, scrunching the top around the baby's chin.

You a loose goose now, he said.

You a real hepcat.

He stepped outside, pausing on the concrete slab at the front of the door to draw deep breaths.

Sarah and Calvin's house won't what you hardly could call a real house. The rooms more like sheds you'd slide together. Pretty flimsy quarters.

Funny thing. He'd growed up thinking them close to rich as oil merchants. It was what his daddy, who hadn't got along with anyone, said.

But his daddy was like to run everybody down.

He see Jesus on the road he'd bite his nose.

But he was the good'un; Mama was worse.

The two hedge bushes Sarah had put in by the door were leaning. They hadn't never bloomed. The Co-Cola clock up above the door was cobwebbed. The clock was working though, or the minute hand was. The hour hand was drooped down on six o'clock, what you could see of that six above the bed of dead flies.

He gave a hello sign to the barking dogs, and jumped the puddles back into the store. The baby felt lighter now, washed, and in this white sack.

How's Sarah? Cal asked him the minute he came in.

Poorly, I'd say.

Don't mind her bellyaches. We've had us a good union.

Unhuh.

You ought to git hitched yourself. Keep you broke and lame, but out of trouble.

So they say.

I had this store, had it from my daddy, you never known him. And she was barefoot and had nothin. Did you know that?

Nawsir.

Childhood sweethearts, we were. And still are, it comes to that. Romance, it will pickle the air.

Yip.

And sweeten the load. A smile lit up Calvin's face. He winked and nudged an elbow into Toker's ribs. Oh. Was a woman was by.

Was?

Good-lookin too. Pretty as a split-rail fence. I got the feelin she knowed you. He was grinning broadly.

How come?

She asked had I seen a scoundrel haulin round a baby in a toesack. You the only one I could think of was.

Toker hurried to the door.

Too late now, Cal said. She's come and gone. On a horse.

Toker scurried out to the road, looking both ways, but the road was empty.

What'd she want? he asked Cal, entering again. Horse, you said?

Unhuh. In them high heels. What she wanted was cheese. I got the idea she was expectin company.

Damn, said Toker. And me washin this baby.

Yip. Wantin cheese. Didn't want no dry cheese, no maggoty cheese, no chicken-flavored cheese or goat cheese. Wanted blue cheese. I tolder cheese didn't come blue lessern it be moldy, and you ought to heard her rake me upside-down.

What was she wearin? Not that robe.

I didn't notice. It won't much of it though, I noticed that. Them stilts she had on most took my breath away. Hair like she'd been wrestlin a bobcat. You and her friends? I guess she's back to claim her old birthplace. I guess you never knowed the awful mess went on up there.

What mess?

Oh, a long time ago. Best forgotten now. Heck, I never even knowed you knowder.

Toker didn't reply. He had a smile on though, trying his best to keep that smile inside. So she was here buying him cheese. Planning a party.

The place smelt of her perfume, now he'd taken wind of it.

He felt like skipping.

I done made an impression on her, he thought. I done got my foot in.

Over the next little while the store had an unusual flurry of customers. The Sprockett woman came by and toured about through Calvin's cloth and apparel section. She wanted a print pattern, she said, fingering the bolts, complaining about the poor light back in that corner. I can't wear solids, she said.

Where's Sarah? she asked. She sees me comin, I know she swoops straight out that back door. No, don't deny it.

No, she told Toker, her hands at fly over her head. No, she won't diddly-squat innerstid in another baby. She'd sooner have her head cut off, she said. If her man came near her one more time she'd flee like a rabbit out of the door. She'd pop a gasket, he tried puttin his hands on her.

Procreation, she said, that's what's doing us all in. And you know yourself that's not what the good Lord meant when he said, Go forth ye and multiply.

She left, buying only a loaf of white bread and a spool of colored thread, counting out her change reluctantly from a deep black purse, and complaining as how she'd thought the rain a while ago never would quit.

I've got toads in my yard, she said to them, departing. They'll hop right inside my kitchen and sit at the table, I don't keep my door latched.

Yes'm, they said. Yes'm. We'll see you now. Nice visitin with you.

Come again.

Someone else was by, wanting a gallon of kerosene, if his credit was good.

A boy with stick legs and a drawn, spent face, a runny nose he wiped on his sleeve, edged inside and for some minutes examined with hostile lethargy the storekeeper's candy rack. A scab festered on his chin, his ears steering wide from his cropped head, those ears raw and stretched where his parents—as Toker recalled his own had—over the years had yanked and tugged.

Where your jawbreakers? the boy finally asked Calvin, his voice a whine thin with malice and his eyes scrappy.

The jawbreakers? Calvin said. Why only last week I chawed the last one myself.

The boy stared at Cal's sty-plagued eyes, his lips curling.

Where's your Wagon Wheels? he asked.

They's there, Calvin said, his voice rising.

Ain't, the boy said. Where's your Mary Janes?

Well, they's in the Mary Jane box, ain't they? Calvin said, clearly wanting done with him.

The boy picked at his scab, rooted a one-cent piece from his pocket, picked up a Mary Jane candy, and bolted on out.

Toker crossed up and shut the flapping door.

Won't that a Looper? he said. One of them Looper boys?

You can forgit them Loopers, Calvin said. Them Loopers already got more youngans than they can count.

How about the Tiddies? They seem a decent kind. Maybe the Tiddies could use a extra hand.

The Tiddies is movin. They's oil lease done run out.

The baby belched. It was down on the tray, a foot up in its mouth.

Cut me a nibble of that cheese, Toker said. Let me see this here baby has a taste for cheese.

A man in a rattly, dirt-splattered black car, hunched low under the wheel and smoking a bent, wrinkled cigarette, drove up by the gas pump and choogered his horn.

The car shuddered there, clucking low on its springs as a setting hen.

He done drove that contraption to earth, Calvin observed. You'd think a honest citizen would take better care of his transport.

The man removed his nubbed smoke, and spat. Then with a grimace reamed a finger inside his mouth.

Look at it hop. That car, said Cal. You'd swear it was a livin thing didn't like its passenger any morn us.

They saw him shift up from his seating hole under the wheel and look, wait and look, with scowling dead-shot eyes, getting impatient and finally choogering his horn again.

He's a snake-faced hombre, said Cal. You'd think he'd know to draw that ethyl his own self.

The man dismounted his vehicle and stood to the car's far side, only his head above it like a floating masticated ruin up from the deep. He had lopsided face, one cheek swollen red, his other darkened with several days growth of beard, though still ashen somehow. He rounded his fender with bent caution. A string of spittle hung thin as spider's thread from his lip to his shoes in that second before he fingered it free. He retreated and slipped a hand through the window and rapped his horn time and again.

Calvin at last moved. You'd think I was slave to the public's every whim, he said.

Toker hauled up the baby and drifted out behind him, curious to check the license plate and determine what origins could so bless a man.

Toothache? he heard Calvin say.

The man only flared his nostrils at him.

You come far? Calvin asked.

The man didn't reply to this either. His black suit, snagged and wrinkled and thin in spots, was covered with dirt and ash. The car plate told Toker nothing, the numbers caked with mud. In mild upheaval down in the backseat foot space resided a few rusting pots and pans and the wicker seat, the slatted backside of a broken chair, various stobs and iron works, and other such miscellany all tied by ropes one to the other. Interlaced within these provisions the few odd, decomposing articles of wear.

Looks like you've about set up housekeepin in that car, Toker said.

The man spun to lacerate him as though under visceral obligation to perform such a task. But his eyes floated on down to the baby and in that instant his hands whipped out of his pockets, his eyes sliced all but shut. He licked his lips, studying on the baby for prolonged seconds before whisking his eyes again up to Toker's face.

Yourn? he asked.

He thumbed his cigarette nub over into a puddle, and snickered softly. Makes me right mushy, he said.

His teeth, Toker noted, were lightly furred, and low in his gums, as though filed.

To see a baby, that is. They's so precious. What's thatern's name?

Toker expelled a long breath, and said nothing.

The gas gurgled and burped up in Calvin's glass tank and the storekeeper jiggled his line.

Pesky rascal, he said. This hose. I'd venture you've come many a mile, this here vehicle draggin so low. You goin far?

The man jerked his head about. The sockets about his eyes seemed to have brightened, almost as if cut there.

I ain't ast you your life story, storekeep, the man said. So you can pass up any curiosity you have in mine.

Calvin hung his hose.

No need to get bristly, he answered. Me and Toker here jist passin the time.

They both stood a minute in bleak regard of the smeared giblets of insects blackening the car's windshield.

Ye can wash that glass, I'd appreciate it, the man said.

Calvin laughed. Lord, he said, washin that windshield would take me thue till Monday. I'd sooner dip my hand in a one-seater.

The stranger grabbed the windshield blade and angrily smote it twice across the screen, before the wiper ripped loose in his hand.

A string of creative invective tore from the driver's mouth.

That's how it always is, laughed Calvin. A man jist can't leave well enough alone.

Toker drifted on over to the car door, feeling the man's gaze peel off and follow his backside.

Git me anothern, the man said. From your stock in there.

Calvin lifted his foot up on the front bumper.

I don't have a one, he said. I've fresh give out.

The stranger looked dumbfounded at him, then off the same way at a distant pole.

But you keep to this road another eighty mile, eighty to ninety, and you might can find blades. You might can.

The man opened his car door and sat on the seat rim, stooped over, both his feet out on the ground. He cupped a flared match in his two hands, lit another of his butts, and puffed a ring of smoke out over his shoes, then lifted his eyes in baleful stare at the infinite universe.

I don't git me new blades, he said, I'm having to git me a new car. One or the other, blades or new car.

That right? replied Calvin. It comes to them is able and can afford it. Me, I can't even afford shoe-leather.

The man alighted again.

You got brakin fluid?

Nope, I'm fresh run out.

Well, what do ye have then, carwise? Do ye have anti-freeze? I won't expectin such a cold spell as I've run into.

Nawsir. My shipment of coolant is held up. But ye could git yourself it a piece down that road.

The man stood for a moment in grave indecision, as did Calvin, as if between the two of them was to be weighed their sore knowledge that the world's supply of all that was valuable had finally run out.

You got a pump? he asked. Tire pump? You can see there I'm ridin low.

Calvin shook his head. Nope. I'm fair give out of pumps. I bin run ragged tryin to keep in stock everthingamabob folks might want, but here comes another one ever time I look up, askin for somethin I never heard of.

The stranger hoisted up his trousers and worked his tongue

over his front teeth and spat. Ye never heard of tire pumps?

Oh, tire pumps now, I'm fresh out.

Calvin was drooped down on one knee, peering under the car. You done seem to have picked up a bush, he said. He unstuck a long, crushed limb and yanked it forth.

The driver snatched it away, yanked open the rear door, and flung the bush onto his backseat. Then he spun back, darting a glance at Calvin so dire of intention the storekeeper flinched in surprise.

I reckon you gone tell me you not got no smokes either.

I don't have the habit myself. Though I might could root up a pack.

Do it then. Camels, goddamn ye.

Calvin went inside, leaving Toker and the man outside warily examining each other and the landscape. In a minute the stranger ventured over, on his face the dreary pretense of a smile.

I'm begging yourn and that child's pardon, he said. For my short fuse. Profanity oughten be the words a child to hear. But I bin motorin all night, east to west, doin my bizness, and now I'm tuckered down to thumb and have this here mean toothache.

Oh, it's a killer, Toker agreed. A toothache.

Pretty youngster, the traveler said.

He made to touch her, but Toker whipped back.

God's breath. That's what they are.

The man was looking owlishly up at him. His slagheap eyes telling him he could deny it if he would.

Precious as honey in a bee's hive.

A sour reek clung to the air about them, Toker wondering would this chatterer never leave, and why it was he felt such discord standing with him.

He felt a sharp tug at his sleeve.

I've got one myself. Yessir, I'm a dingdong daddy of the mountains and slaphappy proud, same as you.

The man sang this out sweet as a ditty, though Toker saw his lips hang in a sneer. Their eyes wavered up over each other in the making of what Toker construed to be some kind of unformed testing his visitor seemed disinclined to resist. In a side-glance each saw the other's fist squeeze.

That tug at his sleeve again.

Me and the little mother both, the man said. On account of we had tried and tried. You see. Yessir. And she could tell you, she was here, the minute our egg joined. I put it inner that day, her sittin out on our porch stuffin crackers inner mouth from a red box. Yessir. I did. We knowed we'd done it, coupled our egg. I knowed it from how her face lit up. But when I put my tool in, you ought to of seen the cracker dust fly.

Toker pressed a hand to the man's chest and pushed him away. Then he relaxed, seein the bastard was half-crazed.

You gone tell us that life story after all, he said.

The man's eyes crossed. He spat another of his wads into the dirt.

Calvin appeared with the cigarettes and gave change to the payment.

The man got into his ratty car, thumped out a new smoke, and sat a while, a disfigurement in the blue haze of his jouncing car. Watching the three of them. Next to bounce slowly over the ruts and scuttle on off, his automobile firing small explosions of wrath, the tail pipe dragging.

The baby coughed.

Hold on now, Toker said. This here jasper is gittin ready to talk.

But the baby was chewing on the white pillowcase, its eyes bright, both hands up to its mouth like munching coon or squirrel.

The flurry was over. That little rush, Cal said, it happens ever time I'm thinkin I can catch a wee rest. But I can't complain, I reckon, as it's my bread and butter. He was a spooky one, that one, won't he?

Unhuh. He'd of stuck knife in both of us, or all three, we turned our back on him.

They Lord knows it.

Well, he's shot off to hell now. We won't see his likeness again.

Oh look ye. Look ye there at your caretaker. Tremble ye at the caretaker and beg for his mercy.

Truman on the road stroked his swollen jaw, a careful brushing of fingertips to cheek, feeling the heat throb against his palm. He gave a grudging look to his face in the mirror and snickered. Tremble ye, he said. Oh tremble, for that cheek is red-hot as a devil's lantern. His nose felt knackered, lopsided, his lips too. Ye ain't never known pain, he said aloud to his haunts, lessern you've known toothache. Do you have toothache? Do ye have spare blade? Do ye have tire pump or coolant and can ye bake me cherry pie? His eyes narrowed, squinting up the road that stretched before him. How are ye? he said. How are ye, and would ye set an extra plate for Truman at your table? Would ye let the night candle burn in your window?

Daylight was harsh, daylight was an affliction.

He never had known no comfort in daylight, and wished now the storm clouds would again blow over. Blow in, douse the night candle, let a good man prop his legs under your table. Oh yes, how are ye, and do ye tremble?

He felt jittery, though he couldn't reason why. And looking for reason was asking for trouble.

He rolled down his window a mite and spat, and saw his spittle cling to the glass and slide down like a slug till the breeze snatched it clear. He sucked up a glob adhering to his lower lip, and flubbed that out into the alien world.

There ye go. Go with my blessins.

There's but the two known geographical abodes, he thought. Hell is the one, and hell on earth the other.

His foot a second later stomped the brake. The car bolted up on its rear axle, slewed about, throwing him forward against the wheel.

He sat in the idling car, hard onto the road, rubbing his chest, pondering his next move.

Now that fresh-face back yonder, holdin that baby. Could be that fresh-face is knowin somethin I ought to should know.

He bent and scratched at his ankle—it swollen too. Something had bit him there, some bug or spider, most likely, and he wished he could place when. But the Lordgod took all forms and shapes, and could be it was the Lordgod hisself in all his glory lancing fang into his ankle bone.

With some irritation he studied his hands on the wheel. Yes, he was skinned up some. His foot on the gas pedal and his othern lying along the brake hadn't yet thawed after cold night. He hadn't never been warm, it seemed to him. But you weren't put in this world to go perfumed and lily-white as a maiden in clover. Now were ye?

He pulled the car over to the roadside, it noisy of its springs, the tail pipe clanging, the engine sputtering with the off-chance disruption. One front tire had a wobble—it won't going to last long.

He alighted from the vehicle, thinking, Now thatern with the baby, was a newborn thatern was, and is it hisn or mine is the question I'd ask you. He swooped over, his back against the surly wind, hands cupped in the lighting of his cigarette. A fresh Camel, and there in the beast's hump the full bedlam, riding the earth on cloven hoof.

If she's mine then that fresh-face won't a dog-lap away from my leavins.

He snuckered in the tangy smoke, wondering in that moment hadn't the Lord bin a smoker. If the Lord won't hisself victim to the habit. Oh yes, he thought, you could see him, the Lord, you looked hard enough. Crouched by the roadside with his woman's hair, draggin on his smoke.

He wondered hadn't the Lord stood by inhaling his weed, relaxing his mind, relishing the state of his affairs, after finishing up another of his miracles.

He closed his eyes now he could all but see the Lord, looking pleased with hisself, enjoying hisself, watching the rabble chomp into the loaves of white bread he'd divided from the one.

The rabble complainin one minute, feastin the next. Miracle or not, the next time belly rubbed backbone they'd be snipin complaints all the faster.

He could see the Lord waving to him.

Come on over, the Lord said. Let's you and me git to know each other. Light up. Me and you's done earned our minute's restjob.

He wondered it won't toothache, or for want of the weed, made his Lord moan and cry out up there on the cross between the four sunken eyes of two rat-hole men.

From his pocket Truman took out a length of dusty fishing line and got it uncoiled. He gave it a pull and it took his weight without snapping.

Now tie that toothpull off. Tie it or kiss my ass. He reamed a finger about inside his mouth, testing one tooth against an-

other. Trouble was they all ached, his gums swollenish and
festery. Tie off the line, pull whichever one out. The ache was
now up inside his head, his jawbone near to popping. So hard
to git that hand inside the mouth. To tie off a throbbing tooth.
But I'll git you, bastard, he told the tooth. No need thinkin
you can escape.

He remembered with dull loathing a time long before he'd
seen God on the road or was come of age, when in his dreams
of nights there'd been a little pygmy-type man crouched in the
dark barn loft, and anothern up beside him furry as a monkey,
the two of them picking mites from the other's hide and
crunching them between they's teeth. God the Father and God
the Son looking after each other as vaguely they weighed
they's handiwork: him scrunched up on hard floor under toe-
sacks, trembling with cold.

He tested the line and his knot held. He tied the other end
to the open car door, then backed up so that he stood above
the gully, the line taut. Without thinking further about it he
lifted his leg and kicked shut the car door hard as he could.

The next second he was slipping in mud, upended, cursing, sprawling on all fours into the rank ditch.

Tooth hadn't cracked off beneath his gums, thank God.

He moved his tongue slowly over the vacated spot.

He spat blood, then dropped to his knees and rooted in the
leafy dirt.

Let's see you, you slack-eyed, four-toed sonofabitch.

There you are.

He wiped the tooth against his pants and dropped it into his
coat pocket.

He spat blood again and slid back inside the car.

Now where'd I put me my durn smoke?

I done stopped here by the road a minute ago, but why?

That baby. Funny, Brightface to carry it in a white pillow-case.

Women could cry out too, and moan for they's plight on this earth—the way thatern last night had—without never obser-vin they's all males crucified and toothachey on Golgotha cross.

Still, he could see some point to a female's tirade, loath though he was to hear it. It was women had made that last supper, had slaved and slavered at it, baking bread, cleaning and cooking fish, mopping the table and laying out the plates. You could lay a dollar that Matthew-Simon-Jude tribe hadn't had a hand in it. So the women had a right to quibble when they were sent to while away the hour in olive field while that other party supped and sipped and awaited the news.

Afore the evenin is done shall one of ye betray me.

I do, Truman said. I do, do, do, he said, and laughed at the sound of his own voice as his fingers slapped out disjointed rhythm on the dash.

I have driven the serpent from my jawbone and come afresh as a gravedigger's white dove to your divine light.

Me and that mink, he said.

He drove on, tunelessly slapping the wheel, his mind crawling backwards *to that time of the mink, when she* . . . come up out of swampy riverbed, and I grabbed holt of her leg and tugged, her skin slidin off ragged and slimy, no morn squatches in my hand, it that old and rotted so long under-water. And, phew the smell! Though I kept on grabbin slimy new holt, tug, tug, and the skin in that one jiffy flyin loose of its frame, flyin up tailbone to headbone, and me flyin back with it kersplash into water over my head, my feet churnin to reach muddy bottom and hollerin won't someone come to save a drownin boy, hep, hep! Though faint the hope there. There,

I say, there, Truman, after a minute. There, now ye can stand up. And I stand up in the current, holdin loose, flimsy-furred skin, it fallin apart like wipin paper, it that smelly and rotted, and me tryin to decide what thing's skeleton bones it is I have holt of in the other hand. Because I have helt onto both parts, you see, in my kersplashin—to the skin in one hand, skull, spine, and limbs in the other, which I chunk to shore.

Me then with a wary searchin eye up and down the glade for who might be spyin, for wicked is the presence about the land, I've bin tole that. I've bin tole that, I've often enough had that drummed into my ears. But I'm safe for the minute, them two guardians got not the least concern for where I am.

Now, where was I? That stink, oh yes, that stink so bad I nearly set down and cried, I won't say I didn't, that hide and hair all dissolvin, flakin away, though I'm still pullin, I've got a new holt now, because there's still more to tug up from that muddy bottom. Let go, goddamn ye, I say. Let go! I done founder, ain't I, fair and square? So I keep yankin and hollerin. Then finally up comes the claw mouth and her with the other limb trapped up to thigh in this iron-jaw leg-holt trap. I wanted me that trap, wanted it bad enough it was a taste in my mouth, so I waded ashore and got me a stick and I pried, I pried, but the stick broke, that durn trap's all rusty corroded, thick with river bottom's sludge and scum. So then I drag up big rocks and gradually I inch the jaws open. I git me my fur laid out, and my skeleton bones, and I study my catch. I study the fur and skin pieces aloose in the water. Mink, that's what she is. Not a shred of meat on her, she's that putrid, but she's mink.

Dear God, I say to myself. Dear God, I've done snared me a mink.

Dear God, Truman. This here is mink.

I take my mink home and I oil me that trap and hide it in

the wagon shed and sleep that last night under my orphan wraps in the barn, my old uncle guardian-man in the front room dyin and his old sister back there in her kitchen rockin chair singin the roll call. Oh, when the roll is called up yonder, when it's called up yonder I'll be there. Like heckfire she will, I'm thinkin, that smoke-eyed, skinflint old woman, no kin of mine either one. I'm seein me out in the world in my lonesome, my trap jaws open. And I can catch me a mink jist like whoever it was caught that mink the first time then never could find it, that mink draggin the trap thue however many miles of river bottom till somethin snags it and the mink stays snagged. Till she falls under my jurisdiction, oh yes. And that night I sneak up to the old man's window, I say, Uncle? Uncle? You in there, Uncle? Uncle, it's me. So I pull that old man out of his sleep. Uncle, I say, what's good bait for mink? But he's raspin ever minute, he don't answer quick she'll be runnin so I crawl half over the sill. I yank at the collar of his longjohns, him smellin of pee, but I tug and tug at that old man. I say, We know you dyin I know it you jist answer you better answer me goddamn ye to hell now tell me I'm askin you fair and straight one last time: What's good bait for mink? What can I bait my new trap with? He's raspin, suckin air, he's tryin to git it or somethin out afore he croaks, the both of us tuggin, him almost yankin me up over sill on that cot atop of him, his eyes poppin, his voice raspin. You better tell me, Uncle, I say, but he jist goes on raspin, makin these dry chokin sounds, by this while all the covers pulled off of him, his bare naked ugly legs knife-blade thin and what I see most amazin is this pile of gnawed chicken bones he's bin hidin under his covers, these bones heaped up on his mattress, these yellow pee stains all around him in yellow circles, and him bolty of spine, raspin like he was suckin stones, a trickle of blood from his nose and them rasps now faster, this gurglin in his thoat like water down a pipe, on the verge of tellin me what bait I can employ. When I hear a scamperin behind the wall, her yellin Lube? Lube, you callin me? Lube? You want me, Lube? Hold on! And then her feet flyin, me droppin down and stealin away.

He ought to of tole me. He ought not to kept it to hisself, that old man.

A few minutes further on up the road Truman's soreness returned. The ache, the throb.

You sorry sonofabitch, he said.

He went on cursing the tooth, his eyes screwed all but shut, for that while he would motor on. Blood trickled at the corner of his mouth; he wiped with a finger and sucked it back.

He seen Jesus jist now, standin by the roadside, his thumb hitched out, Truman would give him a finger and shoot on past.

Hey George, hey Martha! Git down now! Git! I say git! Oh you dogs!

The two dogs, though but pups, were of distinguished character, George lean and long and rarely moody, Martha blondish and brisk in her movements, the both of them smilish. Smilish, and mostly pure, pure to hear Calvin tell it. Your prime travel agency dogs, your number-one, fit-as-fiddle, tracking dogs, ready to leap off the minute they sniffed open gate or could claw tunnel under cyclone fence. Oh, the best dogs on these mountains. But on edge now, near neurotic now, because he, Cal, never could break loose of the store to give them their running nose.

Won't the wife spell you?

Not lessern I've got both legs broke. Not lessern I've got bubonic plague.

Martha streaked along the fence, nose skimming the ground. George nearby, doing the same. Alert, zippity rascals, scenting freedom now.

Cal dropped down their feed into a bowl and they romped to it and him, near lapping up both bowl and Cal, jumping up on him with all eight feet, yodeling as they nipped and crooned at his ears.

Hey George, hey Martha! Git! Git! Oh dammit to hell!

They drove him, stumbling and squalling, through the fence gate which he clapped shut with a bang, and he hung there grinning at Toker, disheveled in his every part and breathing hard.

They's dynamite dogs, he said. Brimmin over with love, and if they don't soon git their run I will have to shoot'um.

The dogs slavered at the gate, whimpering and whining, hiking pathetic nose or quivering rear end Toker's way, in appeal of the friendlier hand who would show them freedom.

Toker was thinking. I bet I could use them dogs. I could shove baby up under their snouts. With them dogs taken to laurel bush, I bet we could track that baby's mama. I bet these go-getters could lead me right up to that poor woman's front door.

Though hard rain might have shot hell out of that theory.

The dogs moaned and slobbered their distress, chewing the cyclone fence, as Toker and Cal, their shoulders touching, ventured back toward the store.

Toker told him his idea.

Unhuh, said Cal. I was wonderin that same thing myself. Worth a try. How much might you pay?

They fixed a price, twenty-five cents each dog, by the day.

But I was you, Cal said, I'd turn that two-bit over to the orphanage home yonder in Plottsburg. Let them knockabouts haver.

I been mullin that point over, Toker said. But I'm not keen to be trudgin two days and back, to that hellhole.

You could hike a day up to Hoop Mountain. They's a telephone there.

I'm done hikin up Hoop Mountain, Toker said.

You a choosy rapscallion, said Cal. Right curious to me. I never known no fatherly instincts to be yourn afore.

Me neither.

Though I know you liked that sister. Otherwise, you was always hell-for-leather.

Unhuh.

A draggy-mouth boy.

Unhuh.

Specially since your kin perished and skedaddled. You don't mind me sayin?

Nope. Not a hangin hell.

Once inside the store Cal fumbled about inside his meat unit and emerged with limp bacon slices folded over his fingers. He gnawed these down to rind and sucked at the grease on his fingers.

You and that baby don't want none? he asked.

Toker shook his head.

You won't be needin no lead, Calvin said. Them dogs will follow hindmost deacon into drabbest habitat.

They stood together a minute by the front door, gauging the sky as though beholding a sorcerer's grubstake.

The air held a light, fresh scent.

Addy-ose then, Calvin said.

Addy-ose.

You go on, Cal said. I'll go un-pen them dogs. They won't have no trouble findin you, they git ready.

Toker and the baby struck off.

🦅

A ring of floating black gnats hung about Toker and the baby's face for a duration, oblivious to his swats, then they swung on off.

Trees here were crippled and struggling, consumed by moss and vines and riddled with webby cocoons huge and silvery in the high boughs.

His shoes were stiff, though still soggy, and rubbing at his raw heels.

The baby rode cradled in his arms now, a soft, bagged lump with stupefied eyes.

Sleep on, Toker said to her. We'll be home briefly. Then my scoutin with George and Martha, and I'm off to nibble cheese with that firecracker Bathroby.

He'd carried Princessanne this way, her a baby like this'un, and him pushing his teens.

Yes, you grew up lost and lonely when a child and that loneliness stamped you, it stayed with you all your born years, makin you weighty and miserable in your outlook as them diseased trees.

All in all, though, she was a sprightly hellion, sister was.

The thing is, baby, he said, you heard the story of your own self tole the way our mama and daddy ever day tole it to us, and the wonder is you'd ever even bother to stand up.

The dogs, first playful at his heels and between his legs, then shot off and disappeared in the woods. Now and then he could see hazy streaks, their darting phantom shapes midst the distant, rising brush.

They weren't barking yet, he noticed, a good sign that they knew their business and were reserving their enthusiasm for the genuine item.

He saw them come out a good quarter mile up the road, by the Frog Eye's turnoff, weighing and debating his coming, then to streak away again.

Jist feelin out their freedom, he said. That's all George and Martha are doin. I'd do the same, I had the sense a dog has.

I got your milk bottle in my pocket, he told the baby. You gone think you bin hit between the eyes.

Here's our lane.

Where Raymond Toker did his housekeeping was in a burnt-out spot high on the Goose Neck range, though to find it you'd have to know Goose from Neck and that a burnt-out site was the place you were looking for. The lane that went on by the Toker burn to one other dwelling a mile further along had been fit for a car as late as last year. This year, to his knowledge, car had yet to try it, nor mule and wagon neither. Old Man Dealer, whose place it was further on, had owned a truck, but the truck gave out. Then Dealer gave out. His shack up there was now abandoned, and likely to remain that way, since it resembled nothing a human being, except those most desperate, might choose to inhabit. Built of sawmill shavings, of tin road signs, and forest salvage, together with whatever else he could plunder, the shack was all but fallen now, which was the way Old Man Dealer, when he had been saying anything, had said he liked it. When Dealer died, or at a point soon after, his head had been found in one space, his body in another. Such, anyway, was the talk, and how, some hours after the discovery—so the talkers insisted—he had been buried. The speculation was that he had dug himself two graves, stood in one, hacked off his head, and somehow in his death agonies flung that head downhill to his second grave. It was the downhill part that people nodded to, for in digging his two graves that way, so that with just a nudge, just by falling, his head would roll on down into the grave intended for it, Dealer was establishing his natural affinity with the mountains and its raw elements.

The place was haunted now by these two deformities, another reason home-hunters, Toker included, looked elsewhere for their happiness.

Toker's own abode was worse. Most days burnout was what you mainly smelt. Electricity didn't reach this far. There was water in the winter and too much of it; in summer the well was dry and the river, a short distance off, but a trickle. There was a near spring—springs, in fact, were all over, which was why, ages ago, the cabin had gone up where it had—but the spring flow at its main source was erratic, and the others mud-colored. The water had a faint stench to it. It had a puerile flavor you had to get used to. Mild exhortations, belches, down in the earth's crust, most said, was the explanation. It was Lucifer down there with hobnailed boots, smoking his cigar. It was Lucifer, pacing. Lucifer had slippery shoes, nighttime slippers he put on, and sometimes he flopped over. This, most said, made your water run foul. It was this that made springs, even lake beds and rivers, dry up or suddenly alter their courses. Look what had happened with that man Frog Eye's old camp. The man dredges, he builds roads, he builds floating docks, he constructs a guest home straight out of a Switzerland magazine, and what happens? Frog Eye wakes one morning, strolls down to throw in a line, and the river isn't there anymore. The river has struck off in another direction. Frog Eye has lost his millions.

It was true one heard of dark nights, and Toker more than most, the odd rumble or quiver. The odd rattle of window. He could stride out of a morning and come across sunken ravine where last week had stretched flat field. He could see trees toppled that had stood a hundred years.

There was something in Toker that relished all this. Here along these nethery miles, up and down these undulating hills, he could bear witness to the world as garden, as garden and stinkpot both, and this had appeal to him.

Days, this past year, he'd climbed the summits and from those heights looked out upon the rivers and valleys, grim in his features as a vulture upon a road wire.

It beat him how you could so much hate what you'd been born to, and so much love it because you had nothing else. He hadn't done anything with his life. He put footstep down, and then another, and knew with each breath his steps led nowhere. Scumwater filled his imprint even as he lifted bleak heel.

One day, though, he thought he might come to open field.

He might would.

Bathroby, for all her acute nakedness, her nipples against wire, seemed to of had.

And this baby, orphaned to dark night, hadn't once issued offended howl.

Sonofabitch.

He'd stood up on the lane's shoulder, on a mound of smoking earth where tree had baroomed down, saying that under his breath. Not believing his eyes.

I be dog.

It was Calvin later that day who had told him about Princessanne's death, about his dogs, his mama's flight.

Now, Toker, you'd best set down.

You'd best hold on.

Princessanne, now. It was the smoke done her in. Smoke is a terrible thing. Terrible, and the mind best not ponder it. You know? But with your flesh sizzlin, maybe smoke is a blessin. Best to look on it that way.

Or maybe she was sleepin and never known what hitter.

We couldn't finder body. Ol' Hindmarch, he poked about in them ashes the whole next day.

You know how it is with these fires.

Oh Toker, son, it was a bitch to behold.

A few bones, that's the gist of the matter. Only enough to know by the size of the bone Princessanne's who it was.

She was charred right smart. You wouldn't want to of seen it, son.

And Mama? Toker said. What about her?

Well, your mama lit right out. God blesser, she'd survived the inferno safe and sound. Out gittin drinkin water, she said. That or somethin. You know how it is, a dozen people askin questions, all in your one ear. Maybe out takin a leak, I forget which. But she didn't ask for no sympathy. Wouldn't have none. She wouldn't stay with any of us offered our roofs for her to stay under.

Right strange, folks thought it was.

Well, she won't her own self. You can imagine the shape she was in.

There won't no reasonin with her.

It was the kerosene heater exploded. That was the best we could come up with.

A spark, that's all it takes, the crackerbox houses round here.

We tooker to the crossroads, waited wither till the bus come. She still had on her charry dress, a black shawl over the shoulder some woman giver.

That shawl, that dress, her sole and solitary goods.

It was me flagged that bus down. You know how hard that is to do, that bus comin down the highway a bat out of hell. I can't tell you the times I've heard of folks havin to chase it, and one time I knowed a man chopped down a big pecan tree, whopped it clean cross the road jist so that bus could must slow down.

Git back to my mama, Toker told him.

I am, jist stop your grumblin at me, Calvin said. Well, she climbed on. We could see her scootin down the aisle, huntin empty seat. Them other passengers they's faces to the window, not wantin to miss a snippet goin on.

Never a word of regard for us takin her to that bus, that bus roarin on off, not so much as a little flap of her hand. In a daze, I guess, the same as you would be. It's shock does it, like beast of the woods, your leg in a trap. My guess is she don't even know yit what's hitter. Don't you see?

I giver myself five dollars straight out of my own pocket, Calvin continued. This was back at the burn, with her standin by the fiery rubble, lookin round like a chicken with its head chopped off. Or wonderin where the fryin pan is. Don't think you ever got to return me that five dollars. I given it out of the goodness of my heart, with no thought to what it cost me. Life is hard up here, at the best of times it is. Us folks have got to stick together, do the good we can.

I pay you back, Toker said. You don't have to worry your head over that.

Well. If you want to. Iffin ever you're able. That ain't why I raised it, son.

Anything else to tell me?

Not that my mind can pull up to, right this second.

She let on she know Princessanne's dead?

They Lord knows.

She mention me?

Well now, son. Now that you ast.

What'd she say?

Well, it was like she thought you won't her own son nohow.

No more and nohow. That was the drift some of us caught. But you got to remember her shock. And Princessanne, well, Princessanne, in her mind it was like your sister never had bin born. A queer thing, I know it, but you know how a mind twists round, how it twists to protect its own self. All your mama knowed for sure was that the time and the place didn't suiter. All she could talk about was catchin that bus.

Unhuh. Every minute I ever lived she was talkin about catchin that bus.

Yes, well, we all do that. Sarah every day. They's gold pots at the end of that line. But your mama was brung out here a little girl, you know. This place never was hern. So she was slinkin off for parts unknown, or maybe goin back to some part she left away from. People will do that.

Unhuh.

You knowed that didn't ye, Toker? That she was brung out here a little girl?

Unhuh. I knowed that.

Well, the way you looked I won't sure.

How soon did folks git here, to the fire?

Old Hindmarch seen it from the store. That's the Toker stompin grounds ablaze, he said, his voice all ahush. And we come runnin. I seen myself the last fateful hours. We all wondered you won't here. You'd of bin, the story might of read different.

What you mean? Goddammit, is that what they's sayin?

Oh forgit it. Forgit I spoke . . .

Your dogs now, they was up in the smokehouse, never had no chance, them sparks everwhere. I guess it was your mama locked them up in there, knowin you was gone, not sure you won't gone for good like your brother and your daddy was, or maybe to muffle up they's hollerin.

Unhuh. My mama never could abide them dogs.
They was right smart, them dogs. You goin to miss them
dogs.

The burn. He'd cleared away what he could of the charred
sidings, the crumbling posts and joists, the rippled tin. He'd
borrowed a mule to do it, and constructed a litter to haul the
debris off to the side, hurl it into the woods.
Let the growth have it. The iron beds, the bed springs, the
cooking stove, the skillets, the tin cans and buckets. So many
tin cans and buckets. So much rubbish. He started another
fire to burn what hadn't been finished off the first time. To
burn what would burn. Thow in the iron beds, the bed
springs, the cooking stove, let it all burn twice. Let it keep on
burning.
So much wouldn't burn. But Princessanne had. In his
mind's eye, of nights even now, one year in the turning, he
could see the house igniting, the roof and sides exploding.
Could see this even as he saw himself on cane chair at the
Crossroads Tavern, a mason jar up to his lips. What am I goin
to do when this jug's done? Git another one. Thow a dead
dog in.
He could hear Princessanne screeching.
She won't but twelve. She hadn't never yet bin kissed or no
one never said they loved her, excepting maybe when she was
little and their mama in her right mind. But Mama never had
a right mind. They hadn't either one, Mama or Daddy, had a
right mind. Maybe when they was little, or when he and his
brother was. Maybe one time in the Garden of Eden. Haha.
Git me another one of them jugs; let these last two dollars see
me thue till dawn. Thow another dead dog in.
Maybe Mama was out taking a leak, having a squat-down,

or heading off for fresh drinking water—or maybe she was out with a stob of lit firewood from the cooking stove, saying, I think I'll set fire to this shack, I think I will.

The time is come.

A little spark is all is needed.

She'd always vowed to. She'd threatened it every minute.

I won't born out here, she said. I didn't come of my own choosin. I was brung. They's no civilization out here. It's not fit for human beins, savin those of your daddy's ilk.

Well, where are you from, Mama?

I don't know. I was that young. But I mean to set fire to all that's here, your daddy first if I can find'm. Then I will.

What was it like, Mama, where you come from?

It won't like nothin, she'd said. It don't now exist to me either. But I know they's a place better, somewhere in this world.

Catch that bus, Mama. Go find it. Ride on thue till the shank of the day.

And while you're at it, Mr. Barkeep, shove me over that jug.

The cellar was all that had been spared, if spared you could call it. The preserve jars down there had busted, the jam and the glass in a cooked tar puddle, the earthen floor still warm to the touch three days later. Shove aside these beams, these curled boards, let me see what else I can find.

Scoop that out.

Yank that over.

Haul away glass and tar.

Haul away tin can.

Haul it all away, let the wild grass have it.

He'd hauled for two days without stopping, had hauled through the night and on into morning, his head down, inching one way and another, clearing out only what was under his nose.

Let your nose be the guide, Toker. Let your nostrils breathe cinder. Let it breathe flesh cookin. Let your spit be black and your eyes be gritty. Let your face blacken, your tongue thicken. Oh Toker, you sonofabitchin Toker. Off to your good times, were you, Toker?

Like daddy like son.

If people came by he didn't see them. If he had help he didn't know it. Now and again he was aware of the mule standing in its traces, standing and waiting. Of the mule neighing. The mule had to be fed. The mule had to have water. Once in a while he saw the mule and remembered that. It won't his mule to treat so sorry. He ought to feed and water that mule.

Ride this mule, Mama. Put your self blind upon it. Go and find what never existed.

He talked to himself, to the mule, and would look up, surprised to see the space empty. Okay, let's git down to it. Let's haul the last ash, haul the last bone.

Haul it away.

Let the wild growth have it.

He got to feeling that once he had the earth cleared, every cinder swept and scraped clean of the ground, he'd come across Princessanne with her face shining, her eyes big, her chest swelling, crying: You're a sight, you are. Hidy there, big brother!

She was all goodness, was Princessanne. Hadn't nothing assailed her.

Once in a great while, when a slice of sunlight stabbed at his eyes, he'd pause and come remotely to his senses. The mule was standing, waiting, the trees were a black ring, drooped and wilting, rubble all over. There won't no way one man working alone was ever going to git the place back to a state you call livable. Livable or reasonable. With air you could breathe.

He was black then himself, black head to toe, carrying the smell of fire, bedecked in a suit of soot and cinder. Hey now, Toker, is that you, son? Is that you I see once was a human bein? He saw black shawl, saw his mama's face at the bus window, grinning at him. Calvin's five dollars folded and clenched tight in her hand. On her way to a place never existed, but pointed the way could be it did.

He saw her somewhere the other side of Crossroads Tavern, some place outside this ring of bluefish mountains, at a little parasol table, eating ice cream, always a relish. Little china teacup to her lips, staring at him over the rim. You Tokers, she'd say. God hep you if only for a minute. I had the Toker name, Lord knows I did, but as the Lord breathes, no, I never was a Toker.

Princessanne screeched each time he ripped out buckled post or yanked up blackened board. She took to talking to him. More than once he'd look up and find her standing beside him. Her white face alien specter in the black-ash air. You weren't goin to leave me were you, Toker? You hadn't wanted to be drinkin that rotgut licker did you, Toker?

Once, when he was hauling a load, she'd placed a wispy hand on his arm. I won't bad, was I, Toker? That won't why I perished, was it, Toker?

It had got so hot, she said, inside that room. That door outside-bolted. Who'd of locked it, Toker? I don't know why my mama would, do you, Toker? She latched up the dogs, Toker. But them dogs were howlin. Them dogs were makin a ruckus. But why'd she latch me up, Toker? Why were we all latched up, and her too, every minute?

He'd drop the shovel, look up, and find her gone. He'd
stoop to pick up flaking board, stop to wipe sweat out of his
eyes, blink, and she'd be back again.

If you can find enough of my bones, then bury me, Toker. I
want a big funeral with all of you cryin. Find my mean daddy
too and bring him back, I want him there, Toker. If I don't
have it then I am doomed ever to flicker and flit like candle
flame.

The dogs he'd buried, together nose to nose the way they'd
liked running, always thinking the other was following the one
pure scent.

Where would he live? Where, once he got round to living
again? Why not down here? Why not indeed? The clay was
hard. Would be warm in winter, cool in summer. Nothing
wrong with clay. Othern that it was killer digging. His hands
swole. The shovel split three handles. Watery in spots and
slippery as hell. It took the whole of one day and on into star-
light to dig out the roots of one bitch tree.

He was going to do it, then? Take up residence down here
in Mama's old root cellar and jam-jar room? In this hole in the
ground?

He cut in seven earthen steps. Ye walked careful, ye could
walk them down. It's Toker, he said, going down into his tomb.
Pull the lid over your head, and crouch down.

But first square off these walls.

Then it rained. It rained for four days without letup, a
round-the-clock rain. His pit filled with water; he sat crouching on the lip, shivering, cursing the rank earth. His mama
smiled grandly at him through the fog of her distant bus window. Git down in it, Toker. Wallow in the best Toker dream.

He dug trenches up on the high slope so the worst of the
downpour could drain. Divert the bastard hurricane. Let the
lowlanders have it. When the rain at last stopped he spent

another day carting water away in leaky buckets. He carted in sawdust to soak up the wet, then shouldered the weighty sawdust into creaking wheelbarrow.

Haul it away. Let the weeds have it.

He laid a slant roof over the deep hole. He hung a door and cut in a shoe-box window. He called it home.

He lived there now, in his pit, within his circle of scorched earth which highland forest was ever threatening to reclaim.

Such was where he took the baby, this damp day.

There it is, baby, he said. Shut your eyes. Home is where the heart sinks down.

𝕏

A cherub was up near his door. A cherub fully growed, without a stitch of clothes on.

A woman, peach-skin nude.

Whoa now. Let's parley on this.

He could hear George and Martha off in thick wood. He could call and they'd come, maybe they would, but for the minute he decided to let them play.

She was sunning herself, stretched out on upslung board. A stomach round as the fullest moon.

Asleep, it seemed.

But ain't the cake hern? No wonder this here sky is blushin.

If it's your mama, he told the baby, she don't seem to be troubled none.

He'd come up over switchback path through the woods. Now he doubled back to the lane, and came on again, putting whistle to his approach.

Cherub wasn't out front now. Had he dreamed her, then?

No, he hadn't, for there to the front lay the cherub's things. Her clothes strewn over the weedy ground. Cherub had got caught in the downpour, it seemed, the same as him. She'd shed her wet belongings, faced them and herself up to the sun. And stayed that way, sleeping, pending arrival of him.

Now he could see her head poking forth at the side of his shed. She had red hair and reddish skin and her eyes were blue. She had a full face, a bloated face, that face strained some now.

She called to him.

I didn't mean no soul to slip up on me. You stay in your tracks, I git somethin pulled on. You the man with the baby, I see. You the one I was waitin for.

Was I waitin for you? he called back. Is it a nude bathin colony I'm runnin here?

Turn your head, she commanded. I don't mean maybe.

He turned, or half-turned, catching sight of a lumbering fat woman out to pluck dress off the weeds and scoot back to the shed's retreat.

She'd had time already, he noticed, to git her bloomers on.

She was swollen up as a cow. Pregnant as thunder.

Maybe seventeen.

You can come up now, she said after a minute.

As it's my place, he replied, I reckon I can.

She was out hopping on one leg, twisting on her shoes.

Careful you don't shake open the gate, he said.

He went on inside and down the seven steps, feeling he knowed her from somewhere but unable to placer.

He put down the sleeping baby on the cot and stood over it a second, shaking his head.

That birthin sure tuckered you out some.

He had skillet and one little and one big pot and the little one he poured water into now from an oaken keg. Or did a youngan gulp it warm? He held hand over the stove ashes where yet he could feel heat. He took the milk bottle out of his pocket and leaned it into the pan water. He pulled a handful of straw out of his mattress and spread that over the ashes, then lay on his cedar kindling and his twigs and finally three split logs. He set this afire and watched it spring alight and spread.

You hold your horses now, he told the baby, which hadn't stirred. You could see her little chest rising and falling. There was a bit of fluff fanning in front of her nose. He turned and spun that off.

She had that toe out again.

He saw Cherub's feet on the stairs, then more of Cherub padded on down.

He placed the pan up on the grill, once the smoke had volumed up. He lifted the bottle out, unscrewed the nipple, smelt the milk, blew on the nipple, and twisted it back on.

Musty, the girl said.

He looked at her.

She was still up on the steps, stooped some and holding on. She looked right normal in her clothes, excepting for the balloons under them.

I never knowed no man lived down no gopher hole.

You don't know one now. Looks to me you could have it any minute, he said.

That's my trouble, she said. I can't. It's why I've come to see you.

She hadn't come so much to see him. That was his thought as he watched her career straight over to cot and baby. She unwrapped it. She felt its arms and legs, felt between its legs, rolled it over and studied its spine. She looked into its ears. Then she rolled it over again and pried open its mouth.

It's sound, she said. Though I had my hopes on a boy.

You and Kingdom Come, he said. Everybody and his brother think we got females comin out of our ears. How come I can't git me one?

She wrinkled her nose, sniffing the air. Throwing a half-smile back at him.

I bet you can and do all the time, she said. Smells burnt in here.

He removed the pan from the fire, held and examined the bottle. Then he poked the baby. It came up out of its sleep slowly, with a rueful grimace, stretching its limbs and yawning.

No need to say please, he told it. Not one please and not one goddamn.

Hush, the girl said.

He swung the baby over to his lap. The nipple grazed the baby's lips and immediately she pitched her belly, flung her arms wildly, taking greedily to sucking, the eyes bulging, intent on him.

Whoa. Whoa now.

It's a strong'un, he said after a minute. I can't hardly lift out this bottle.

The girl had one eye out for his baby-tending, the other eye out for the place she'd walked into. Taking inventory. Deciding what he had in here that she wouldn't want or have, her nose every second wrinkling. She studied his shelves, his bare walls, his cupboard. She curled her lips, as much as saying You don't even have a table. Why it's like a hermit's hole in here. She took special interest in the teensy window: only the one pane, shoe-box size and up on end like one. She counted his three shirts on the nail and his pants folded in the fruit crate and looked a while at his spare shoes. They were Sunday shoes, her look said, with a high shine, and that took some studyin.

She punched his shoulder. I thought you had a woman here, she run off or you run her off, but I see now you never had one'ud live in this dirt hole. Your name's Raymun, ain't it?

Yes'm.

Raymun Toker?

Both parts right, he said, but I got no cigar to give.

She punched his shoulder again, bobbing her head.

You the one lit up the Crossroads, ain't you?

He kept silent on this. Crossroads Tavern seemed a long time ago.

Beat up two deputies, I heard, and tore up a bawdy house.

He stayed silent.

The warrant still out, I'm tole.

He looked from the baby to her, wondering that a pregnant girl in the woods away up here had heard all that.

He said nothing.

Put two more in the hospital at a dice-hot game?

No, he said, I didn't. It was one. And him already a cripple afore I busted his arm.

Unhuh, she said, pleased that he had spoken. Now you got that baby.

She was gitting to it now. He'd been wondering when.

Yes'm.

What I want is to swap.

Huh?

The baby was grabbing at the bottle. He upended it again and the baby stopped thrashing. Its eyes seemed about to pop out.

Mine that's comin, she said, for the one that's here.

I declare. Now why's that?

She laced her hands under her stomach, and seemed to

shift that stomach, or what was in that stomach, over to another side.

It's kickin, she said. It's the kickenest thing you ever looked at. I wishen myself I could kick it into next week.

She scratched behind her neck, scrunched up her shoulders better to get at the itch, then sat down, crossing her legs. She had right trim ankles for one in her condition. It seemed to Toker it was his sweet day for trim ankles.

She had this little fall of hair over her eyes she kept blowing at.

Around one eye was a faint blue tinge, like not long ago it had been blackened.

She had teensy lips narrow as pine needles.

You ain't ast me why I want that swap, she said.

She rolled her eyes, poking a finger into her tummy.

Why? Why is because my own I'm carryin will come way late and my husband will know the real one ain't his.

Toker pondered this.

You know what I can't see, she exclaimed, slapping her brow. And never will? It's why they don't git mixed up, the seeds, I mean, and nobody know who's planted what. I tell you, it's plenty mixed up in my mind. I don't know whether the daddy of this one is light or dark, long or short, has red hair or no hair. But he sure thowed me a curveball.

She bit her thumbnail and smoothed out the wrinkles on her shirt front.

You know what else I don't see? she said. Why it would matter to a man whose it is, since they don't raise them anyhow. Now do they?

Toker was still pondering.

Maybe you best ketch me up, he said. I've not quite got the hang of why it is you want to swap babies.

You're slow, she said. Not to insult you.

She fixed a long look on him.

My husband's up in Gripper Falls jail, she said. Bin there eight months. My baby's due in anothern or two, right round the time he gits out.

They hell.

He'll likely kill me he finds I bin playin round. See, I can git rid of this'un and claim that'un and say it was hisn planted by his own self afore he got sent up. See? Then I'm sittin pretty.

What's he up at Gripper Falls jail for?

Do I ever know! she said, her voice rising. He's up to his meanness every day he's breathin and I can't hardly keep count.

You wouldn't be Esther Jeff's wife, would you?

He had her placed now. That's who he'd seen her with, old Esther Jeff, but slimmer in them days.

She bit her lower lip, looking up at him with a smile. Yes, Esther Jeff, she said proudly. Ain't he ever bit a fool!

I don't know he's that much a fool that he's goin to take this here girl-wonder I'm holdin for one of his own.

She got briefly excited, seeing her plans steered awry. She shot herself up, tugging at his sleeve.

I got to have it, your youngan, she said, else Esther Jeff will cut my thoat! That man, he's jealous inside and out, his ever bone is. I can't take me a pee, he's not peering thue the floorboards.

She started crying, her shoulders rocking up and down. Toker didn't know how much was put on.

I tell you, it's driven me to wrack and ruin, she sobbed. Nobody knows yit my sorrowful condition but my mama. I done done everything I could. I done prayed myself black and blue. Twice I done pitched myself off a high hill but all it did

was put a soreness in my left elbow. Somebody done tole me
you drink lye, lye would do it. You think lye would?

Where you and Esther livin now? asked Toker.

Me and Esther Jeff never had us our own place yit. Now
he's in jail I'm up with my mama up Devon Creek way, past
the Rancy Heights turnoff.

Up round where that sawmill was?

Unhuh, but way on past it.

I know it, he said. I've gone huntin up there.

She waited for him to say more but he didn't. She stared
moist-eyed at him and the baby. She couldn't figure whether
they were striking a deal or not. But she knew she hadn't yet
offered much inducement. She wiped her eyes with a clump
of skirt and let a slow light trickle into them; she did something with her lips. Her dress hem slowly inched up.

I got no money to give you, she said, her voice low.

Her hands stole out and grabbed his.

I be willin to give you anything else you want though.

She moved well down on her knees in front of him, her face
up close. He didn't know he'd call it flirtin now. He'd call it
oats in the feed bucket or his head in the trough.

I be willin to do it any way you want it, she said. I ain't hard
to git along with.

I can see that.

I give you the best time you ever had, you say the word. My
baggage don't slow me down one whippit, don't think that.

He squared the baby up higher in his arms. The baby's eyes
were half-drooping shut. Its own belly had rounded some.

I bin poked left right and center since the day I could
stand, she said. One more poke don't bother me none.

She laid her hand gently over his crotch and stared at that
hand on his crotch with her eyes up close. Her bottom lip was
out thick, her lids fluttering half-down just like the baby's.

Say the word, one word, and I gobble you up like a lamp-post. It's risin and wants to, I can feel it does.

He could feel it too. He lifted one leg over her head, stood, and crossed with the baby to the stove.

It's heated up some in here, he said. All the same, I think I'll have me a Nescafé. You want one?

She sagged forward, bringing her head to rest on the cot. Ain't that somethin, she murmured. I never bin turn down before. I didn't reckon no woman ever had.

Well, I wish I could hep you, he said.

She squared around and let her buttocks sink gloomily to the floor.

I knew you wouldn't. When you didn't grab me naked in the yard I knew it then. I said to myself, my head pokin out from your shed, Sorrel, you done wasted this trip. But tell me? she said.

Yes? He was pouring tepid water into his Nescafé.

Is it my belly? I had no belly would you of said yes then? Is it on account of your livin in this hole in the earth?

He could see she wanted him to say yes now. That she needed his lie. Needed to see herself pretty and sassy and wanted again.

He said yes. Yes, he said, I would of chased you naked up every tree on this kingdom. I would of come at you like a bear after spring honey.

She raised herself up, pushing against the cot. She straightened her clothes and seemed to search around for a looking glass.

You're cute too, she said. I wasn't in my condition, I wasn't worried how Esther was goin to kill me, I'd eat you alive. I'd have you doin me Sunday to Sunday.

The baby's bottle was drained empty. She was sucking at

the shrunk nipple, beating her curled fist against air, heaving her body up and down.

Lord, what do I do now? he asked. I only brought it the one.

The girl slipped the blouse low on her shoulder. She reached in and brought the one breast out. She had tugboat ones, he'd already seen that.

I ain't wet yit, she said, or I'd be pleased to letter have her turn after yourn.

She gave a bounce to the thing.

They's big ain't they? I can see you can't stop lookin.

Toker was looking, but trying to look everywhere else.

My mama now, the girl said, she's flat as a board. But you see here?

Her head was scrunched down, both hands pushing up the one breast. You see here? Esther Jeff plays this here nipple like you would a guitar.

She was pinching the nipple between two fingers.

You strum this here left nipple and do it right and this here right nipple will near sing you a song.

She made to bring the other breast out.

The Lord's truth it will, she said. Now watch.

She flopped the second one out. She tweaked the left nipple, pinched it between her fingers, and the right nipple instantly popped up, high and hard.

Her tongue was out between her lips, her face in dire concentration.

Then she laughed. Ain't that a hoot?

She leveled another glance at Toker's crotch, and laughed the more.

I can raise'um all, she said. Within a distance of five miles. My mama claims I can raise the dead.

Toker laughed too. He felt his face getting warm.

I pass a graveyard in the night you can hear the stones upliftin.

She covered herself and for the next minute looked his way with a vacant gaze.

I knowed your brother, she said.

Toker shrugged feebly. Did?

Or, that is, a friend of mine did. She done gone away with him.

Toker hadn't heard that. There was little he knew of his brother's life and not many who had openly confessed to friendship with him.

He done lefter, the girl said. Done abandoned her on the street over in Laversburg. I'm not tellin you what that friend of mine had to do to work herself back here.

Toker nodded glumly.

Don't mind me, she said sorrowfully. I got a brother I can't stand either.

The two of them sat a moment in dreamy reverie, contemplating the hardship of families, the waywardness of lost brothers.

She dropped her head down woefully on Toker's shoulder and for a minute played tiddly-finger with the baby.

I don't have no milk yit, she said. But still it could suckle, you wanted me to let it. I know the baby would enjoy it.

She had a soft look, saying that, maybe seeing there against her breast her own child suckling.

She looks plain sweet as cuddly puppy.

This woman was right nice, Toker decided, you got to knower.

Well, she said, rising, giving the hoist to her belly. I'm off then, we can't make us no deal. Water in a bottle with a sprinkle of sugar, that'd keeper quiet till you got more milk.

Me, I bet mine's a hell-raiser. I bet Esther Jeff will want to shoot it.

She was up hunting for anything that might delay her departure. She located his little compact shaving mirror over hanging on a post, and for some lost seconds studied her face, then went up close to squeeze at a blackhead or pimple on her chin.

You git pregnant, she said, your skin you can't do nothin a-tall with. Don't let no one tell you different. This belly of mine, sometimes I feel like a jackknife truck.

He was rinsing the milk bottle, splashing whitish liquid into his drain corner.

It comes to me, he said, I don't have no sugar.

You got honey?

He didn't have honey.

Molasses then, she said. Try sweet molasses.

She was flouncing all around him, butter-heeled fluttery.

Practicing her neighborly qualities.

She was a nice, decent person, and if Esther Jeff had any sense he would take whatever gift she give him.

Lord, she said, now I got to go down your squishy lane to that road, walk or hitch myself a ride with a total stranger. You wouldn't think it to look at me but sometimes I think Why go on?

She was talking to cheer herself up. He'd done the same, Toker thought. Done it a thousand times.

Though now she was leaving, she looked weary.

He stood with Sorrel out in the burnt yard. It would be getting on toward dark soon, and he hadn't yet made his ground search. He hadn't yet got to think about when he could be hot-footing it to Roby's.

He called George and Martha, called them a good many

minutes, but he heard nothing. Them dogs might could be in China by now. They might could be skiing on a Swiss alp.

Sorrel, by his side, looked up with a shy smile, and let her one hand fold into his. To fold her hand there like a child would.

Together they listened to the silence.

I love this earth, she said then. I love it to my very most marrow. Don't you?

A few scraggly bushes had come back, and weeds, and what remained of leafy melon vine up over one of his refuse piles. He had four trees, of a sizable sort, killed by the heat, and yet to bring down.

That burn smell, she said, it won't never leave this place. Like you come to know early or first sorrow, it never to unfasten from your bones, though your way be thue thick or thin.

She lingered there beside him one last minute.

My mama'd take it, she said. Take my baby. She's offered herself. She's not but forty-eight, be forty-nine by the time I have it.

Unhuh, Toker said. That might work.

She's willin to say it's hern. She claims she'll swear it to Esther Jeff's face, and anyone else asts. Or she says I can claim to Esther I was raped, that I was gang-raped, which I have bin.

She paused by the side of his lane, looking both ways. He saw her shiver some little bit.

Me and my mama, she said. We bin all around the horn on these questions.

That's nice to have, he said. Your mama's company and wisdom, I mean.

Oh, she's smart. She's a saint, Mama is. I never got no worries, no real ones, so long as she's on the scene. We'll hatch up somethin, her and me will.

This here I take it is your first child?

Lordy no, though it's the first I've offered for trade. I had me one dead at the barn door and anothern Mama already has.

You ought to hang yourself iron gate over that door.

I ought to, she said. But what would be the fun in that?

All right then.

She was already moving down the lane, going gingerly, her legs wide apart, the two hands flapping up at the wrists like small wings the wind stirred.

Further on, she turned and called.

It's them nasty rubbers I can't stand. They's mostly the reason the trouble I'm in. I like to git right up inside with the warmth of the thing and some sweet-talker like Esther Jeff blowin in my ear. She laughed contentedly. You sure you're not innerstid?

Not this day. This day I'm all tuckered out.

You don't look it. You look like you could.

You too, he said.

I git it from my mama, she called back. Mama's a randy old hen. Anybody goes up agin her, she'll pluck their feathers.

She laughed harder, waving, and passed on down the mountainside.

He won't worried about her none. She'd come thue.

And, anyway, Esther Jeff be back in jail most the minute he got out, the bad nature he had slung on him.

Sorrel, he told the baby. That's what that lady's name is. You might of bin a Jeff you didn't have me here to brighten your load.

In a minute, laid out on his wire cot, the baby sailed off into sleep again. Her stomach bloated, her hands curled, the bottle adrift under one cheek. Not a lick left in it. The nipple

scrunched flat, gone whitish from her fierce sucking. He held
ear to her breath; she was whirring away like a blowtorch.

He flapped woolly cover over her.

A minute later he heard raucous barking from a far distance, these intermixed the next second with a woman's livid
shrieks.

He ran to his lane and couldn't see either woman or dogs,
though the shrieks didn't lessen.

Sorrel. His pups only saying hello. Such friendly dogs.

He called them again, and heard silence. Then crackling
bush, thumping paws, their hurried approach.

George and Martha charged in, panting for breath, snarling
playfully about his feet, snorting and bullyish, jumping and
licking—eventually to plop over on their backsides and wait
for the lash.

Bad dogs, Toker said. Bad dogs!

Then the dogs to take notice his voice was a pleasantry; to
wallow up then in smooch of his face.

Toker rubbed their scalps and thumped their sides and
tickled their bellies as they rolled over, forelegs folded. Grinning at him.

Good dogs, he said. Good dogs. Now on your feet. Let's go
to work.

The sky had that special light now, the special darkening light
that hung over the earth like shade under a sunbonnet. It
might hang so for another hour. Then full dark. They'd have
to hurry.

Come on, he told the dogs. Let me show you that laurel
bush.

The dogs running ahead of him, he struck off on a path beat

down every season, though for the moment still springy, then circled off along the ravine and down its turning past one of his rabbit traps. Rabbit trap, but no rabbit. They were getting smarter, them hares.

He went on.

His mama one time, by the back porch-step, had squoze him between her legs as she slit knife along a rabbit's belly, as she peeled back the fur. Now, she said, you'll know how to slit it the next time I tell you to and you'll skin it how I tell you to and you'll stop squallin this minute or I'll box your ears.

On down and across this here cleared spot, then up over gully, up past this rotted tree stump, now this high bank, and on thue them tall weeds yonder. Not far. Hardly morn a rock's throw from my front door.

Now which way? Thue here, as I recall. Now swerve south and angle myself creekwise.

Watch out for them thorns. Watch your foot don't slip. Watch that limb don't swish you.

Now up this incline.

So far so good. We got all my cylinders clickin. We gittin close now.

The dogs held close by as well, apparently liking the sound of his voice. Yes, dogs liked it, you talked to yourself. It flared their ears up, it kept their tails pointed. Periodically now, George and Martha licked his hand, whining their curiosity. Eager to see what mission he had for them.

That mother. She's drivin by, she sees my lane, she says to herself, There's a nice deserted spot, I can hide my baby there.

Does so, then she's long gone.

But why break her backside haulin that baby thue so much killer terrain? And it nighttime, her not to know where she was goin? What branch she'd slap into, or what cliff she'd fall over. Mighty thick thue here. Or here's somethin we don't know: maybe mother hadn't had her baby yit. Maybe she's having her baby in these very woods. Maybe right here.

Hold up, dogs.

Here. Yes, here. Beneath this very laurel bush.

Toker dropped to his heels. He searched the ground. No blood. No beat weeds where a woman had groaned and bucked and bit the cord. Nothin here.

George and Martha quivered at his elbow, excited, waiting his permission they could slide in their noses, capture the scent. He clawed up a clump of grass from beneath the bush, smelt it himself, then floated the clump under their snouts.

Do it, dogs. Capture the scent.

The dogs flashed in. Their noses swept the ground. In a second they were moaning and dancing. Such a frenzy of scent.

Yes, Toker said, I know was a baby here. Find the other scent. The other one. Show me. Show me the mother's trail.

They licked his face. They yelped. They flung their noses down again and spun them like whirling bees over the ground.

The next second both broke. They whirled, their yelps throaty now.

They were off. Both following the same zigzag course.

Toker flung himself up and in a trot followed their swinging rear ends.

But not blind himself. He could be tracker too. Not for nothin, all those years: Because, hold up! Look here. What's this?

A heel print. And anothern over here. Not his print either. Too small.

And what's this?

Well now. Had there bin a third party out here? Someone chasin that mother? So it looked like. The trail seemed to say as much, then to take it back. Broken bush, dead leaves whipped about, footprints all about the place. Scuffed earth, like someone had fought here.

The dogs yelped, looking back. Come on, they said. What's holdin you up? Can't you see we've caught a good scent?

They zigzagged on, noses cruising the ground.

Toker retraced his trail. Peered at the cracked twigs, the footprints, the scuffed earth.

He crouched down. Hold on, he said. Don't let your mind run riot. You best study on this.

He was still crouched, probing at a man's heel print in the leafy soil, when he heard Martha's padded feet, her proud wheeze. He looked up and there she was, a few steps away. Bright-eyed, her head high, her lips wide: a woman's white cloth shoe dangling by its string from her teeth.

And further on, out of sight, way over through the woods about where his daddy's old junked Hudson would be, George barking out the news of his find. George saying, Come here! Shake a leg! Forget Martha! Come see what I've got!

No need to think you're walkin on eggs.

No ghosts about.

No one here but us chickens.

This Toker told himself. But it seemed to him, moving briskly toward George's call, watching Martha streak on ahead, that the world about him, other than dogs, was in a strange hush. Disabled. Holding its breath.

The light dim through here. The light dimming all over. Full darkness soon to swoop down.

His skin prickled. He looked at the woman's faded dirty

shoe, carried in one hand, and wondered, filled with forebodings. You could hide away baby. But would you leave behind shoe?

That lace still tied. Had she run right out of that shoe? In so much a hurry that she would?

His stomach grumbled. Won't he ever goin to find chance to drop biscuit into his mouth? Had he give up wine? Roby would be waitin.

He shivered, coming upon that spot where the old Hudson, down on its axles, had been rusting out here a good twenty years: young and old growth embracing the wreck, boot and engine lid raised, a pine sapling growing up out of grassy boot space. Stripped down to all but frame, the glass milky-blue and shattered, that front door flung open, a rotted seat angling out through the absent windshield.

But oughten that back door be open too? Hadn't that back door bin open all these years?

George was in slant away from that back door—slung his way, hair up, ears laid back. Emitting low snarl. Ready to spring.

Somethin was in there.

Easy does it. Easy now.

Toker, advancing, told this to himself. Easy. Python snake's not goin to shoot out at you.

As he stooped to peer inside his knee brushed the metal. The door gave a squeak, and opened a crack.

A woman's naked foot plopped down.

She was in there, her throat slit.

Best he could Toker removed blood from her face.

Pick it off with a fingernail.

Now look close, Toker. Do you knower?

No. She won't no one known to him. No one ever seen around here.

No ring, I see. Too tight, the sonofabitch who did this to her, to buy her one.

How old? Well, you couldn't tell that either. Young. You could say that much.

No, you couldn't tell nothin about her, only that she was dead.

The shoe on her left foot was the match of the one Martha had found. Blood coverin much of that shoe. That dress bunched up high around her waist.

No panties.

That dress a godawful mess.

Briar scratches runnin up and down her legs. Hands and face too.

Well. Think on this.

If her throat is cut, and it is, is she holdin in her hand a clump of scalp belongin to the sonofabitch done her in.

No. Not that he could see.

But, dammit to hell, it was gettin dark. It most was dark. Gettin on toward colder too.

Her out here like this the whole day.

Tug down her dress, Toker. Tug it down.

Well, look. Look there. Them leaves caught in her hair. What's that shinin?

I be dog.

He held the object in his hand, studying that object. What a whimsical piece. A little blue glass hairpin bow in a butterfly shape. Funny thing her to have. A little girl's bow.

Put that back, Toker.

Somebody might can one day recognize that bow.

No, no, wipe your fingerprints off it first.

He backed out of the car, scooping fresh air down into his lungs. He was sweating. He felt giddy. His legs wavy. He crouched on his haunches in the weeds, his eyes closed, his head down. The two dogs slid their heads into his lap and he absentmindedly stroked and patted them.

What next? What do I do now? Do I call the law? After I've bin troupin all over the land with the murdered woman's baby in my arms the whole day? If I tell the law the law will say, Well, Raymond Toker, air you the scoundrel done her in? You have your fun wither first? Was she juicy, Toker? Raymond Toker the crime is yourn.

He knelt so, a long time, on into full dark.

Here's how he saw it.

Someone was after her and she hides that baby up near where she's seen my light, then she thinks to hide herself, but X finds her and X slits her throat. X drags her here to this car and parks her in that car, probably a married man coverin his tracks, or she says to him, Now you got to marry me, and he says, I will, here's the minister right here, and the sonofa-bitch, like that, slices her throat. He leaves here thinkin, Now that bitch never be found, that bitch who tried to motherfuck and hog-tie me.

And goes home easy of mind, thinkin, I got out of that fix. I pull that one off. Hoop-de-doo.

I ought to cover her.

Toker moved over to take another look. To tug that dress another inch down. He measured Martha's found shoe against the sole of her foot and saw that it fit.

But why, if he's chasin her and she's seen my light, why didn't she come to my door, callin for help?

Here's why. Because she can't hide baby and do both. Be-cause that X sonofabitch is hot on her heels.

And likely she wouldn't know these woods from Adam anyhow.

So she's thinkin, If I can't save myself how can I save this
baby? How can I saver from that bastard's knife?

That knife now, come to that. You bein the X sonofabitch,
what would you do with the knife? Okay, you've slitter throat,
then would you wipe the blade on the grass, on the seat of
your pants? Would you fold that knife blade back, drop knife
into your pocket, lick your lips, and steal away? Or would you
want to git rid of that knife. Would ye jist fling it anywhere?

Let's look.

Toker looked.

He looked on past full dark—sometimes not looking, only
forlornly pacing the ground or rooted to it in abject consider-
ation of these inevitabilities: Your luck run out, the road not
taken, the crime that could catch you while you won't
lookin—your life's blind sides, your body at peril, your luck
straggly at the best of times—oh, life the way it was up here.
Then he remembered he had unprotected baby asleep on his
cot, and he gave up his wanderings, spoke softly to the dogs,
and hastened on back.

Turning over in his mind who the dead woman was, and
who was X, and how the baby might fare, in what manner she
might survive, with such tidings as this.

Truman knelt by a shallow stream away in a highland bower, splashing up icy water over his face and in the disturbance addressing his image. He'd not slept or eaten for two days and this was going to be the second night, and though he felt adrift in his bones and ragged of flesh, in spirit he knew neither weariness nor solitude. Nor was any weight of pain or affliction upon him, though his brow burned with fever and a side of his face was swollen with tooththrob. A vein pulsed bright as embered stick along his hairline, though he took no notice. Oh my heart is at plenty, he said to the rippling current, and from the very earth's udders have I suckled. He shivered with the run of icy water down his neck, lifting bloodshot eyes to take in his surroundings, though it be darkening, for darkness was not in the habit of keeping much from him. Here was creek and running creekwater, and what, he asked himself, has steered my footsteps to this wayward location? What, indeed. I sojourn over no visible road, I go where wagon nor mule has trod. I deploy myself without weather vane or compass, all according to need and all according to God's laws, which are few and of my own choosing, these seeded unto my

brow like trinkets hurled into whirlwind. Let sulfurous fumes
ascend and the very earth be at quake. Will ye not tremble
and beg a caretaker his mercy?

His incantation done, his eyes slewed, spun inwards, and
for some minutes he hopped froglike along the shore, wheezing a ragged breath, butting his head against the pebbled
ground. He wrenched at his hair and clawed finger along his
fiery gum, emitting stridulous croak, the sweat on his forehead ajitter and coursing warm into his eyes. He flailed his
arms in hot-footed dance over his construed field of quaking
sulfur, wagged and sucked his tongue and made as though to
yank it from its roots.

He raised himself from these antics, laughing.

Can ye not play? he said aloud to the heavens. Can ye not
be the fool?

He opened his mouth to sing and the voice that issued from
him was the voice of a woman: We shall gather at the river.
The beautiful, beautiful river.

If ye cannot sing, if ye cannot play, he said, then the caretaker's mercy will be slick upon your hide as grease upon the
greasepole. Slide ye down it to the fiery furnace.

Then he laughed more, for the woman's voice in which he
found he could sing was the voice of his old and ancient
guardian.

Let us gather at the river. The beautiful, beautiful river.

Grab holt of Jesus, his old guardian-woman had said, and
she'd doused him in and held his head achoke under.

Truman's temple vein flared and pulsed anew, and he
dropped again to his knees, and in supplicant's crawl the old
woman's own direful solfeggio dropped out for a time the
chirping water, and his memory.

Oh bathe ye my feet, Truman said, splashing his head again
into the stream. Bathe ye my feet in pan of warmest water.

Then Truman wiped his face with his garments, stretched himself out upon the pebbles, closed his eyes, and slept.

In his dream there was a woman running her hands through his hair and she would not stop it. In his dream there was a woman who placed her lips upon his and bore her lips down and she would not stop it. In his dream there was a woman who pressed her body against his and she would not stop it.

In his dream he clutched at a hiding girl's play pocketbook and she slapped at his hands and said, Now, you stop it.

In a few minutes he waked, nervous and sweaty, his body afire with fever, and for a moment he wept, wept silently, hands up over his ears, his head burrowed, seeing himself of dark night a boy on a barn pallet by the pig shed, the plopping about of hooves in thick mud, the black movement of sundry, whispering beasts in their cramped enclosures. Then he scrabbled up with a low curse, in abolishment of these loathsome tears, his eyes alert, searching the darkness for intruders.

But intruders were none, and he went with willed serenity to his car hidden away under heavy swoop of limbs and from the trunk took out the paper bag containing his strop-razor, his witch hazel, and a cracked wedge of soap turned brick hard. How are ye, how are ye? he said. He spat, and stood a moment grinning at the bloody glob loosened from him.

He returned to the stream and again knelt down, wetting the soap and smearing it over his face. He sharpened the razor over his trouser leg, soaped his face anew, and swept the blade skillfully over cheekbone, under nose, about his chin, then, with tilted head and his eyes closed, skimmed the tool down and up his neck, now dousing that tool and its refuse into the rippling water.

Can ye walk, then? he asked. Can ye run? Can ye make mud pie or know right shoe from left?

How are ye, how are ye? The graves shall open and the corpses jiggle.

Git me out razor, strop, and witch hazel. Git me out your pots and pans. Rinse me in your best springwater. Bore ye washcloth into the left ear and into the right ear. Snip me off all dirt and hangnails, and mind ye don't miss the neck now.

He doused himself, boring and snipping and cleaning.

How are ye, how are ye?

He went on with his preaching, as he did with his cleaning: swooshing up water over his face, soaping the flesh, stropping his razor. Even with his face immersed under water, bubbles of air broke to surface and burst or floated away with the easy current his aggrieved tidings: How are ye, how are ye? Is it ashen bag to carry your head, or my love to wheel you thue all eternity?

He laughed his merriment, then to plunge his head yet again into icy water.

For some little while longer he preached to his imagined flock, there by the dark stream.

How are ye today, brother, and how are ye, sister? How are ye all, sisters and brothers and even strangers to one another?

Oh there is black crow, my brethren, awatch upon the road wire.

How are ye?

Be there vultures aspin above your rooftops and snakes aslide down your chimney.

Eel and rodent alike take balmy rest inside your kidney.

Go ye without tardiness to your rabbit-box destiny. For is not the rotting your ultimate and foremost charter?

How are ye, how are ye? How are ye?

The Lordgod is your Doctor of Darkness. He liveth in pike and mire, he liveth in feral, he abideth under your scalp like maggots unto sheep-rot. And time, my brethren, is the fish net, it is cod and haddock on the same plate, on the same table with the same three legs, where you might once of seen the chosen thirteen in assembly at the book's last supper.

He went to the car again, to lean his body under the lifted trunk and pry his hand under the worn spare wheel, though that spare not of a size would fit his car.

He retrieved the girl's purse.

He rooted among the sparseness inside that purse, took from it what might be counted as worth keeping, and came down again to the creekwater, there to wedge rock inside and to throw the purse into the dappling stream.

Float ye on down.

Tremble ye, my children, at the caretaker's mercy.

I do, he said.

She done pledged to me her monandrous vow.

I done rightfully wedded her, and me a father now.

He looked a while at the folded handkerchief taken from the girl's purse. Then he wrenched away a lacy edge, wet it in the water, made wad of it, and wedged the wad to sore tooth and gum.

It came to him that somewhere he had a man's watch and a wallet and the man's shoes buried. Under the straw beneath a pine tree somewhere, but he couldn't think now in what county that tree was or whether the man who had once owned wallet and shoe was buried in that same spot, or another.

He had need to bury last night's one, and yet meant to, though first he'd have to find shovel.

He returned to his car and stared a while at the ball-peen hammer in his trunk, wondering had he the nerve to rap that bad tooth out. He could take pliers to it, that was done often enough, but he had no pliers.

He searched inside his car's housekeeping, wishing he might find his hat of old, but he could not find his hat.

He made a circuit of his car, computing its wear and giving rough estimate as to its future utility. The tires were bald and one wobbly up front had a blistered hump on the side. The rubber stretched so thin he could glimpse red inner tube. He went to his trunk, upended the debris, and emerged holding a dusty tape-roll. He spooled this over the wounded tire. Then he took up rusted bucket and filled his radiator from the stream. He had hanging wire he'd brace up his tail pipe, but wire for now was come and gone.

The man whose car this once used to be had tended it better than him.

But there won't no cause to level complaint over something a body had no time for.

No, I must to my flock. I must to my Amens.

He thought of curling up in the backseat for a moment's rest, ached to do so, but reckoned that would be erroneous choosing.

There was the law, no doubt, running their blind circles of old. But a wise man needn't tempt them or give snooty nose to fate's steady gaze.

He hadn't had no wedded bride in white dress with lacy veil, and he regretted that. He wanted her to have jump-rope and play pocketbook and black shiny shoes, though she hadn't had that.

She had bow, though, and that was good.

He sat a minute under the wheel of his car, looking out over the darkness of this place.

He lit a cigarette.

He wished he had whiskey to sipple at.

He cranked the motor then, pulled away from his hiding place, and rode onwards in silent speculation through high hills into low and on through these and the dark.

He wriggled loose his overburdened ashtray and held it to

the window, in his rearview watching to see could he glimpse the white nubs there leapfrogging like hail in the night.

A short time later, under beam of jiggly headlights, he sighted an old man trudging the roadside with bowed head, his shoulders level as an ironing board. He saw the old man stop, to watch him pass. He hadn't no fuss with old people, he thought. They'd come thue the fiery furnace and not let the blaze topple them. Excepting his old uncle, there with his stoup of chicken bones.

Soon he was pulling into the store called Cal's Place, bringing his car to geared halt just as the storekeeper was whipping the last chain over his door.

The storekeeper stayed in place, his hands limp on the chains, studying with sullen indetermination the vehicle's shadowy driver.

Truman rolled down his passenger window and leaned across the seat.

Looks like I caught you in the nick of time, he said. Be sworn if I ain't.

Cal looked from the man's swollen face to his bolted chains.

Looks to me you're a mite late, he said. You takin up residence in these parts?

Truman gave him a mirthless grin. He crawled on over the seat and got smartly out.

Cal backed up a smidgen, keeping wary gauge on this latecomer.

You don't have no headache pills, do ye?

Not on me, I ain't.

You'd open up for a stranger in trouble, wouldn't ye? I won't take a minute of your time.

Cal grumbled and began unlocking the door. You git that tire pump yit? he asked.

Nope.

Or your wiper? I remember you was wantin wipers.

Nawsir. Didn't find wiper either. Folks was all run out.

One chain thumped to earth and Calvin kicked it aside. He looked over at the man hobbled up close beside him, hand up nursing a bloated cheek. A breath of vile air blew the storekeeper's way, and he hastily set to work on the second chain.

I'm jist visitin up the road, Truman said. But now I've done bin overcome with this mighty toothache.

Unhuh, Cal said. What's their name, these friends? If they's up or down the road they know Cal, and will tell you I run a good honest place.

He watched the man grab at his brow and double over and wind about with tortured lament.

What's your line? Calvin asked. All this visitin you're doin, a man might think you had none.

Oh, I been preachin, Truman said. Here and there.

You a holy man, are ye?

Well, we all is. Ain't that the hope?

These friends you're visitin, don't they have no headache tablets of their own?

The second chain clattered down and Cal ushered in his customer and poked over to give the pull to the light string.

Nawsir. They've fresh run out. Them dogs git whiny and sore-bellied, they jist lap them up. Can't keep no tablets in the house.

Calvin considered this report with obvious distaste.

You want the sixteen-pill tin or my economy one-hundred size?

The tin'll do me.

Unhuh, Cal said. It does most people, I find.

He reached to his shelf and slapped the aspirin tin neatly on the counter.

Twelve cent, he said. Anything else?

I could use me a can of somethin to eat, you could open it for me. Maybe sardines?

Cal got the sardines and plunked them down.

Truman looked hard at the tin.

I don't know, he said. My jaw won't hardly open. But my insides swirly-lizard hungry and I ought to of pack somethin in.

Make up your mind, Cal said, weary of tone. But he took another look at the man's blistery cheek and softened his manner some little bit. I was you, he said, I'd crush up me a mess of them tablets in a cloth and wad the cloth right up next to the bothersome molar. You might try that anyhow.

I mean to, Truman said.

He pulled from his back pocket a lacy woman's handkerchief and ripped off a strip. He took from his side coat pocket a knife, set the pills on the cloth, and rapped them hard.

It's far-gone, I can see that, Cal said. You was good with your hands I might say you'll soon have to lance the gum. If that knife's sharp, I mean.

It's sharp.

Truman jiggled the tablet dust into a pile and twirled the cloth about. He tongued about in his mouth and spat onto the floor at his feet a bloody wad. Then he took the new wad and poked a finger about inside his mouth until he found what he consented would be its ideal resting place.

Feelin better already, he said, smiling his smile. A dentist fella I know claims attitude is half the battle. You treat yourself good and the Lord will do the same.

Cal leaned his arms up on the counter, too out of sorts to

respond civilly to this. The wad chinkered up the visitor's mouth and imparted an odd sibilance to his speech.

Truman flipped over the sardine tin, noted the turnkey attached to the bottom, and flicked the slim staple into his pocket.

That'll be thirty-three cent it come to, Calvin said.

But the man now had seen something in the dim rear of the store that interested him. He strode on back and next turned, holding up a trap.

This here's mink, ain't it? he called. A mink trap?

Calvin got a flustered look. He'd left the door open and a cold wind was shooting in.

Truman approached, the trap clanking its chain, the metal jaws blinking faintly blue in the cord light.

It's mink, Truman said. I used to of had me one.

They could hear the car still chugging away outside, jittering side to side, the headlights tracing paths dim and fading before they reached the trees. Beyond that, the dark.

I'll have it, Truman said. This here mink trap, it's not too steep.

It's all steep these days, Calvin told him. That's six-dollar steep, that there one is. You plannin on trappin mink, up the road there where you're visitin these no-name friends?

Truman worked open the trap, placed the contraption on the counter and set the spring. Its teeth were cut large and soldered in pointy triangles thick as a thumb, its gaping jaw large enough to take a man's head.

Put your arm in there, Truman said. I bet itterd snap the bone in half.

Cal picked up from the window ledge a thin, dusty board. He whapped it against the counter edge to show its strength, then pitched the board into the trap, which closed with an instant explosive clang and jumped to the floor, where it seemed to crawl, startling them so that both men scooted back.

Yessir, Truman said. Snapped that board right in half. I believe I done bought me a mink trap.

He peeled from his pockets several tightly folded bills.

And a pack of them Camels, Truman said. I go me thue my smokes the way a washerwoman splashes thue her laundry piles.

You don't buy them but the one pack at the time then, do ye?

Nawsir. I'm tryin to quit. Tobacky'll drive you to death's door quickern snakebite.

He picked up his smokes, his tablet tin, his trap, and made it to the door before twisting back. He turned on Cal a bored, treacherous gaze.

That there good-lookin fella was here with the baby today? he said. He your son?

Calvin shook his head, puzzled by the notion. Nawsir. Though he's a good enough boy.

Calvin watched the man cogitate a while on this news, wiping sloops of saliva on his sleeve.

Reminded me of someone I knowed, he finally said. Though when I knowed him he won't holdin no child. Looked a newborn infant, thatern did. That baby. They's a pretty thing, babies. Gladdens the heart. The mother, I reckon, must be right proud.

Calvin dipped his head noncommittally. He veered over from his counter and yanked the light string.

The store swooped to black. Truman didn't move. Calvin held his breath, watching the man's hulk dimly shadowed by the carlights to his rear. His flesh pebbled. With a certainty that froze him to his own tracks he judged that this figure swept up out of dark and rootless night meant to lunge at him, swinging his trap or stabbing his blade.

Then the floor creaked and a snickered laugh broke the silence.

Jist curious, Truman said, I see a baby my spirits rise like a biscuitcake. I had me one I could call my own I'd crow like a rooster, that I would.

Grunting, Calvin stepped forward to usher the man out into the night.

Though still he hung there.

Say. Ye don't have no shovel I could borry, do ye? Nor one I could rent?

Calvin sent him on his way.

Afterwards, he stood outside the door, his chains muted, his skin clammy, watching the car jostle over his ruts and, tail pipe dragging, buck away.

Over the past year, since he'd had this car, Truman had slept any number of nights here under the steering wheel, his legs either bent up by his rump, or spread out to the far floorboards, a coat wadded up behind his head and a rug pulled up over his chest. When it got too cold he'd snag something else from his jumble in the back, and cover that over him, or he'd run the car engine until the heater made him toasty warm. But tonight the heater won't working, would only blow cold air, his tooth thudded, his head too, and first there was him feverish and then him chilled. At the minute he had all he could find from that backseat heaped up over him, but he was still shivering.

He won't going to git any sleep, he could see that.

He turned on his radio and listened a spell to the crackle, then switched the radio off again.

He drew out his mink trap and for another minute took pleasure in its manufacturing.

That, he said aloud, is the best six dollars ever I spent.

He was parked in the trees about two hundred yards up from that man Calvin's store. He considered how he could later on in the steep of night go back to that store and see he could break in. Against this was the storekeep already wary, and on top of that there was the matter of them dogs.

He could steal by and lay out a plate of poison, he had any.

Though he hadn't heard dogs this last visit, and he counted that curious.

Now why, he asked the dark, would a man have dogs, and then not have them?

He fiddled with the heater buttons and stomped the element with his foot, but cold air kept blowing.

He tossed his covers from him and stepped out into the night, flaring up match under another cigarette.

The thing is, he said, I'm a man needs to keep busy. Ye can't sleep, then you don't stay there wallowin.

He'd seen a lane back there a ways, and now he walked it, he could see yonder on the rise a house with a lighted window.

No harm in checkin that out, he said.

Anything useful pop up, he'd grab it.

Truman thumped out a cigarette for himself, and offered one. He explained that his car had give out. It had give out down on the main road, and he figured he'd give that car a rest before trying again. It was shot to its mud flaps, he said, and hadn't bin for a good while actin up to par anyhow.

The woman up in shadowy light on the front porch, her

hands stiff behind her, refused his cigarette. She refused that just as she'd refused a minute ago to answer smile with smile.

She was standing there now wrapped in flimsy green bathrobe asking him if she looked like she was running a garage. Asking him in a rough whorey voice if he'd seen a goddamn sign announcing she was open for car-repair business. She was ready to spin inside any second, and slam that door, he could see that.

So, short of strong-arming her, he'd best quickly perk her innerist. He had no qualms about strong-arming her—he wouldn't of minded it a nickel because he could see her detestation of him and see that personal fear won't a part of her mixture, no, she was above that—but although he'd scouted the place and peered an overlong time through her windows before rapping, he won't too sure what help she'd have inside.

Ye wouldn't know a doctor-feller, would ye? he asked.

He'd dropped down in the dark of the yard after knocking. Now he ventured out into the pooled light, going two steps up to the porch. He wanted her to see he was ragged and poorly. That he was no morn harmless urchin. He stroked his fiery cheek and wiped a hand over his hot brow and sagged there.

Hereabouts? he said. A tooth-doctor, I mean. Could look here at this troublin tooth of mine?

But already she was asking was it a garage or a doctor he wanted or was it both? What the slam-hell was it he wanted, or was he no morn a goddamn sonofabitch standing on her porch steps making sorry excuses.

He peered around her to see if anybody was in there with her, but she shifted each time he did.

She looked to him right wanton.

He could hear some kind of soft music from inside her door.

He wondered how much money she'd have hid in there.

He hobbled sorrowfully back out into the dark.

Well, he said. If this's how you'd treat needy stranger.

She came on full out of the house then. She stood out on the porch, regarding him with hard suspicion. With the light behind her he could see her nakedness through the gown.

What is it you want? she said. You look to me like pure sorriness up to no good bizness.

He saw she had a tongue on her could cut wire.

He made to climb the steps, and would have, but one of her arms flew up and inside the fist was a long knife.

Back up, she said. Back up and haul ass.

Truman backed up.

Sorry to bother you, he said. You ought to could look at me and see I wouldn't offer a body no harm. I will say though that you got a hard mouth.

She darted forward. That knife fist slashed up.

You'd eat raw buzzard, she said. You'd eat it, and if that didn't satisfy, you'd flap and cluck your own self. Now git the hell away from here.

He could rusher. He could try it. But that knife was at the ready and she'd get one good slash in.

He paused before dropping away into full dark, listening a second to the low swim of music from inside. It won't fiddle but could be violin. Quite a splash of them catgut instruments. An organ somewhere way to the rear, like a thing under water. Cat-fight music.

I like a good tune my own self, he said, grinning. Well. Ye won't hep me, I say goodnight to ye then.

She watched him go from the yard and when next he looked she won't there.

He floogered his tooth wad into dirt and stayed on a minute in the dark, watching.

He saw her whisk past the window and a moment later the table lamp went off. The house went black.

He heard someone's step among the bushes and whipped around to the sound.

He could dimly see an old man rooted there, a shotgun crisscross the arms.

Truman spat, faded quickly on away into the night.

The old man came out onto the road, to see he did.

Oh little sister, are ye cold? Are ye hungry and adrift and are ye weary? Would ye pause a while in the caretaker's mercy?

She'd had image of her sister, periodically.

Mostly Sister was a ghostly phantom, skewered to her brain like burled knot upon a tree, that tree phantomish as well. Though she'd had good sighting of her, periodically.

Last night she'd felt relief in her body of a kind that all but amazed her, and had halted in the roadside's blackness to appraise the new condition. She'd seen her sister unbinding herself of tight cloth. She'd seen her astreak through forest in close to full nakedness.

Later, she'd seen Sister clutch hands to her knees and keel over.

She'd seen that driverman's face aswirl in dark mist, and felt him claw up upon her.

She'd seen the car time and time again shuddering upon dark road, and once or twice heard the mutter of voices.

Once she'd glimpsed a man, another man this was, walking a road with what seemed like a baby.

She could clench her eyes shut now, her head athrob as

though beaten with branches, and see inside her head the black mud of what might be black river, and perceive under her eyelids a derelict dwelling, though Sister was absent and in all other regard that space empty.

She was cold now, and hungry. She'd had to leave home without taking a coat, that to avoid raising suspicion. She'd grabbed unfinished bread out of the griddle pan, to take that, but that doughy substance long since no more than a clawing rake in her belly.

She'd walked through the night and on through full day and now it was night again and she was resting.

She wouldn't stay at it long, she told herself.

But her feet were so swollen and hurtish.

She wished she had food.

She wished she could be home asleep on her pallet bed and her sister asleep on the floor beside her.

No, not long, she said to the dark, and her eyes lidded and she slept.

She'd come in her journey that day up over a knoll and there to her front stretched three hovel cabins laid the width of one, and in a front yard a woman under a sunbonnet was spreading seed to an emblazonment of clucking hens, some few Rhode Island reds, the most no more than pullets atilt under yellow feather, the others Dominoes, one more dusty and ragged than the next, as many as a hundred or two hundred strutters, all told. Some were at roost up in the branches of two deformed and bark-ravaged trees, their heads cocked like sentries awatch over the heavens for scabbard sail.

In late afternoon this was, a cold sun concealed behind clabbered sky, if there at all. Under the hat, the woman wore a red satin dress and stockings half up her legs. Mounted over on the middle porch was a high, stark bush killed by freeze, it in a painted bucket, and five or six other buckets overturned up by the door. Beyond the corner of the last hovel stood a wagon with a broken tongue. Way out there on an open field was a mule grazing and a small boy holding a hat on his head with both hands. Staring her way. A fox hide was pegged up to dry against each of the three front hovel doors, their fox heads intact, and glassy eyes studying the floor beneath them as if to specify the last footsteps of the huntsman or huntswoman who had nailed them there. Over to the side, given wide shift by the prowling chickens, streamed a black iron workaday pot fired by a crisscross of smoldering logs, and beside this set twin galvanized tubs in which floated ladle and scrub board and an ill abundance of sheets and clothes. Nearby was strung a clothesline with nothing yet upon it.

The woman saw her but did not speak until the girl was a good piece past her on the road.

That ain't the way.

It was this that she called, and when the girl turned to espy her she was waving her sun hat at one of the birds clucking in her tree.

The girl wondered was the woman's words meant for her or for feathered flock, and she turned again and padded her footsteps on. At the bottom of the hill she screwed a look over her shoulder another time, and there was the woman out in the road still waving her hat and hollering out the same report.

That ain't the way.

The girl started running then and for the next hundred or two hundred yards the woman with the hat seemed to be trampling after her, and the boy from the field running along too.

The woman calling this out all the while, through huff and puff of breath: That ain't the way. That ain't a road you can go down. There's nothin but ruination down that road. I come from down that road and I ought to know. Don't say later you won't warned. That there road will kill anything comes up it or goes down. You come back up this road agin won't solitary soul recognize you. You better hear me. It ain't the way. What I'm tellin you I'm tellin you for your own good.

She went on calling such words long after the girl had pushed on out of her sight, and even some ten or fifteen minutes later the girl believed she could still glimpse intermittent flare of red dress through the trees, and hear the hatted woman's voice echoing brokenly over the distance.

Later on she had come to a burnt house, burnt of old, naught but stone chimney at stand, and piled rubble, and here she briefly lingered to poke among the curious heap. From the chimney hearth she picked up wormy, uncharred board, and there beneath it coiled to cowpat size slumbered a bed of rattlersnakes, some four or five. She jostled them with the toe of her shoe and as they disembraced to lazy, cheerless wakefulness she abandoned them to their solitude and steered her way along.

Later still she came to a divide in the road, the one route no more worn by traffic than the next, and both weedy in the middle so as to be little more than cart or wagon trail, but she leaned without caution to that right-most one, taking that pathway which angled down into wide fold of valleys out of which rose vast miles of green expanse, some of these many curvatures shaded by dark, oppressive cloud and many another astream with milky fluid.

Eventually she arrived at a kind of draw in which bestirred three strange people, the each garbed with numerous coats so that they stood thick as bears, and shouting a tide of excited exclamations at her, and one, most oddly, giving hurried chase after her.

She hadn't reckoned the world could be so enormous, so unrestrained in its turbulent character. She had expected she would find spidery network of paved roads, them all lined with an affliction of moneyed people streaming heel against heel.

It was a jimcracky, hodgepodge of universe, she determined, as all said.

But that lane terminated soon. She stood for a time in weedy field the growth of which topped her shoulder blades, here weighing the hours to be lost if she reversed herself, and mindful of the bog's slow creep up her shoes and the hungry suck of mire about her ankles if she straggled on. She rested her hands palm down upon her head and thought what she must do. An awesome silence stretched about her and in this unstruck terminus she was aware of a good many crouching woodland creatures stilled as she was herself stilled, and all awaiting her movement, since it was her own that would determine theirs. She wondered she wasn't the first person in the world ever to be venturing here.

She did not know how it was or by what queerness of divination this path she had been taking seemed to her the one path to be on.

A bird on a far tree swooped in quick downward flight and squawked its displeasure before its wide white wings caught air and it flapped in direct pilgrimage between two gapped ridges, and could be that was a sign.

Could be she was meant to go that way.

But she took deep breath and strung her same way along. She was not unaccustomed to weed or thicket, and reasoned that what was sour bog in open field one minute would turn hard floor and open road the next.

She hoped she didn't cripple down, or her way through this wilderness be versed with delirium.

Over time the sky fomented a gun-barrel blue, which color darkened as she marched, and she thought she could see distant rain, though these storm clouds for the most part stayed wide of her. She only got thin switches of rain, and these brief. A cold wind stirred up and with that she was glad to have the company of birds, and traipsing hare, and once a squirrel which flew. Now and then she came upon goat trails, though the trails not new and, for a duration, if they suited her purposes, she trod one or another of these. She came upon the gutted carcass of a furry beast, its bones disassembled, and wondered what engagement had defeated it and ought a thing's parts be left to rot out in the elements that way.

At another point she found a warped wagon wheel decomposing in muck and it bothered her the absence of any recognizable entry or transport for this vestige of other worlds.

She wondered no ruined city, no Indian encampment, or jungle emporium, or gypsy wagon, or lost gold mine had marked her travels. She wondered there weren't cabin or grave or church any bit this way. She had feared dark cave or twisty canyon in which she would lose her bearings, but until this hour had witnessed none. She'd seen things magnificent, but little she would call unusual.

On toward dusk she came upon a river, it roaring at mighty caterwaul along eroded clay walls, the depths beclouded and the surface aswirl with foam. Here she trekked the shore nosewards past rocky undulation leading to high, thundering waterfalls amid twin peaks, which she lingered a minute to study with rapt breath, and from there her way was downward until a rotted, fallen log provided her safe passage across and thence she followed for a time the river's other, now meandering, shore.

She awoke from her sleep with a start and looked about at the dark. She wondered how much time had elapsed, and whether it was night of the same day or was it the dark morning of another.

Her teeth chattered and she could not stop her shivering.
She started again on.

She was nearer to her sister, not yet so near as to satisfy
her, but nearer, and this chanting to herself of that fact was
calming in its influence. Her heart could thud, and her flesh
shiver, but she knew she was nearer. If the man had harmed
her sister, she would, if she could, she thought, slay him. If
her sister was dead she would bury her. If Sister by chance
was alive she would bring her back to home—not by this
route, for her sister would not tread it—or the two of them
chart mutual course through more favorable wilderness to another, and more foreign, place.

She was drowsy, and hungry in her belly, and her legs and
her feet were awhack with ache. Her shoulders were weary, so
weary, and her feet near raw. Her flesh stung with myriad
bites, the many cratered and blistery, puckerish. From time
to time as terrain allowed she smeared mud about her limbs.

She felt fright for her sister, but experienced little for herself. It seemed to her she'd made this journey before, this or
another equal in its demand, in another life, as some would
say, and she therefore saw in it scant novelty or hardship beyond her scope of measurement. It was why she'd been born:
to wade behind her sister and take unto her own flesh the
portion of punishment otherwise her sister must bear. Such
sharing, she reasoned, was necessary, for without it portioned
out to the two of them neither would have survived to this
hour.

It amazed her that Lena had never appeared to know this.
It saddened her as well, for there was a sweetness in the sharing, and such good strength to her heart that the sweetness
gave, and now Sister might never come to know this. How it
felt so good, and sure enough better than any feelings she'd
get from the hands of that smoker in his black car. Her flesh

won't like her sister's, though Sister said one day it would be. One day she'd want a man's flesh pressing her own, Sister said; she'd want to sling herself against whoever that man might turn out to be, and go at it like lizards.

She could love her sister, she thought, but it would be God's sin to want to be her. It seemed to her that her sister's life, the way she looked at things, was such that reproaches were not unwarranted. For the one thing, Sister was vain. Sister was misguided. Sister would trust the first man blinked eye her way. Like had happened. No, she wouldn't want to be Sister. Not because of the fix she'd now got herself into, but because her sister's yearnings, her impatience to claim for her life something better, were not in accord with the heart's pure journey. Her mistakes, her crooning love, and giving herself to corpsy-eyed stranger, had made of her a piteous creature. It had made her stupid. But she hadn't ought to have to die for it.

Toker had slept a fitful sleep, what there was of it. Frequently during the night he had been disturbed by sketches of dream, a car door squeaking open and a woman's white foot plopping down, and had waked to hot sweat over his body. To the sight of the baby softly breathing beside him. Then he'd dreamed the baby squished up under him, dead, and he'd waked with the sweat again. So there were those dreams to trouble him. Frequently, too, in his sleep he had heard the dogs scratching at his door to be let in, then squabbling among themselves, and later their howls over distant-flung hills together with the muted response of other canines on the prowl away off there. Then he'd heard George and Martha no more and knew they were roaming again, roaming far, catching up on the miles they'd missed while penned-up down at Cal's. He didn't expect he'd see them again until they got hungry or their curiosity about things here got the best of them.

It was the baby, and the baby's wetness, that finally waked him proper. Waked him, though without whimper or cry of neglect, the trickle of her fingers over his face. He got up

then, sore of joint and rubbing his eyes, and crept on bare feet
to his shoe-box window, there peering out into a darkness in
which could be glimpsed the odd whip of fine mist. He judged
it to be close on to daybreak.

He lay again on his cot, in play with the baby.

She was entranced, it seemed, by the blinking of his eyelash. By his ears, his hair, his hands, his nose.

Time and time again her small curled hands slapped at
these, or clawed at them, or she wriggled to get them into her
mouth.

He won't in no hurry to rise and get on with what must be
got on with.

You stuck a finger in the baby's belly she went all giggly.
You tickled her feet she went all zany.

You looked one way her eyes would slice off the same way,
then she'd dart hers back and slap that hand up again in your
face and ream fingers inside your ear, your eyes, your mouth.

She had a ring of dirt, of crusty milk, around that mouth.
That wet pool under her bottom.

She ought to be washed, but he won't her mama.

What's that? For he next was sitting up, straining his ears,
hearing hushed voices, skulking movement, outside. Pans
rattling together.

God in heaven.

He whipped up, grabbing clothes with one hand, reaching
for shotgun with the other. But that space bare where his hand
fell. No shotgun, that shotgun gone in the fire, the way everything else was. More voices, whispers, out there now. Someone up by the side of the house. Another one running. He
wished he had a watch, that he did know the time. It won't no
reasonable hour for friends, what few he had, to be dropping
by. And what was out there didn't sound friendly. He pried his

face up to the shoe-box pane, but saw nothing. Trees, that was all. Black sky, that was all. The night with a nose the same as his.

Not the law already. The law wouldn't come in the dark anyhow. And when they did come, if they meant to, it would be in a passel, with bullhorn and bulldozers and yelping dogs.

But maybe some anonymous informant had give them the news.

Still as a grave out there now. All but pitch dark.

Or was it X the throatslitter, with his ratpack, come back to finish his work?

Toker rushed his pants on. No time to think now about shoes or shirt.

The baby was uncovered, with a stern look that said, What's the fuss? He dipped back, throwing cover on. Hide that dodger.

Can't have you gittin no croup.

Something was hoving into view now, coming up slowly, thick as a tree stump. Swinging a lantern. Specter with an orangey hue. Rattling with each step what sounded like those pots and pans.

The figure stopped some forty feet from his door. It brought the lantern up to the side of its face.

Hallohhh! it called.

An old woman's spookified voice.

Toker moved up the steps, the earth cool to his feet. He cracked open the door, slid out, and kept on sliding, taking up his watch in a crouch near the shed's corner.

Hallohhh! the figure said again.

Then: Don't think I can't see you.

Toker knew she couldn't, not with lantern up to her face. Not looking off as she was, the wrong way. But whatever was still and shadowy and now running bent over and hoppity be-

hind her might could. She had somebody back there. She
hadn't come up here alone, in the night, armed only with her
lantern and good will.

You Mr. Taper? the voice said.

Toker, he replied. I bin known to be.

The one behind her stopped and plopped down.

The woman advanced a portion, hand cupping her eyes, the
lantern still carried high. She seemed to have about a thousand clothes on. Topmost was a man's thick overcoat, which
dragged at her heels. She was transporting a slew of pots and
pans.

I thought I was lost, he heard her say. What's that smell.

Toker watched the form behind her dart up and away.

We had us a fire, he said. We had us a little burn-down.

Unhuh, she said. I thoughten it so. None perished, I hope.

He thought he spotted a third one now, off slinking to the
side.

He wondered what the tomfool they wanted.

The woman advanced a few more timid steps, her eyes
searching the dark. Agitated, as though them behind her
might shoot her in the back, she didn't press on with her mission. She stooped, placing the lantern by her feet. Her pots
and pans clanged. A garment flapped up and covered her
face.

Fire's the menace, she said. It's the one true peril. It goin
to swoop over the earth one day, east to west, and not one
man, woman, or child escape.

You can see I'm a woman, she added. That I can't give you
no harm and don't mean any.

Toker stayed crouched. Them behind her were getting
braver now, creeping on up. He extended his stick out over
his knee. Let them think it a gun barrel, they wanted to.

We—she halted on that word and he heard a string of clear

cusswords behind her—I bin walkin all day. Since midday, about there.

Unhuh, Toker said. And you lost, the whole of that time?

No, she said. I had the way pointed out to me. I had it scribbled down.

Someone giggled in the darkness. An idiot's giggle. Over to the right. By that dying hedge. Now skulking again. Toker saw him stagger and fall and heard his curse. He saw him getting up, hobbling.

The woman picked up her lantern and nosed forward, still trying to draw a bead on his hiding place.

Toker counted about six coats on her, buttoned and unbuttoned, and some held shut by wire. Assorted rags hung from her pockets. A kind of bird-cage contraption rode high on her backside. On her feet were boots of different sizes and colors.

The talk on the road is, she said, that you have a baby under your roost.

A baby? His voice thinned in the lift, he was that surprised.

That's what the talk is. I mean to see it.

Why's that?

The woman flung out her arms. You best hand it over, she said. Iffin it ain't the one I want, then it ends right here.

Toker wondered what could end that hadn't hardly started. He wondered she didn't swelter in all them coats.

The idiot one hobbled up to her side, giggling and hawking up spit. The woman turned wrathfully upon him.

Ain't I tole you to stay low? she cried. Ain't I tole you to clamp a hand over that fool mouth?

The third one cussed. He cussed in a rage, bursting up out of the darkness, just barreling up to stop wide of the woman, leveling his rifle on Toker's door. He stopped cussing then.

Another coat dealer.

Housekeeping utensils were roped to his waist. His mismatched boots alike to those the woman was wearing. He was gimpy, Toker noted, in the one leg.

Hidy-do, he said, bowing. Mr. Taper?

It ain't Taper, grumbled the woman. It's Toker, he says.

Where's he at? the man asked.

His rifle swayed; he wasn't none too sure of his target behind that door. A felt hat with a brim was pulled low over his brows and over the ears. Under that, another one. His head looked way small inside the piled coats, the hats. His legs spindly. He was chawing on a stick. He too looked orangish in the lantern's dim light, though Toker noticed now that the sky was lifted some little bit. He could see the ground's frost cover and mist rising from it as though heated.

The idiot boy standing near them wore boots of a jungly wrap-around kind climbing to his crotch. He had on a white sailor hat.

Ast him he got any licker, that one said. Ast him he got a jug.

The woman whopped her foot against ground. Hush up about licker, she said. To Toker adding, as she spun finger to ear, He's not right.

They won't none were, Toker thought. We'se all at the same fish fry.

The older man lumbered forward, giving a belly laugh as he made to fold down into a friendly crouch. Like he had in mind squatting on his haunches for a quiet confab. Then the knee sprung up and he was sighting his rifle hard at Toker's shoe-box window.

Dead in my sights, he said. One move and you're horse-flesh.

Toker laughed out loud. The durn fools hadn't yit figured out where he was. Would he shoot at a window?

Then fire away.

But hold on, he thought. I got me a baby in there.

He wondered where was George and Martha, now he needed them.

We don't mean you no trouble, the woman said, shambling cumbersomely forward, dropping a heavy hand on the man's gun barrel. We mean to have a gander at your baby though. Aye, we do mean that.

No, no trouble, the man said. He spat, and slapped her hand away, rocked lower on his heels, realigned his rifle.

Lessern you want it, the idiot one sang. His left arm was cocked back to throw whatever it was he might have in his hands to throw.

A rock? They meant attacking him with rocks now?

This baby you're talking on? asked Toker. Is it yourn?

That waits to be seen, the woman said. We won't know till we study on it, will we?

You could come in daylight.

We come now, the man with the rifle said.

The idiot boy snickered. Let's git him, Pa, he said. Let's scatter his brains.

He reared back and threw. The rock looped up, disappearing into the dark. Then he slipped. Toker saw his feet fly up, saw the idiot's tumble. Surprised, the man leapt up with a whoop and as he did so his gun went off. It went off high into the trees, reverberating, the kick of the shot knocking the man to the ground, his goods flying each which way.

They all cowered, Toker among them, the shot seeming to echo and blap again and again through the mountains.

A second later Toker could hear the dogs. They seemed to be about a mile away, barking venomously and running his way hard as they could.

Toker's visitors lifted themselves up slowly, with chagrin

and mortification, touching themselves to see they remained alive.

Air he dead? asked the man. I ain't heard no grunt.

Hallohhh! the woman called. Air ye croaked?

Toker jumped out from his hiding spot, shaking his stick. Startled, the three collided in a huddle, cowering more.

You are everone damn fools! he shouted. You want my baby? Then take it!

The woman took offense at this.

That waits to be seen, she said. Of the minute, all needed is we study on it.

She came on springy, ready for business.

Where's it at?

Come on in, Toker told her. I swear to hell.

He could hear George and Martha nearer now, barking and galloping.

The man and the idiot with him heard them too and seemed to be searching for a place they could hide.

Toker got the lamp lit. He pointed at his bed, where four limbs were flashing.

The woman crept down, not trusting the steps, wrinkling her nose at the burnt odor. Toker judged her to be on the mean side of sixty, with her humpbacked coats and her red nose and three scarves knotted at her neck.

A hand flew to the woman's mouth. Her eyes went big. She seemed not to like what she saw.

Toker yanked the bedcovers back.

Iffin she's yourn, he said, I want to see proof.

A few tears spotted the woman's eyes. Some of her breath rushed out and she had a spent, forsaken look in that second before she stumbled back against the lower step, slapping hands over her face.

She wiped her eyes, gathering herself. Turned and hollered up through the open door.

It ain't ourn, Pa.

Not yourn? Toker said.

He could hear outside the dogs thundering in, whirling and snarling, and salvos of terror, shrieks, a wild thudding about, from the two men up there.

The woman was rooting under her coats, now posting a hand up inside her dress. She pulled out a rat-eared snapshot in a tin frame and looked from it to the baby. She seemed to study both a considerable minute.

No, it's not ourn, she called again.

She didn't seem to notice the dogs.

The two men were jammed in the doorway, kicking at the dogs and issuing the odd appeal for help.

Toker hurried up the stairs and called off the dogs, who hopped up on him, licking his hands, happy again. Bearing no grudge against anyone.

The woman came out, her steps dragging.

How old is it? the one called Pa asked.

It's teensy, the woman said.

You don't wanter anyhow? the idiot one asked. But Martha growled, her legs set to spring, and he fell quiet.

The woman took up her lantern. She trudged off into the dark.

We'se licked agin, she said.

Sorry for troublin you, Pa said. We ain't bad folks. We jist chasin what's ourn.

How old would yourn be? asked Toker, thinking he'd never set eyes on a more pathetic bunch.

Come to twelve, the man said. Our baby'd be bout twelve now, give or take.

Twelve?

Yip. Bout that. We been huntin her now four years, nigh on. Four or five, give or take.

Toker studied the man's earnest face.

Run off or drove off or stole, the man added. Likely stole.

His eyes wavered, he peered by Toker down into the grim hole.

You ain't got nothin you don't need, do ye? That I could swap ye for? I'd let go my best duds here, ye had a good leg-hold trap.

No, Toker said. I got nothin you'd want.

The man snapped a look at the dogs.

I've got me a bag of washers I could swap ye, he said. For either one or both of them dogs.

No, Toker said, I don't need no washers.

The man nodded.

Mine run off, the man said. He hesitated. He was backing on off now. Everthing I tetch does. We'se tried to run him off— here he jabbed an arm toward the idiot one up on the lane— but he won't budge.

Toker listened to the idiot and the woman, up there on his lane, in argument about something. He saw her raise the globe on the lantern, and the boy bending to blow the wick out.

The sky was near light now.

The man joined them.

I wishen you the best, Toker told him.

The three waved.

The man stepped back haltingly from Toker's way, and Toker watched him gyrate a second there with open mouth.

We did come cross us one earlier in the day, he said.

One what? Toker asked.

Oh, female, the man said. She was that.

Toker felt his skin crawl. His knees went buckly.

Wherebouts?

The man huffed his collars up around his head and stared wide of Toker's head, as though searching his mind for the forgotten spot.

In a draw, the man said. We seed her in a draw not morn a tinker's smell from here. But maybe it was yestiddy we seener, now I think on it. She was right stick-legged. Harm here give chase, my son Harm—raise your hand, Harm.

Harm, smiling from the lane, raised his hand.

Come on, Spigot, the woman said.

He give chase, the man continued, but she near run him to his kneecaps. We could see she weren't ourn.

Toker didn't reply.

The man stood roping and tying at the waist his many coats.

A stray, I reckon, he said. Right whipped lookin, she was. But she could run.

He paused, and in the silence eyed Toker cagily, his face slewed into a man-to-man leer.

Ye could likely catcher, ye needed extra one. I've always held that ever man does.

The woman cursed him, and shied on down the lane, driving the idiot boy before her.

I can't innerist ye in no washers, I'll be seein you then, the man said. In heaven, if not afore.

Soon the mist, ghostly in hue, swallowed up their scraggly shapes, and the space was empty again.

Y

Some short while later Toker stole alone through the woods in the early light, having told George and Martha to mind the baby and mind her good. He'd left all three together in a pile on the cot, all sleeping and drooling, limbs and snouts slung one upon the other.

He'd brought along the shovel, not knowing what use he intended for it.

The woman's foot was still slung down out of the door and for some minutes he wavered there in silent speculation, undecided about what was expected of him. What he might do.

He was feeling sorry for hisself, that a feeling of old, and he liked it no better now. You let that feeling in once, just once, and it seemed to lap you up whole, mowing you down from within and leaving you no more capable of action or decision than two-toed sloth or simmering chicken in a pot.

He'd brought an old wrapper down and he flapped this quickly over the woman's body, not this morning able to do more than glance at her. To glance and see was her throat still slit.

It was a shame to leaver here. A shame not to giver a decent burial.

He prodded his shovel into earth and thought about that. Thought about what would be said now if he reported this crime to the law or even mentioned the matter to them from whom he might could expect friendship. They'd have suspicions, even as he would, him in their shoes.

Ladies and gentlemen of the jury, this man tells us he finds in bright mornin a baby in his woods. But that day slides by and then the night, and only the next day does he come forward to report the findin of a dead body not a stone's throw from his mole-house door. Ladies and gentlemen, I ast you, is that the way an innocent man would behave? No, he have sliced that woman's throat same as he would take razor to yourn or mine, then he have gone out with a shovel to fix unto black earth his sorry misdeed.

Guilty, judge and jury would say.

Raymond Toker, we condemn you.

For a while he looked on his lane for tire tracks, ruts, tell-tale signs where a car might have pulled in or attempted a turnaround, assuming the killer had come up here by auto-mobile, as he must have done. But he saw nothing. For a while longer he tramped up and down his woods, thinking he might find something—the knife, the woman's purse, any-thing—but aside from a few cigarettes, the tips yellowish with spit, a few rusted tin cans, a few dirt-packed bottles and the odd scrap of corroded iron, and other such rubbish, he found nothing.

He trudged back to his pit in the earth, the shovel still on his shoulder, having determined nothing, and when he en-tered it was to find the dogs and the baby still curled together on the cot. Martha was gnawing on something, however, with low growls meant to keep George at bay, and when he man-aged to wrestle the object from her he saw it was the woman's cloth shoe, chewed into raggy bits, only the rubber sole to any degree intact.

He was, he figured, as good as hanged.

Soon after that he fed the baby and the dogs as best he could manage, dressed the baby in the best of his shirts, slid her into the pillowcase, summoned George and Martha to his heels, and hit the trail.

The sky still starry. The ground frosty, the air swarthy, thick with a ghostly mist.

A horseman astride his mount appeared out of the mist, leading riderless mule, and reined up as the girl sat with locked eyes under a tree by the side of a paved road.

Have you gone lame? he asked.

She was too cold to speak and could scarcely tilt her head to determine who was addressing her.

The rider dismounted and slung his coat off and placed it over the chilled girl's shoulders.

She stayed on so seated, her knees knocking together and her jaw rattling. Icy slithers lay along her lashes and when she could turn her head she could see him only as dark shadow through these slithers, for she could not make her eyes open.

He crouched before her and buttoned the coat about her chest. He lifted her hands from her thighs and warmed them between his own. He lifted her feet into his lap and removed her shoes, and briskly and for a good many minutes rubbed her feet. He placed his hands over her face and pressed the warmth of his flesh into her own.

Later, when speech again was a property she could claim and her eyes once again knew normalcy, she addressed him and saw by his method of reply, as by the dislocation of his stare and by the curious milkiness of his eyes, that he was a blind man.

I've come from afar, she said. And she gave study to his body, to see if the rest of his parts were whole.

So have we all, the man said.

He was back upon his mount now, a tall, high figure, and he leaned from the saddle with his arm extending toward her.

The girl pondered this invitation and by degrees stood.

I ain't said I wanted ride.

The man nodded silence to this, and calmly enfolded his hand about her wrist and lifted her behind him.

He gave a click to his lips and the horse broke off a last bit of grass, looked inquiringly back at him, and began slow clip-clop down the road into the dark.

The girl fitted her arms around the man's middle, staring back at the riderless mule.

It's old, the blind man said. I wouldn't want no one should ride him.

Where you taking that mule?

Only for companionable stroll.

A stroll where?

Oh, the man said. Over to new pasture or down to water. Whichever one the one we're ridin might choose.

The girl huddled herself to him and watched the frost sparkle under the stars and the mist sweep around them and sometimes part as they passed through.

She was warm now.

Do you mean me to keep this coat? the girl asked.

She waited for an answer, though none came.

Had I worked for it or were you kin I could keep it, she said, but as it is . . .

She unbuttoned the coat and was about to slide it from her shoulders when the hind legs of their horse began a sprightly dance beneath her, and she had to hug the man's middle to keep from falling.

The blind man laughed and rose up a little from the saddle, in the patting of his mount's long neck, and the girl said no more about the coat.

I'm lookin for someone, the girl said.

She saw the rider nod.

I'm lookin my sister, she said. Her and the man in a dusty beat-up black car she's with.

I've seen'um, the man replied. I've seen'um all my life. Sometimes they holler and wave, though I will say it's her who has best reason to holler most.

She did not understand his meaning, though she could think no question in probe of this oblique reply.

They continued their slow pace down the road in the dark, in the mist, and she wondered how soon it would be before the earth brightened and would she be awake to see the frost vanish and the mist thin away into nothing.

It's some bit misty this mornin, the girl said. Now I can see it.

The blind man did not answer.

How long the girl rode with the blind man she couldn't say, for the most part dozing against his backside. After one of her sleeps she looked back and saw the mule no longer was with them. Here they stopped and the man slung one leg over the horse's head, dismounting in such way as not to disturb her.

He pulled a red apple from his pocket and slooshed it up between the horse's teeth. He bit into another himself and then passed a third over to her.

Were you born blind? she asked.

What's sighted in one is blindness in another, he said.

She didn't know whether in such manner he spoke of his own two eyes, or of affairs peculiar to their race.

Where's the mule?

The man laughed. Oh, I traded him.

She looked about this person and probed the near terrain, though she saw nothing the man might have traded his mule for.

They went on then and the darkness didn't lift and she wondered she'd had no recent vision.

They rounded a curve after long straightaway and she heard the rider make that clucking noise again. The horse veered off from roadway into a lip of trees, and down a steep hill, and at the bottom of the hill they came to a channel cut with strange contour through the mountain, out upon its black route trapped formations astagger in the vaporous dawn.

What's this? the girl asked.

River without water, the rider said.

They started their way across this, soon the horse's hooves sinking into mud, the sounds sucking ones as it lifted hoof out, though the rider and his mount seemed to take no notice.

A faint odor of newly unleashed sourness drifted along with them.

Up ahead she saw in the mist an abandoned building with wrecked sidings and a leaning, though still vaulted, ceiling, and strung along the bank collapsed footings once in support of a variety of docks, these now as blackened teeth hanging out over nothing.

A fetid smell enveloped the place.

By this dilapidation the blind man gave small tug to the reins, and horse swiveled its head to him and halted.

The blind man swung her over, loosening his grip that she might slide his leg to easy ground.

I'll keep it then, she said. This coat.

The man smiled at her and said he had many.

He then clicked his tongue to the horse and went on through the dark mist and in a minute she didn't see him.

She tracked uneasy of mind up among the ruins. She'd seen this place before, in dream or vision, and was not surprised to see it now a second time.

She wondered her sister had come to such a dreadful place and whether she was still to be found here.

Near seven, Toker was down at Cal's Place waiting for it to open. He tried the door and beat on the windows, knowing the store was empty. Cursing Calvin who was not a soul you could ever in this world rely on to open when his own sign said he would.

That floorwalker'd sleep thue to Sunday if you let him, he told the baby. How he can squeak out a livin and call hisself well-off is way beyond me. You can't count on him for a hole in the ground.

He went around to the back and tucked the dogs inside their pen, the two whining, stiffening their legs so that he had to drop down behind them and shove their rumps in.

Oh yes, he said, you chew my evidence into rags and not once a sign of repentance from you.

Cal and Sarah's squat abode was shut up tight, not even a light on.

They's in there, he told the baby. They's jist too tight to let a light bulb burn. That lard can be out directly, Sarah'll see to that.

As he walked away the dogs began howling.

That'll turn them over, he said.

Back to the front again, he saw a car hurtling zipperdy-dash along the roadway, plunking up gravel; it washed on out of sight, its hiked rear end a rank snub to anyone saw it.

Abel Enal Wright. Acy's hobnail son. That sonofabitch. Now what, Toker asked himself, is that sorry sonofabitch up to so early in the mornin?

Maybe that sorryass is the one done it.

He hadn't never bin able to stand sight of that high-nosed sorryass, and wouldn't put it one bit past him.

The mountains were misted over, the sun locked out.

More rain comin, if God up there didn't die of guilt and heartbreak first.

The baby pulled at his hair, and Toker slapped at her hand.

Stop that, he said. Then when the baby scrunched up her face to cry he held her to him, rocking the poor lost thing.

Sorry, he said. Sorry, baby. My mood today is rotten.

The baby trickled its fingers into his mouth, now gurgling such crooning sounds he was made to laugh.

One of the old men, Wallace, came in a slow gait up the road and turned in. Toker could hear him scolding the ground. He had a rolled cigarette pinched up between his lips, smoked down to the last quarter inch. He hobbled up beside Toker and they stood together in modest silence beside the kerosene tank. Then a freckly-faced boy with flaming red hair came along, hopping on one leg, dragging a bare foot. He stopped as he saw Toker and the old man gazing his way, and just stood there by the road.

Ye hurt yeself, boy? asked the old man, but the boy drooped his head and didn't reply.

Wallace took a final squinty drag of his cigarette, then pitched the nub down to grind it under heel. He looked at Toker.

Not open yit?

Nope. Not yit a while.

A lazy dropass, ain't he?

He is that.

The old man cackled, then went into a wheeze. He tipped over and blew snot onto the ground.

I've knowd'um was too lazy to lift hand to face, the old man said. Jist petered out, they was that lazy.

Yessir.

Had me a cousin afflicted that way.

Unhuh, Toker agreed. Lots is.

You the Toker boy, ain't you?

Toker nodded. This old man had asked him that question near each day of his life.

That baby walk yit?

Nope. Not yit.

He ain't lost nothin then. Be better off if he never try.

She's a she.

The old man regarded the baby more attentively, as if coming upon her for the first time.

It ain't often I see a she this close, he said. Not to know what I was lookin at. But she was older, I could tell.

I reckon you could.

The old man stared off into space, momentarily lost in his thoughts, as Toker was in his. Then Wallace felt into his pockets, pulled out a plug of tobacco and with difficulty gummed off a healthy chaw into his mouth.

Yessir, he said, she was older I'd of knowed right off. But them days are past me now and I thank the Lord. I've bin able to give up thinkin of suicide, now I don't notice the women no more. That's the sole advantage of a man's old age.

He laughed and Toker politely laughed with him.

You gone raiser?

I hope to gracious not.

You raiser a Christian. Otherwise the raisin don't count. You see that car? The one come a tick ago? Acy Enal Wright's woodpecker son.

I seen'm. It would make me feel good one day to give him boot up his rear end would rupture his tailbone.

The old man regarded him closely.

Yip. He's a sorry one. Him and Acy both got their fingers up their rear ends the full day long. I remember now your daddy and them Wrights never did git along. Of course, though, most couldn't stand your daddy either.

He wiped his mouth and spat.

It's a chaw keeps me young now, he said. Tobacky and hell-raisin and paregoric when I can git my hands on it. Wonder what's keepin ol' Trout and Hindmarch. They's usually here by now.

He stepped out, peering up and down the road.

The freckly, red-haired boy, whimpering as he bent in caress of his naked foot, hopped back to stand on the one leg as Toker and the old man looked at him. The boy had small white circles on his cheeks, his red hair showing a fresh bowl cut, the skin white up round his bald ears and neck.

The old man nudged Toker.

I wager that boy ain't bin wormed yit. Them worms now, I've pulled slimy worm out of my rear end long as a fence-post. My daddy said it come from humping mules, but I've never had that pleasure, did ye?

He cackled laughter, spewing tobacco juice out over his clothes and shoes.

A woman hove into view, trudging along the highway shoulder, a wicker hamper full of chickens resting over her head. Toker and Wallace and the boy watched the occasional flutter of wings, watched to see would she turn in. Behind the woman appeared a long, lean man with pipe-stem legs, stooped a bit, his head thrust forward as if a rope hitched him to the creature in front.

I never seen them afore, the old man said. Not either one.

Me neither.

Not much spring to her step, the old man added. Lively as a sleepin gypsy. Though I wouldn't turner down, she offered herself.

That cackle again.

The pair passed on by without looking their way, the chickens throwing up a mild squawk of dismay.

Folks streamin by ever minute, Wallace said. Soon this here county gone be run over with new womenfolk and me never seen the dovepatch of a single one.

He turned leaky yellow eyes on Toker. But I bet a half-dollar you have.

Toker grinned back to him. Nope. I'm Joseph's own brother in that regard.

The old man looked away, lifting a flimsy hand onto Toker's arm. Here come that cranky bastard, he said. You reckon Sarah gave him his breakfast spankin yit?

Calvin was approaching from the far side, stomach riding out over his belt, unlaced shoes flopping on his feet, a set of jangly keys spinning on one finger. Ain't you the early birds, he said.

He went from one to the other of his locks, some eight or ten, grumbling to find the proper keys. He unlooped his several thick chains.

Good to see I ain't bin broke into, he said.

The old man poked Toker and asked him what he had worth stealing.

Only my virginity, Calvin said, and I'm holdin onto that hard as I'm able.

Shoot, said Wallace. I losten mine afore I was six years old.

I losten it to a full-grown snaggled-toothed woman said I was the best she ever had.

They laughed, gathered by the door, the boy hobbling across the gravel toward them with a stricken face.

The door swung open with a snarly scrape and ripple, then its ping.

Calvin went through, turning on this and that pale hanging light streaked with cobwebs and the corpses of numerous flies. The old man spat out his glob into a bucket and withdrew a Diamond Lil from the drink box before taking up his usual position by the stove. The boy hopped in and leaned against the door frame, one leg drawn up behind him.

They all looked at him as he cleared his throat.

Yawl seen my daddy? he asked, his voice wavery.

Calvin said, Nope. Nope, and hope not to.

They saw the boy slump his head and scratch at the worm rings on his face.

Toker went behind the counter, exiting a minute later with crackers and a wedge of cheese.

Tote that up, he told Cal. Call it a cash sale.

Calvin did so. It come to thirty-three cent, he said, includin the soft drink you gone have.

Toker paid him. His spending money was getting close to zero and pretty soon he'd have to hike up Mignon Ferry Road and offer hisself up to sawmill employment, there was any. Usually there won't.

How'd my dogs do? asked Calvin. They have any luck sniffin out that trail?

Toker's throat locked up. He batted his eyes at the storekeeper, and felt them go wet. He couldn't say anything.

I wishen I could eat a hearty breakfast, Calvin went on. But peptobismal, that's all goes in and all comes out. It's like my insides is speedy as a torpedo shot.

He opened a jar of jam from the shelf, took out his pocket-knife, wiped the blade on his pants leg, and presented jar and knife to Toker. Try that on your wizard, he said. That rascal will think it's July Four.

Toker jabbed jam onto the blade and stuck the blade into the baby's mouth.

Look at that jasper go, laughed the storekeeper. What'd I tell you.

The baby was thumping for more.

They's monkeys you could train to set at a table and eat Sunday cookin, I've heard, said Calvin. I've heard that. I once knowed a man would eat flies, you paid him to.

One of the older men had come in. He'd got his drink from the box, and his Goody's headache powder from the rack, and gone over to hunker down with Wallace. He now mumbled something to Wallace and they both cackled.

Trout here says he'd eat'um too, Wallace said. They come smeared in pussy goo.

They slapped their knees, bent over and quaking with their horrendous mirth.

Calvin appraised the silent boy by the door.

You want somethin, Early? he said.

The boy hesitated a moment, wetting his lips as he considered the question.

I'm lookin for Daddy, he then said. Mama said me to.

Well, I'm not married to him, Calvin replied. You best take your lookin up to where I'm not sayin.

I've done looked there, the boy said. But Bertha done kicked him out too.

The boy hopped to the drink box and wiggled his bottom up over it. His brow was sweaty now, his face ashen white.

Toker watched him a minute, then strode over and

crouched beneath him. He lifted the boy's swollen foot and whistled.

Would ye look at this, he said.

A long nail was protruding from the blackened sole.

Calvin circled his counter, the two old men shuffled over and in a jiffy all were assembled around the boy, oohing and aahing.

That there's why I bin huntin Daddy, the boy said. Mama said I was to ask him he'd pull it out.

I bin huntin him all night, the boy added.

The boy's foot was hot, the skin puckered ugly around the nail.

Git your pliers, Toker told Calvin. We best operate.

The boy whimpered. His red hair seemed to redden more, his nose went suddenly drippy.

It'll hurt, he said, trying to wrench his foot free.

Pliers, grumbled Calvin. Next they gone be askin for the dirt behind my ears. For my very tonsils, I had any.

He plowed on off in search of pliers.

Toker crouched by the boy. That's what comes of bein born without shoes, he told the baby. I git you a pair the minute I'm able.

He stood up, tousling the boy's hair, smiling at him.

It won't give you much hurt, he said. I've had twenty-penny up mine and I hardly even noticed. Ain't that right, Wallace?

Wallace said he'd had railroad spike up both his feet and a day later won a race against the county's fastest thoroughbred.

Cal returned with the pliers.

They's sunlight round every bend, he told the boy. And mercy on God's every twig. You don't screech none as Toker tugs that whangamajig out, I'll give you a marble bag and the best candy I have.

The boy looked surprised at Calvin, and in that second the nail was out.

He had to have more food for the baby, Toker told Cal. Didn't he have no applesauce? Did he have canned peas he could maybe smunch up and spoon into this youngan's starvin mouth?

She already put a deep hole in this jam jar, you can see that. Did he have diapers by chance? Talcum powder, I know you've got talcum powder. For this baby's bottom is red as a berrypicker's tongue. Do you have ointment?

Well, we had ointment, Calvin said, but it was for the dogs. For their mange. Though it'll do the job, I reckon. Here's fresh milk iffin it ain't spoilt. Take a sniff, see what you think. Here, let old Wallace fill the bottle. Talcum now, I'm runnin over with talcum. I do move me a heap of talcum. You look right puffy in the eyeballs, son. Snakes under your bed? You're lookin nearby mangled as was that rat-ear come here last night.

Toker fed the baby without answering, taking time out to gobble a mouthful or two himself. A wedge of baloney, a slice of white bread.

The boy with the nail-foot watched him chew, and Toker nudged the bread and meat over.

I ain't hungry, the boy said.

Toker poked the food more his way and the boy quickly plucked up four or five bread slices and filled his mouth.

They watched him hop himself on away.

Have you dwelt more on what you mean to do with that tyke? asked Calvin.

I have, though I ain't seen daylight.

She don't resemble none around here, Calvin continued.

Nine times a day you have to change a baby's bottom. I read that somewheres. Or fourteen, I forgit which. But from this'un's complexion I'd say the mama was right fair-skinned and she won't no midget.

Toker heaved the baby over his shoulder and belched her.

A good belch make the day, Calvin said.

Toker slung her down on the counter, spread her legs, and sprinkled talcum thick over her hide.

Could be a German, Calvin said. How white she is. We had us a German fella up here once, after the war.

Which war? one of the old men asked.

There won't but the one, the other said.

They fell into a debate on the war question and on what had come of that German fellow. Then next reminiscing over who else in their time had come and gone, and under what straggly conditions, for instance poor ol' Frog Eye. About the dire consequences of life in general, and how birth itself won't worse than being rear-ended by a pickup truck, and how an old crony of theirs had plunged forty feet down a well, only to climb back up and be struck by lightning.

They talked on and on, Toker standing by Calvin and listening to them, wishing he could get the storekeeper off to himself so as to have his ear about the dead woman up in his woods.

I had me a uncle once was hit over the head by a hail pellet.

Was?

Big as a bucket, that pellet was, and he never again opened his eyes.

Didn't? Well, my sister now, she had herself a boyfriend could eat bob-wire.

Could?

And he's livin today healthy as a jackrabbit.

Is?

While she's nine year under the ground her own self, who could eat nothin.

You don't say. Then listen to this. I knowed me this woman in Elgin Springs had three legs and a box between the each of them just as nice as you ever looked at.

Did? Lawdy me.

Ye tire of one ye jist roll on over to number two.

Unhuh. She had breasts and no hangnails, I bet she could of made a killin.

Calvin? Toker asked.

But the door pinged and a stocky figure was standing in the entranceway. She had on a faded print dress over her wide frame and a man's tatty peacoat up shielding her face.

Looky there, wheezed Wallace. Air that the one?

Naw, said Trout. Hotdamn, you are not worth talkin to since your eyesight went.

Her wicker crate was put down on the floor before Toker recognized her as the chicken woman passing earlier on the road. He could see her man outside waiting by the gas pump, his head slung low, lighting up a cigarette.

How much for these chickens? the woman asked, addressing this to any one of them.

Calvin remained behind his counter, stern of composure.

Chicken is dime a dozen, he said. I can't eat a one. It streams right out of my rear end.

The woman lifted malevolent eyes at the baby, at Toker, and at the old men. Dregs of the world, her look said.

Name me a price, she said.

Calvin uncrossed his arms and pondered her haul. They's plumb scraggly, he then said. I don't know I would even call them chickens.

How much? barked the woman, again staring at the baby.

She didn't venture any deeper into the store, her head shifting on her neck, standing with one foot clawed up on the other, as a chicken might. She had a boil or a growth up high on one cheek. A rash of darkish welts dotted her forehead. She kept one hand bunched fist-tight at her chest, like she was holding her last nickel.

I can't move me no chickens, Calvin explained. Folks they grow their own pullets round here.

Air they fed on butterballs? demanded the woman. Air their yard swept clean mornin and night? You not got but the one good eye. God has two, I thank the Lord. Now stop gawkin and let's settle. I ain't got all day, my man is waitin.

Yes'm, said Calvin. I can see he is. I can see he gone blow us all to high hell, he ain't careful with that smoke next to my ethyl pump.

Be nothin lost, the woman said. She swiveled and cocked her head, squinting down at the baby's chin.

Toker wiped drool away from there. He heisted the baby higher on his knee.

You can have my chickens at a bargain, the woman informed Calvin. I don't want morn my fair profit.

Calvin reluctantly crossed over and knelt down to study the clucking poultry.

They's a tiddybit past your spring stage, he said. I see they won't lay. You eat them they'd wear your gums raw.

Hush, the woman said. You're not talkin a lick of sense. There ain't nobody can tell me about chickens, lessern it's God on High.

Calvin stood up. He had that pained look he always wore when being asked to shell out money.

The most I can give you is twenty cent a head. Even then I'm losin my shirt.

I'll take it, the woman said.

She watched him count the birds, count them twice, her lips flat across her teeth, then she watched him go and dip his fingers into the money box.

The wicker cage is extra, she said.

I thought so. I didn't reckon I had no need for it anyhow.

Menfolks, she said. They sicken me to my innards.

She turned to her husband, whose face now was pressed up against the outside screen, peering inside.

Git in here, she said.

He limped in, glancing up and frowning at the door's ping. His bewhiskered face had a strangled look, his shoulders droopy as a casketmaker's.

Tell me what you see, the woman said to him.

Nothin, he said, fidgeting uneasily.

Nothin, you say? She pointed at Toker. That there bubble-headed boy is the one found that baby we heard of, she said. And that there droolin baby on his knee is the one was found. Have you ever seen a sorrier sight than either?

The man slunk back some, jostling the screen door. He looked up, waiting to see would it ping.

It don't look a minute old, she said. It ain't got nary mother in this world.

Calvin was trying to give her the money owed, but she kept slapping his hand back.

I see that, the man said. But.

Hush your buts, she said. She thrust out a thickish arm at Toker. Why don't it speak? It ain't gabbled once in all the time I'm standin here.

It just et, Toker said.

If it et that baloney I see, than I can't blame it. Baloney ain't nothin but cooked rat. I wouldn't feed a horsefly baloney.

The two old men laughed, then got hit by a spell of coughing.

Let's go, Dolly, the husband said.

But the woman bore down on Toker.

Or air ye willin to pay me to take him off your hands? she said. I could give him a decent upbringin and meld a prizeable human bein out of him.

It ain't a him, Toker said, rising.

Hell's bells, she said.

The husband edged out of the door.

A female is worst to holt of than a wrigglin snake, she said. You can't make a thing out of them, othern somethin a lowly sex fiend might want.

She looked down at her chickens.

Still, I might go high as two or three dollar. I'd up that but she might die on me. I've had two did, jist when I thought I'd known the worst.

Dolly? the husband said.

The woman strode over and snatched the baby out of Toker's arms.

The baby's eyes whirled and she let out a startled squawk.

Dammit, said Toker. Now you gone maker cry.

The baby squiggled to get back with him.

Everybody, the woman's husband included, pressed rapt-eyed about.

I swap you the chickens for her, the woman said, plopping the baby down briskly to one hip. I swap you even.

Calvin shot forward. Hey, he said, you and me done already cut a deal on these chickens.

The two old men seesawed back and forth, guffawing, slapping their knees.

The woman crossed with the baby toward the door, as Toker hurried behind her.

I don't know how come I can't quit stop thinkin it's a him, she said. I could raiser one and hardly a soul know the difference.

Toker strode past her and flung out his arms in guard of the door.

I got me one livin I done that way, she added. He's good hep, too, as polite as Sunday.

The baby let out a small peal of pleasure.

The woman's husband shoved in. He'd picked up a stick from somewhere and had it raised.

Let's go, Dolly, he said. Give the stranger here his baby.

He shook the stick.

The woman's face took on a blanched, enfeebled expression.

The baby, the man said. That fella here wants back his baby.

Oh, the woman said. Her eyes fluttered, then lidded like a sleepwalker's. She began trembling. She staggered back, her arms loose, and Toker reached out quickly to grab the baby.

A female can breed, the woman said, her voice low with melancholy. They's useless otherwise, and a burden to talk to, but they can breed. I've got me one now I want to breed, but I can't find no one willin.

Sender to my doorstep, called out old Wallace.

Calvin counted off a few dollars in change into the husband's palm.

The clunk of change revived the woman. Here now! she cried. Them chickens was mine! She stomped forward, tugging at the husband's hand in claim of her money. Then she started to tremble again.

The husband steered her outside. He hiked up her peacoat around her neck and brushed off the odd feather. He settled the wicker cage in her hands and steered her past the gas pump and around the puddle holes up to the road. There the woman took the lead and the two paced woefully on out of sight.

Calvin and the two old men crowded at the doorway to
watch them go.

They's the Bellhops, Calvin said. You seener on a good day.

Toker was scolding the baby.

I never meant won't someone would finally take you, he
said. You didn't have to look so all-fired happy.

The baby reamed a finger into his ear. Then the baby's face
plopped against his cheek and she gnawed there.

Acy Enal Wright's son Abel could be seen cruising by at a
slow pace, his dour eyes turned to the store. Now he slung his
Ford about and roared in, his tires churning, coming to a
slide-stop by the gas pump. He got out and raised the hood,
spending some minutes checking the oil, the radiator, feeling
at this and that hose, though all the time they could see his
eyes aslit, scouring the store's insides.

Your lifelong enemy, observed Calvin. Ain't nobody could
ever stand that boy, includin his own self.

Toker couldn't. Not since first grade when Abel Enal had
chunked a rock thue a school window and left him standing,
with a rock in his own hand, to take the blame. If it hadn't bin
Abel Enal climbing on him each day since, then it was one of
Abel Enal's scrungy sidekicks.

If his daddy won't stinking rich, Abel Enal would of bin in
jail for a hundred years by this time.

It was said now that he had an archery rig in his car trunk
and liked to go about shooting his arrows at cows grazing in a
field.

Toker didn't mind a bit that he was the one said it.

Now Abel Enal entered the store, looking over the occu-
pants with dire scorn for everyone, picking a finger over his

lips. He was dressed in his Sunday-go-to-meeting suit, the tie
knotted so tight under his chin he looked choked. He didn't
say anything, just lounged back against the drink box. He had
this sour secretive look, one hand twisted deep inside his
pocket, a single fresh scar slashing his cheek.

You looked at Abel Enal Wright—Anal Anus, Toker was
like to call him—you wanted to see him hanging from a hook
in a smokehouse.

Hidy, Anal, Toker said, grinning.

Abel Enal ignored this challenge.

You want anything? Calvin asked him.

Abel Enal shook his head.

Unhuh, said Calvin. You jist browsin then.

After an interval Abel Enal reached into the drink cooler
and pulled out an RC Cola. He picked up a Goody's headache
powder off Cal's rack, formed the wrapper into a spout, tilted
back his head, and tapped the powder down on his tongue.

He floated down a dollar onto Cal's counter and waved away
the change. Then he hung there, guzzling his cola, and sneer-
ing his disdain.

A poker stiff up his rear end.

After a minute he banged down his empty bottle onto the
drink box.

Some slimyass broke into my car the other night, he said.

His voice seemed to come from somewhere down his neck,
which was engorged with fury.

Cal inquired what night that might of been.

Night afore last, said Abel Enal. Friday night. They rifled
my glove compartment and took my tools layin about and siphoned off each inch of my gas.

Oh well, Cal said. Lots of ruffians about.

I find who did it, I'll crank his butt.

The baby spasmed its back, crowing, all but tumbling from Toker's arms.

That's a stupidass-lookin baby, Abel Enal said to Toker. That's what I think. You want to do anything about it?

Toker laughed. It had been a long time since Abel Enal Wright could handle him.

Abel Enal stared a minute at Toker and the baby, then went on out. A second later they could hear him gunning the engine, the car vibrating, the little naked-breasted Hawaiian woman up mounted on his dashboard doing the hula in her grass skirt. Then he spun his tires and roared away.

Funny, said Cal. Funny his thief didn't take that hula babe. You notice them scratches up on his face? Peers to me a woman have said no to him.

Or tried to, Toker said.

The thing was, that sonofabitch Abel Enal wouldn't of killed a woman in this county. He'd of done it elsewhere, in another county, and his daddy would have been over in that county this minute, folding money into some sheriff's or judge's hand.

Out on the road a mule and wagon rattled by, conveying a manure load heaped high, and up on the manure a wooden icebox, its weight lowering the rear. The rider, upright on spread legs, reins folding loosely over one shoulder, kept his sight glued on the mule's swaying rear, as did the stiff-necked woman in black seated by him.

Churchgoers, snorted Calvin. Soon they be troopin by here like soup bones to a scaldin pot. That rascal driver don't know me now, but come tomorry he'll show up askin is his credit still good. Reminds me of Lorinda Hodson, that icebox does, who went three years in one like it afore she was found. She won't but two years old, Lorinda won't, five when found, and her mama and daddy scoutin up and down and all over. Come to find out they'd never once looked inside that icebox, and it parked right the whole time on their front porch. Now wouldn't you have?

I wanted ice, I might have, Toker said.

Shootfire, said Calvin. You're so surly today a man can't talk to you. He prodded over and slung an arm onto Toker's shoulder. Didn't you like that high-heels' cheese?

Toker didn't say anything.

Worse than Sarah, Calvin went on. She was a pressure cooker she'd already of exploded. Back there now cookin herself down to shinbone. You look like you're about to your own self.

What's Sarah's trouble?

Nothin my early demise won't cure. She wants to see you, you ever get time enough on your hands.

I'm right busy, Toker said.

Calvin lifted his arm from Toker's shoulder and steered on away to put Abel Enal's empty into the rack.

Toker was of a mind now to tell Calvin about the dead woman. But he kept throwing up trifles to keep hisself from it. And some matters not so trifling. They'd think he done it. There was still some who half-believed, or half-said, he'd set that fire. He'd be the first one the law locked up. They'd look to see what woman he'd been messing about with. They wouldn't find anyone, but still they'd look. In the meantime they'd have his hide in jail. And with him there, what was the point of looking elsewhere?

Guilty! Let the bastard hang!

He wouldn't never git to taste Roby's cheese, or to see this baby had proper home.

·   ·   ·

Toker knocked, heard Sarah's faint cry, and went on in, the baby under his arm.

In here, she murmured, as he stumbled against a chair. Mind the chair.

The rooms were in darkness. You could see an outline of window, where window was, though that was all. He bumped an end table, heard it scrape. Something else clinked. His finger touched lace doily and he yanked his hand back, thinking spider. His face nudged some hanging thing. The light cord. His general sense was that things inside the house had been overnight rearranged. Put asunder. Tidiness gone in one swoop of bellyache rage. A knock-down and drag-out scrape: such was his feeling.

What tender hearts could wreak, you gave them reason.

The place had a musty, closed-up odor. You could smell cabbage too, and the bacon in which that cabbage had cooked.

His mama had quit cooking once his daddy left. Forage for yourselves, she'd told his sister and him. Set food on the table and she'd never, so long as you watched, nibble a bite.

That food dumped, beneath a swarm of flies, the next time you looked up.

Scissors ever at the ready by his mama's plate. To stab your daddy, his mama said, if she spoke at all, the second he shows his face.

You took up residence inside anothern's skin, Toker thought, you might could know what was goin on. But he had his doubts. It would be foreign territory, he guessed, whether you were inside somebody else's frame, or tryin to see daylight from your own.

Something crunched underneath his shoe. He had roller skates on, he'd of come through with less noise.

In the bedroom, Toker, he heard Sarah say.

Hers a resigned voice, like she was threading a needle and the thread wouldn't fit. The clumsiness of men one more irritation a woman had to put up with.

She was propped up in bed. Her leg up on the same crate as yesterday, with the same pillow to soften its ride. Wearing that same thow-me-out gown. Her hair down. Toker never had seen Sarah with her hair down. Lying there in the dark.

You like the dark, Sarah?

You'd be the last to complain about dark, I'd surmise, she said, her voice miffed.

You wanted to see me?

He reached down to pick up one of the many magazines stacked on the floor by her bedside, but her arm shot out and snared his wrist.

She yanked his hand up to her chest, then to hold it with both hands, her chest throbbing. Her body was trembling.

I've got to talk to someone, she said. All I can hope is you'll do.

Toker marveled.

It seemed he was everyone's valentine this week. Killer, sweethearts, and the bedridden, they were all coming to his door.

A woman needs a strong man to hold onto, she said, but all I've had was one didn't know spit from curl.

Toker grimaced. It was a hard-luck story each cheek he turned.

Could you spare a smoke, Toker?

You don't smoke and you know I've give up.

Would you have strychnine?

Toker groaned. The county was afilled with comics, and it the Sabbath.

Pull up a chair, Toker.

This'un?

Thatern will do well as any other.

Yes'm.

A silence fell, though she continued to imprison his hand. She was going to smoosh it right down over her breast, she didn't watch out.

I've had premonitions, Toker.

About what?

That the whole earth is endin tomorry.

Oh come now. Soon you be walkin the road in a black suit and a pie hat, thumpin out prophecy's grinnin last plague.

It comes over you, I guess, when you're feelin that poorly about your own future. The way I am mine.

You got to speak up, Sarah. I can't hardly hear you. You mind I pull on that light?

I do mind.

All right then.

If I end tomorry, or this very day, will Calvin end? Will his meanness come to blind halt?

I've not seen much of his meanness, Sarah. I don't know it's ever blind, either.

He heard her suck in her sniffles, not liking his disagreements with her.

You was a woman I could talk to you, she said. But your gruesome gender wants everything closed. Never, never open the door. Keep it all sealed up and save it, like a Christmas puddin. Do you think your heart's worth is a Christmas puddin, Toker?

I never had no Christmas puddin.

Maybe that's it. You never had none.

I was had at age five by my brothers, she said. Did you know that, Toker? Do I seal that up? And I can't tell Calvin, nor even tell him it was one reason I made myself available. I had a sister, I could have tole her. I tole him, tole Calvin, he'd say it was my own fault, whether five or twenty. The same as you are thinkin.

I'm not thinkin, Sarah. I'm thunk out, on the vissitude's front. Though I'm sorry you had such trouble.

He's not climbed over on me in three months. Maybe he knows.

Knows what, Sarah?

Knows I was damaged goods. Knows he don't like me. The same as you will go out of here thinkin.

Toker started to rise, but she yanked him down again.

You set still, she said.

He did, and a minute later he could hear her breath ride even.

You don't have to like what you hear, she said. All you have to do is listen.

I'm listenin, he said.

You're like everybody else. You think nobody else's troubles can stack up one widget against your own.

He remained silent. He could see the baby in the dark switching her gaze from one to the other.

I want you to promise me somethin, Toker. Promise me you'll come to my funeral. Though I dare say you'd be the only soul present.

He tried rising again, but she yanked so hard he heard his shirtsleeve tear.

Was I younger I'd ask you to climb in this bed with me. Not jist to git me warm either.

How old are you?

Forty-two.

Toker looked down at her dark figure, surprised.

I can tell that stuns you, she said. I bet you'd of guessed I was sixty.

I wouldn't of guessed no such thing. I'd of guessed forty-two.

He heard her laugh.

You're shocked, she said, still laughing. A wrecked hag like me, talkin this way.

She squirreled up a bit, taking a new grasp of his hand and pressing it down over one breast.

Talk to me the way a woman would, she said. Try.

Toker squirmed. Not a word came to him.

You're not tryin. Are ye? she asked.

I'm tryin, he said. I'm thinkin I might ask your recipe for scalloped potatoes.

He laughed, but wriggled about uneasily as she said nothing.

She pressed his hand down harder.

What's travelin thue your mind now, Toker?

I was wonderin will my own life be more plentiful, will it have more nourishment, I ever hit forty-two myself.

She studied that answer, then said: Yes, yes. I can see another woman might of said that. Now try again. Say somethin else. The sort of thing a woman would.

Toker couldn't come up with anything. He could think of several remarks Roby might say to him, but they didn't seem appropriate.

What do you feel, Toker? Your hand on my breast? What do you feel?

Nothin. You done cut off the blood supply, holdin it so tight.

You're blushin, she said. I do believe that in every respect you're nearabouts as innocent as that baby. There now, you can have your hand back.

Toker took back his hand and put both around the baby.

For a time neither spoke.

Yes, she said then. I can see you held that baby long enough, you'd holder how a woman would. You set there long enough, holdin her, you might could talk to me. Yes, she said, I'd ask you to climb inside this bed with me, I was younger and didn't have Cal to shoot me if you did. You're a good-lookin boy, Toker. Though maybe he wouldn't care. You reckon he would?

I reckon. I reckon he'd shoot us both, we didn't die first of the shame.

That baby. Its skin glows some in the dark, don't it?

Unhuh. This here's a special baby.

Could I hold it, Toker? Could I? But don't tell him I did.

Fine by me. Mind you don't hurt it now.

I know how to hold a baby, Toker.

She squirmed up on her pillows and held the baby on her chest.

The baby began slapping its little hands up in her face.

Why don't you git up out of that bed, Sarah?

I was lame and I could not walk. I was bereft and I could not see. That's why I don't git up.

Toker picked up one of the magazines and looked at the cover. In the dark he couldn't see what it was.

Let me hold this baby a minute more, Toker. I never had one I could call my own. Never wanted one, Calvin would say. But what has a man ever known?

I don't know, Sarah. We are both prisoners in that regard.

I'll holder then. She's snuggly. I feel my strength returnin, her up close to me like this. It seems she radiates a certain power.

Unhuh. I've felt the same.

Toker listened to her play with the baby.

Read to me, Toker, she next said. Switch back that window curtain and read to me out of one of them magazines by your foot.

Toker got up and swung the curtain open and sat back down.

Which one?

Read *Hollywood Detective*, I like that one. Yarns to stand your hair on end, tales to tie your limbs in knots. Ain't that what the copy says?

Unhuh.

Then read. Read to me and the baby. I never bin read to, except the labels off cans, and I know this baby won't have. I'll just cuddle her here. While you read.

That's nice, Toker. Look here, you done put this baby to sleep. You got a good readin voice, Toker. You'd make some woman a good husband. But you need takin better care of yourself. To start with, you need gittin up out of that hole you live in. Then you need a haircut.

What else?

You ought ever day to buy your wife flowers. I never known a woman to git flowers, 'cept in *Hollywood Detective*. There they git truckloads.

That's right. But you can see here in this story I read how their lives are empty and they got no moral turpitude and they end up berserk in castle towers. You remember how in thatern I read the man sent flowers sent poison spiders hid in they's blossoms.

Well, said Sarah, maybe that's bettern nothin. Can I keeper, Toker? This baby? I'll keeper and giver all God gives me and never look back from this day forward, you let me haver.

How's my opposite? Calvin asked Toker when he entered.

I do believe she's sleepin.

You were gone a long time. I thought you'd fell in. She'll be tryin God's patience, she don't git up soon.

Toker was of a mind to inform Calvin of Sarah's wanting his baby. She'd cried and begged and promised to look after it with her every fiber.

Likely, she'd make this baby a good mother.

The baby would be well looked after. She could grow up and run this store, the building didn't fall down.

You studied this baby in the store's coffee-colored light, you could see that glow Sarah had mentioned.

She won't no ordinary baby you'd leave in a ditch for the first one who come along wanted her to taker and haver.

Cal was decent enough and what you'd call a straight-faced friend, but somehow you looked at him you didn't see Daddy wrote on him. He wouldn't giver the hugs and kisses a good baby required.

He'd feeder succotash and raw bacon rind and turner into a fat, lazy creature had no horizon to shoot for.

One of the old men asked didn't anyone know Cecil Thorpe. You knowed him, didn't you, Toker? Or your daddy did. And when they said no, or said nothing in fact, simply stood about in a quandary of polite rumination, the old man said they were damn fools then. Everone knew Cecil Thorpe, who owned a pet crow could only fly backwards.

Cackle cackle.

Now I knowed a Horace Thorpe, the Wallace one said. Had a two-seater buggy he use to whip about here in.

Did?

Yip. Got swallowed by a mud slide, him and buggy both, down Mignon Ferry way. You don't mean Horace Thorpe, do ye?

God in hell no.

They discussed mud slide and flood and famine and any number of other mortifications the flesh was heir to; they considered others of their acquaintance, those craven by night and crucified by day, those struck down by drink and disease, by leaky kidney or foul disposition or by the general misery and ill-appreciation of old age.

No, I'm not worth much now. You, Trout?

Not a dog's breath.

Wonder where old Hindmarch is today. I don't know he's missed a day at Cal's Place in a score and some years.

Off his feed, I reckon. Come to think on it, won't he lookin poorly yesterday?

He was that. I set here myself lookin at the thin wire holdin him to earth.

Be gone afore the first elk appears in spring, he don't perk up.

They's truth there. Now he could have that baby's hand in marriage he might could hold on.

Cackle cackle.

Then they got out their checkerboard and sat quarreling about the advantages and disadvantages of first move, and who was the champeen.

A car pulled in by the gas pump and the driver gave three beeps. Calvin was in back trying to stop up a hole mice had chewed in one of his seed bags.

I'll gitter, Toker told him.

It was the Godder car. The Godder brother and sister, middle-aged and twins, sat erect in the backseat, holding hands, and looking off joyfully through the windshield in that way they had. The older brother, twin to a fourth, absent Godder, was up front behind the wheel.

Empty my pockets, he told Toker, nodding toward the pump. Only then seeing the baby in Toker's arm.

Jiggers, a baby! the brother declared. A baby will save the world!

The two in back beamed anew at all they surveyed.

A baby will lead us into paradise, the brother said, his head out the window. Ridin a white pony.

Mine's takin lessons, Toker told him. You on your way to church?

Comin from it.

The two in back nodded their shining agreement and a second later all three broke into joyous song.

Toker filled the Godder tank and asked for two dollars.

The two in back sat with all four hands abounce on the sister's lap, their knees together, their faces identical, even their hats, except for a splash of bird feathers in the sister's. All were rollicking with laughter as they finished their song.

Yessir, smiled the driver. We will come rejoicin, bringin in the sheep. Come to see us now. Can ye make it to supper tonight?

What time?

We eat by the bell-ring, six o'clock.

That's late, but I'll see I can make it.

Hidy ho.

The car chugged away, the three breaking into another riotous chorus.

George and Martha out back were throwing up fitful, singsongy yelps.

Did them Goddams ast us to dinner? Calvin inquired, taking the crumpled bills. I'm takin them up on the call one of these days. See for myself what keeps them Joes so happy.

Trout hobbled to the door and blew a string of snot from his nose, then hobbled on out to the road, looked it up and down a while, then hobbled on back to his poke by the stove.

Ol' Hindmarch got us scratchin our heads, Wallace offered. We can't figure where that shirttail has got to. Maybe someone should check on him. I'd go, and Trout here would, but we'se not spiry enough to grapple that slope he lives on.

Oh, he'll show up directly, Calvin said. No need you boys to be pullin out your hair.

What hair? they said.

Toker filled the baby's bottle with fresh milk from the cooler. He bought two cans of Carnation condensed, together with a few other provisions. Honey, he needed honey. Some canned goods. Stew beef, beans, sardines. Would a baby eat stew beef? Bag of marshmallows maybe? She could chew her gums good on marshmallow, and him laugh to see it, he won't in jail by then.

Ladies and gentlemen of the jury this scoundrel let that woman's corpse rot in junked car. While he went on with his merrymakin. Hang the bastard!

You don't have no gift candy, do ye? he asked. A nice gift box?

Well, I do, said Calvin, but it's Sacred Heart Valentine. And old. But I got me a Whitman's Sampler from last Easter here somewhere.

He rousted among his lower shelves, lifting out rags and tin cans and wooden boxes piled with rusty hardware. A sack of washers. Calendars yellowed with age.

He rose, blowing the dust from a Whitman's box, it shaped

in the form of a yellow heart. Here 'tis, he said. You want it?

Toker nodded.

Or I could pack up some PayDay bars and tie them off with a bow. You want them too?

I reckon. What the hell.

You goin courtin?

Maybe, Toker said. To keep my hand in.

The storekeeper dropped five PayDays into a paper bag, then, to Toker's eyeblinks, dropped in five more.

What was that cheese she wanted?

Blue. But I don't have blue. Anyway, you don't want cheese. She done bought already enough cheese to feed a chain gang.

The storekeeper regarded him with a look of sly, mischievous conniving.

Next thing I know we'll have you hitched up to a hitchin post.

Toker examined his shoes.

I'll scurry back to the house, then, Cal said. See if I can cough up a bow to dress up your love offerin.

The old men took in this development with mute and rapt attention. A moment later Wallace steered over and wrapped a near-weightless arm around Toker's shoulders.

It's a wonderment to behold, he said. A man commits hisself to another, why my breath jist catches in my thoat to see it. Don't it yourn, Trout?

Trout puttered up and slung his arm on.

Yessir, ye gits our age, it's a rare day when ye can see life is still goin on and the generation behind ye ain't shot home the bolt. Good luck to you, boy.

They shook hands, Wallace's fragile and warm and Trout's patting his head.

Be true to your sweetheart, Trout said, and ye won't never regret it. They's heaven on earth, a body would jist accept it at face value and give it its proper turn. Ain't that the truth, Wallace.

My durn very words.

Toker turned away to hide his wet eyes. Calvin reappeared and placed his bowed purchase in his hands.

Addy-ose partner, Calvin said, smiling, pretending for both their sakes he saw no wetness there.

The three saw him to the door, and over the next minute clung there, yelling out their sundry advice, and the variety of perils he might watch out for.

Truman, for the moment again on foot and breathing hard from his climb, stared across a cold dimension of space at an elderly figure, man or woman, seated stock-still on a slab-board seat in front of a bevel-edged aluminum trailer baked dingy on its cinder blocks, a shovel sideways over the knees.

Yawl don't have a drop a man could drink, do ye? he called.

The figure answered nothing, only looked his way, as if at empty space.

Truman narrowed his distance and noted it was an old man ruled this clearing a God's breath up in these deep woods. He seemed to be near a hundred, the old man did, with caulkered eye and none too civil.

He called again, louder this time.

Iffin you're dry yourself, maybe you could point me the way?

The figure stayed as found, studying the same formless region.

Deaf, maybe.

It was such a place as a man might come away to die in,

your life hadn't chalked up nothing even a graveside speaker could plaudit you with.

I'd pay top price for it, Truman called. You could direct me. He'd heard there was licker to be had somewhere up here and he meant to get it.

Gnats spun at the old man's face or something did, because Truman saw the figure lift and slowly waddle his hand about.

You don't mind me comin on up to your yard, do ye?

The old man's head snapped up. He appeared to nod.

Truman pitched down his cigarette and ground it under heel, then came on up by the creek path and entered the yard clearing, content to dawdle a while. He'd have to, he saw, if he meant gitting anything out of this swoony old man.

Up to the side of the trailer, on sloping ground, he could see the result of his host's digging, though not the ultimate purpose such labor seemed contrived to advance.

What you diggin there? Truman asked. Plantin a tree? Or lookin for lost potato patch?

The old man pulled himself slowly upright, then to shift about perilously on his feet before leaning his weight against a yard sapling pole and for a spell contemplating that mound of earth his shovel had scooped up.

Valuables, the old man said, his voice bemoaning and low. I was thinkin I'd lay me my earthly valuables down there.

Well, Truman said. I've heard of pirates as have done that. He walked up an incline to the dig and saw the old man had spaded out from the wild grass and rubbishy bushes a shape would roughly fit a man pronewise.

I reckon this here's pretty smart diggin, he said. So long as ye don't aim to crawl down in it your own self. It ain't your grave you're diggin, is it?

About a twelve-foot space separated them now and he could

see the old man taking a hard look at him, his eyes squinted.

Ain't I seen you afore? the old man asked. Didn't I see you last night?

Where last night?

Like skulkin thief? I didn't see you?

Truman smiled. Nawsir. Not me. I'm stranger to these parts.

The old man lifted feeble hands, then nodded. A chest wheeze hit him and for the next seconds he dealt with that, holding onto the sapling so as to remain upright.

Yes, well, he said, croaking this out. We all are, it comes to that. What can I do ye for?

He beckoned Truman on up.

Truman sat down on the vacated slab bench, noting the old man's whittling slithers scattered wide before him.

He wondered a second he hadn't made a mistake venturing up here. But there won't many mistakes he'd made he could saddle hisself with or not make good with the next move.

Now ye mention it, he said, could be I did see you last night. Out on that road yonder where I was stoppin in to see was a fella I'd heard of was livin there.

Unhuh, the old man said. I reckoned I had. Seen you, I mean.

The old man examined him warily, before consenting to speak again.

And was he? That friend.

Nawsir. Seems I'd come to the wrong house.

Truman's eyes lifted to a spider web above his head, the spider motionless there, it a mean redback. A black widow, it be called. The shells of numerous insects entombed in the strands fluted up now and again in the soft wind.

He got up and hunkered down a few feet opposite, where he could keep an eye on both spider and this hobbly old man.

Yessir, he said. You're lookin at a stranger. But I might buy me some land up here, I seen such to my likin, and hang up my hat. That's another thing I was doin last night. Lookin up good property.

The old man ignored these remarks. He'd trudged over to his dig and was haunched there now, peering down.

I've done most things in my life, he said in his low voice. Wouldn't be no need not to dig grave, I mean. If I had a mind to and retained the prowess. It don't require but the one size to fit us all, worse be the luck. You'd think a body's works on earth would alter that, wouldn't ye?

Truman studied him. He hadn't never known or heard of a man digging his own grave lessern he was made to.

The old man's eyes slumbered up over him. And stayed there, swimmy of gaze. It won't an experience Truman was familiar with, and he skitched his eyes again to see what the redback was doing.

Ye never know, the old man said. Ye come to the end of your tether, ye never know what that end will find you doin. Now do ye? I'd say they's mysterious scale between a body's first breath and his last. Wouldn't ye? Lessern you be privy to morn I am.

The old man's sight floated on up to take in spider and web and then swept on to something beyond. What's the other fella look like? he asked.

Truman blinked, not understanding.

The old man pulled up a bucket, and by degrees lowered himself down.

That swellin on your face, I mean. I can see somebody done got in a good lick.

Oh, Truman said, crossing his legs. That's toothache. But the soreness is halfway gone on its vacation now. I pulled out one with fishin string, it the wrong one, yesterday that was, so this mornin I've dug the right one out with knife tip. You keep at a thing you'll soonern later git it right. That's my motto anyhow.

The old man's sight swam on from Truman to one thing or another. Not listening to him.

Truman wet his lips. He ought not to of come up here. But a boy down on the road had pointed off up these mountains when he'd asked him where a body might find a drink.

He got out his cigarettes and thumped up a few.

Do ye smoke? he asked.

The old man shook his head. Can't say I do. I quit, oh a hind's leg back, when they went up to twenty cent the pack.

What's your name?

If his old uncle had lived, Truman was reckoning—that one grabbing up over windowsill way back when—he'd of had run about this old codger's many miles.

Hindmarch, the man said. Had that name all my life. Can't say what I might of done without it. He paused, both hands lifting in a flap at his knees.

Truman could see the old man was now working his way toward a talkative stride. He could let the string run out or he could strive to alter the tide. He lit his cigarette and sucked in the smoke, still crouched down on his heels.

Ye ain't seen that man with the baby around, have ye? Truman asked.

But the old man slapped his knees again and went on. Yessir, they's much in a name, he said. I'd say it and I reckon your Rockyfella would too.

He took his shovel up again across his lap, working finger over the sharpness of blade.

Truman dug into his pocket and wiped the lacy cloth over his brow. He'd had a hellacious night with that tooth and he wondered he won't now coming down with a fever again.

I'm lookin him, he said. That man with—

But the old man's speech headed him off.

This here shovel my daddy gave me. Was all he give me, this shovel, and with the claim that itterd be enough. I'd surmise he was right too. He cocked his head, reaming a finger into his ear and looking at the tip for what came out. What'd your daddy leave you?

Truman scrunched forward and spat between his shoes. His eyes grabbed at the old man's then fell again back to his spit.

He ain't left me even that much, Truman said. I've never set eyes on him. Never wanted to neither.

The old man nodded.

That's the sorry truth, he said. There's men born ever day will amount to no morn you claim for him. Your mama, though. I reckon you knowed her?

Truman didn't answer, and the two sat in silence, both examining the spit glob, as if divining that a strange deity might any second ascend from it.

I was thinkin you could tell me where that man with the infant lives, Truman said. I need me to have a quick chat with him.

The old man's head sagged between his knees. For a minute or two he didn't move or speak.

Truman watched the spider. The redback had crawled over to a winged thing stuck there and was now spinning its silk up over the squirming shape.

I was jist settin here thinkin when you came up, the old man said. His voice was weary. He looked about to plunge over.

Thinkin what?

Oh, rememberin the time.

The time what?

Truman took off his shoe and banged that down at the spider. But the spider shot off and disappeared into a corner. He slipped his foot back into the shoe, mindless of the clinging web.

Them widows eat the male, he said.

Hindmarch gave no notice he'd spoken.

I was seein that child hangin, he said. Hangin by tree limb. Over on yonder road this was. Over that ridge. Near twenty years ago. The sister is livin now on the place it happened at. She come back finally, I don't know why. That child hung there a night and high part of the next day. Funny, we're here talkin daddies now, me jist then thinkin on that child hangin, when you come up. His daddy took mad-dog mad and went at that child and hung it and stood by with shotgun keepin the wife and little girl from takin the little boy down. I said that, a little boy, though he was maybe ten or twelve when his daddy took him up from the supper table and went out and hung'm. Was the sister, her who's back now, who finally run and got help. Run down to Cal's store.

You can see her out by her house most mornins, struttin the fields in that gown, or riding that horse, and never even think to yourself she's the same one.

Her daddy stayed by the tree holdin us off.

I had me my gun and wanted to shoot the boy's daddy but his wife kept runnin up and pushin my hands down and cryin. That boy up there swayin from the limb the whole time. That limb creakin.

To this day I can hear that limb creakin.

And the little girl shriekin and runnin. Us too, I guess, since we won't none of us had ever seen such afore. The daddy was ravin. Ravin the whole time. Standin us off. He put a shotgun blast thue both the front windows, reloadin the double-barrel while we was still duckin and scramblin. A new tinkle of glass, or somebody'd step on a twig, and we'd duck

agin. I don't know what any of us would of done he finally
hadn't put his gun up under his chin and blowed his own
brains out. Won't but six of us there and I'm near the last one
left. We done hushed it up best we could. See, they'd had a
good name, up to the minute he strung up the boy. I was
thinkin on that a minute ago when we was talkin on names.
Rockyfella now, I'd 'spect he's had his stoup of troubles, same
as us. Silver spoon don't keep it from ye. With ourn it won't
no need to bring the law in, we figured. Jist more trouble.
Yessir, funny me thinkin that, rememberin, when you come
up. And thinkin the same earlier, when I had me my shovel-
work goin. It's hard work in hard ground, that shovelin. I'm
goin to be some spell finishin and for the minute my hurry is
absent. It's funny what any brain can hatch up, it come to
that.

Wouldn't ye say? I was settin here thinkin that when you
named your spit no morn what you claim your parentfolks
were. But it's your spit and it could be they had not a hand in
its creation.

The wife won't never would ever say why her man done it.
Kilt that boy. Probably no morn some squabble was how it
started. Then you know how things mount up. It's like ants,
they git haulin a thing they won't stop till they's hauled out.
Trouble's like that, I mean. It gits started, well, you can't
stomp it out, it jist keeps comin. Any evil form, I reckon it's
the same. You scrape and you scrape till your arm falls off and
still they'll be a drop of it left to go on and start its new trouble
later. Times was scab-hard then. It's heap better now, or anyway some folks seem to have means to shoot off in their automobiles and kayaks wherever heart's wing wants to take'um.

The girl child she wouldn't say word one, not even a hidy,
you said that to her. Her too young to know why it come about
anyhow. About six she was, I reckon. No morn six. I ast her

the other day how old she was now, and all she'd say to me
was that she was old enough to know better. That's what I was
thinkin on when you came hollerin up. Hearin these limbs
creak here, and thinkin on that one way back when.

We buried that boy out on a hill some ways down from the
house. I used to walk there sometimes and study the ground.
Study that tree too. That limb. Though you won't find it
standin now. I don't think it was nothin that boy done wrong.
I think likely it was the daddy won't livin up to the honor-
picture he had for his own self, and knew he won't never goin
to, so somethin goes twist inside and caterwaul is all he hears.
It's his own self he thinks he's slingin up from that table. No,
he won't one you'd think to take mad. Hellfire, he was out
plowin a widow-woman's field only the previous day. It smarts
my eyes to think of that.

So we buried the daddy right beside him, beside the boy,
which'us how the wife wanted it. Though the little girl didn't.
She ranted and raved and one of us had to taker off shakin and
try holdin her down. A sight it was, I tell you. Jist screamin
the godawfullest injury out at her mama for where she was
layin his body and at her daddy for . . . well, I won't go into
that part. I do know I seener myself, later on scrabblin her
fingers over the daddy's gravesite. Wantin to dig him up and
move him away from her brother's side, I'd witness. She was
right smart fond of that brother. Him older, you know. One
she'd look up to. The other children still as stones, they were,
hardly an age to know what was transpirin. I don't know who
she has to look up to now and maybe she's better off not havin
the need.

The wife stayed on no morn a month or two. Then she run
off. By herself I mean, won't any man she'd of run off with.
Won't never one she'd of let herself come near to. Not in that

manner, I mean. Ain't nobody knows she's gone for the longest time. It was a man sellin watermelons off a wagonback tole me. Then kin went up there to look in on them. That little girl's got one little brother under one arm and one under another, and a mop and broom between her legs. She's bin feedin and washin them youngans, lookin after them, since the day her mama took off. And the house is so clean you can see yourself, that kin said. Her six years old.

And she went on raisin them youngans practically by her lonesome year on into year. Till they got of an age she could strike off. She's done good by herself, she has. It's here tole she went bad a while up in the city, but I'd listen to that story with caution. It might mean she done no morn eat donuts of a Sunday. Anyway, it done my eyes good to see she finally come back, shed of her grudge. Shed of all what must have ailed her. That's a good thing, the sheddin, if you can jist plow thue to the shedded hour. I was thinkin that a minute ago, lookin at you with that spitball between your shoe. How you done made of your unknown parentfolks the worst invention, and never shedded nothin. It's bein mean-spirited, is what it comes down to.

He fell silent, though Truman could see his mind went on remembering, or that the tale he'd told had no end he'd yet come to. Truman stood up. He wiped a hand across his face. His flared cheek had set some, was less heated now, though his gum cuts sent off shooting pain whenever his tongue touched there. He picked the two teeth from his pocket and studied them.

But you was wantin somethin, the old man said, stirring, his face swaying up to ponder Truman's hot eyes. You come up askin about somethin and I never paid your request the smallest attention. What was it you'd ast for? Was it water?

Nawsir. It don't matter. I'll chase him down anyhow.

The old man nodded, absently. He reached down and scribbled something meaningless in the dirt with a stiff finger.

My car's broke, Truman said. Spurting this out in a dash of pent-up anger. I've throttled it and choked it and near broke my toe kickin the wheels. But she still won't chooger.

The old man considered. Probably jist as well, he then said. The same stiff finger lifted and shook at something up over the horizon. In my day it took three people to motor a car. Ye had to have one with red flag trudgin up front and another luggin spare tire in the rear. That'us by day. By night ye had both troupin with red lantern, and hell it was to pay, ye didn't start early.

You goin now? the old man said.

Truman was pacing.

Hindmarch stood up as well. He was about to offer his hand in polite shake, then measured Truman anew and seemed to think better of it. For the next few seconds they held their places like paired strangers at a civic meeting.

That won't the most heartfelt adventure befallen me in my lifetime, Hindmarch said. Though it come close.

And with that the old man sat back down again on his pail, his eyes brightened by the flood of some new memory.

Truman didn't speak. His mouth was dry and he hadn't yet managed any new forage in his pilgrimage along toward liquor.

The old man's tale hadn't touched him none. He figured the man spoken of had good reason for what he done, hanging that boy, and if you first let him explain it you might see his side. He didn't credit nothing having to do with the two females' place in the picture. It wouldn't've happened nohow, that hanging, the daddy had stayed away from the women.

Hindmarch's sight was holding onto something over to his

rear. Pausing, Truman guessed, to get whatever new story oc-
cupied him rearranged in his mind to his liking.

Truman lit up another cigarette. His old uncle hadn't never
been a storyteller like this old man. Ye asked that bastard
something and he'd slap off your head.

Was a black man I had once workin for me, Hindmarch
began. He got cut up somehow and his innards fallin out. That
black man. Still, he worked the full week at my sawmill that
way, his haulin plank or kickin log with one hand while stuffin
his innards back with the other. He won't slowed down one
dart of one smidgen. Ye couldn't eat your lunch, or I couldn't,
or swallow water, without seein his trouble. I kept tellin him
to go on home, to git it looked after, but he claimed the labor
come first. He claimed first come the honest sweat for his
wages.

Was his wife finally stitched him up on the weekend. She
come to me to borry the needle. Gunnysack needle was all I
had and she took that. I plugged along behind and watched
her stich'm. She tied his hands to the bedstead and had me
anchor his feet. He wanted his best hat over his face and we
done that. That hat never fell off the whole time he jiggled and
howled and near yanked the bedframe into Sunday but otherwise he give no complaint. Though you could see his arms
and feet go blue with the strain. My knuckles near cracked
keepin his feet pinned to mattress. I hepped her wash the
wound. Long as my hand that wound was, and some of his innards left out, near as I could see. But could of bin it was gore.
No, it was gore, it's jist I can't hep it, throwin that part in.

When the chore was done he got up and trod sore over to
this mirror they had hangin and he put the hat on his head
and studied his likeness in the mirror. Laughin. He was a
good-lookin man and he had that hat tilted rakish as leanin
chimney. He said to me, This here hat is good as a bossman's

hat, ain't it? I allowed as how it was. I said he could wear that hat on the job, he wanted to, and I'd thow away mine and do any lick of work he requested. The woman was up huggin him. He said to her, Now are ye ready to go dancin? And durn if they didn't hucklebuck a minute or two. They was a pretty pair, her every inch up to his level. Maybe over his level, because one thing I've witnessed in my time is that women do seek to the higher level. It's plain to the eye as after long rain ye see water along the riverbank steady risin. I told him to git his rest long as needed and his employment would ever be waitin, but come Monday mornin he was back on the job. Yessir, the hardest worker ever I've seen. Often the time I wonder what happened with him. I never did git me my needle back.

They sat in silence, both looking about vaguely, in the weighing of this story.

Truman could see no point to it his own self. He couldn't see how any such stories hinged on him, or why the old man would dredge them up.

It's a sorrowful tale, Truman said, hoping by this comment to halt it. Don't ye have no happy ones?

The old man looked surprised. The remark even seemed to startle him.

I thought thatern happy, he said. I've lived my whole life thinkin it was. But I see your side of it now. Yessir, if you focus only on the knifin, on the pain involved, on his squishy innards and the woman's backwards doctorin, I reckon I'd agree it's got its sad notes. I like that hat part, though. I can't wear one tomorry, I won't remember that man.

They hell, said Truman. Ain't no job worth as much as that man thought, save you're commanded to it by God on High.

Hindmarch drew up from his bucket and crossed over to his slat seat. He steered the shovel over his knees and waddled about a hand before his face.

Well. I don't know nothin about commandments from above. Though they's been worse ones, I'd think, than one sayin honest work was what held heart and soul together and kept your home fires burnin.

The old man looked overhead at the ruined web.

They do eat'um, he said. Though you won't find no lesson in that.

He sighed down, as though done with talking for a while. His eyes watery now.

What you wantin with Toker? he asked. It's that baby you're after, I'd warrant.

Truman shuffled his feet in the dirt.

What baby? Nawsir, I've jist got my bizness with him.

I knowed I'd seen you, Hindmarch said. Seen you last night. Out on that woman's lane. I see you got meanness writ on you bold as a hoofprint. I expect under them trousers you're even wearin a tail. Or hope to will. You'd sell your soul for a biscuit, and anyone else for butter went in it. Wouldn't ye?

Truman sniggered. Ye don't know nothin, he said. You a batty old man got nothin left but to bury hisself.

Oh, you're mean, Hindmarch said. But I'd warn you away from that boy's quarters. I'd warn you to scurry back to your own dark side.

Why's that?

Why? Because he means to hold onto that baby sure as that man I told you about did his cut innards. Morn that, he's got jist enough sense to knock you flat.

His eyes sighted up at Truman, steady and clear. I won't ast ye what ye did with the woman. I'd git lie to your very last breath. Wouldn't I?

Truman crouched down and calmly tied off the laces on his webbed shoe.

What woman? he said.

Over by the way was a stream dribbling weak defiance of its forced contours. It was the one sound he heard, save his own footpads, stealing away from there.

Whip me along, bright rider. Whip me along, O my care-taker, like you done in my dream-house hour.

A dervish of wind raked the valleys and combed each purlieu and harbor, and yet spun on its grave tillage under pilot of no recognizable theodicy. The girl in her cove by shining water shivered and sucked the wind's rutting into malign and fuliginous dream that found no end within the space of the vision-keeper's orbit. What housed or contained one housed or contained the other and in neither could it be said there existed any trace of a caretaker's mercy, or any hope of a permutable future. The wind brought with it her sister's scream and collected her own, and so the dervish coiled and spun and would not release her from it. Her fists clenched at her brow, and in her brain there her dead sister was prone and stiff in the shadows and could beg no mercy. She was beyond all providence, now as in the beginning.

Hit and bleed me, dark runner. Cozen and devour us here among your dwarf-elders.

She moved in a half-trance from her shrub cove out into a briary thicket and through that over a field charred with the remnants of burnt cornfield and through that to a grassless pathway that led up to narrow cart trail and on down that toward whatever might soon beckon as her terminus. Billowed by wind, snagged at by weed and briar, curtain flowed behind her. Sister's unwrappings, dingy wet gauze found that morning midst the sulfurous fumes of the decaying camp by the dried-up river.

A dog with a lame hind leg and sorrowful eyes appeared out of the brush and for a merciful time loped along with her. Her brow unknotted and her stride quickened.

The winds quieted and the sky above her turned glacial, a vitriform imbecility hoarfrosted to inexorable span its godless authority.

Then the sun shoved this coldness away and the day turned November civil.

Her pathway took her by woodland one-room white-painted church from which she could hear a parched whisper of song, and see six dilapidated cars haphazardly parked, but she hastened on by.

She passed a clapboard house in a trove of maple trees and there saw white sheets strung on a line and a man in the front yard burrowed up under a tractor.

Later she heard a horseman at slow clop on the road behind her and she scuttled quickly off into foliage. Then to crawl flat into low, pooled water, and lay with her ear to the wetness, listening in the stilled silence to her heartbeat and the clopping horse.

The hooves slowed. She clenched her eyes and buried herself deeper.

The clopping halted beside her.

A voice familiar in its remote softness addressed that space where she hid.

Yo. Are ye there?

She lifted her head and there on his mount, the mule now again tethered behind him, was the blind man.

She scrambled afoot and approached him and he lifted her up.

Yo now, he said to the horse. He clucked his lips and the horse flared its mane, and they rode on.

Sister's dead, Lena is, she told him, and pulled from her coat pocket the wrappings that had bound her sister.

Where are you takin that mule now? she asked the rider, and he answered that he was taking the mule home.

Where's home? she asked, but the blind man said nothing.

They rode for brief interval down that road and then down hard road, and then the horse turned and clopped a few steps along an unkept, beweathered lane heading up into a wilderness of mountain.

Here the horse halted and though the man nudged it with his legs the horse did not move.

Far up the curvy lane she could see what looked like an old man trudging along, his backside to them.

What's up that lane? the girl asked, and she made as to slide from the animal's flanks, but the beast skittered and she had to hold on to rider or fall off.

It's bin up that road earlier, the blind man said. It won't go the same way twice, 'cept it's a return journey.

He dismounted his horse and fed each and all from his pocket of apples.

Then he slid his hands under her arms and lifted her to the ground.

I thank ye, she said.

'Tis little enough, he said. And no bargain.

Then he took to his horse and, in the minute, rode on.

Ye can't hide, thought the girl. Ye can't nothin hide. I known I would finder.

She wrapped the blind man's coat about her and started up the lane.

After leaving the store Toker climbed Roby's road for a good thirty minutes before connecting with Hindmarch's worn path to and from Cal's Place, the ascent steep even for him. He paused there, then to scamper up on high rock and sight along the treetops for glimpse of smoking chimney where Hindmarch's trailer would be.

In a minute he made out thin puffs rising from the boughs and fading invisibly into the sky, this to his mind sufficient proof that the old man was still alive and kicking, and no need his sidekicks to dribble away with worry.

He strode onwards, wondering a dodger like Hindmarch would trek that path each day of his life and not be confounded by the niggardly rewards awaiting at both ends. He wondered your steps wouldn't finally betray you and the day come when you wouldn't bother rising from bed.

Though them old boys could be spry enough, they had reason to be, and you couldn't discredit their way of finding fun in the smallest toad that jumped.

You don't say nothin to Roby when we git there, he advised the baby. Not a peep. I mean to give that beauty my best shot.

She'd thrown the cheese out onto the porch. She'd emptied half her closets and thrown that out too. She'd thrown out mop and bucket. But she wouldn't come out herself.

He went about the porch and yard, picking up her things, placing them neatly by her front door.

Don't you come in! she shouted.

No, he won't about to go in.

She flung insults out as well, one after the other, and to each of them he said, Yes. Yes, I am that. I am every kind of low-down sorry name you can think to call me. You shot me I wouldn't blame you the one fatal wound.

She was wearing that same green robe, her hair a pile of snaky loops, her red fingernails back there slashing and stabbing.

Try that hangdog look on your other women, she said. If you think I was expectin you last night you got it comin out of your hindquarters.

She had a mouth would scald water.

I tried to come, he said. I even washed and put a part in my hair. You should of seen the polish on my shoes. But they's bin comin at me with rock and pistol, underground and over-ground, swearin they'd trade me my baby for so little as a crate of chickens. I hit the trail to see you, here would come somethin else. And that was the story of the whole of last night.

He kept saying such things, and finally it was quiet in there.

He fell quiet too.

He had a dead woman on his hands, and this one who already believed the worst of him. What would come thue the door if he told her the truth?

Put her down, she said. I can't stand seein a grown man holdin no snot child like it was the Prince of Grace. I'm surprised you had the balls to show up with her. Or at all.

Toker lowered the baby down on yard grass. The fracas hadn't seemed to upset the baby's countenance one gibbet.

If you flipped that thing over to the stomach so its rump was high and you put an apple in its mouth she'd look like a pig on a plate.

Roby was up on the porch by the upright, that hip slung. Her eyes cutting him in half.

I'd of thought you'd turned her over to the law or the welfare by now.

I'd have to answer a thousand questions. They'd be actin like I'd blowed up the First National.

Knowin you, she said.

Ladies and gents of the jury, here is vermin of the lowest order. Hang'm!

She was prancing the front porch, uneasy in her truce. Even her kneecaps aquiver.

You don't have no coffee, do ye? he asked.

My coffee is reserved for friends. I had me a full pot reserved for one last night but the sonofabitch never come. I take it the sonofabitch was too busy. I take it the Don Wan sonofabitch had his nose up another skirt.

He could see she won't never going to forgive him. Chip on her shoulder long as a flatbed truck.

If you think I was here pinin for you, she said, you've taken a turn up Crock Alley. I went out and had me a hot time. They were fallin all over me, good-lookin men would make you look like a wrapped turkey. The day I stay home and wait for a philanderin sonofabitch can't keep his word will be the day they pull the covers up over my face.

She was a real toe-grabber, Toker saw. She had tongue would melt enamel off a bucket.

I'll git you your coffee, she said, it killing her to spit it out. Though it's the only thing you'll be gittin out of me this lifetime.

She trounced off huffy of chin, that green robe sailing.

Now where'd he stashed them presents? In the baby's pillowcase sack? He'd git them, slide them inside her door.

No. Hide them away here under the step, for the minute.

Now she's busy, maybe I'll have me a little poke-around.

Toker crossed the yard to the side of the house. Here was that stump. With a team of horses, and six months, she could pry that out.

Seemed she'd tried putting in a grass lawn, though the grass hadn't taken. But she was trying again because a load of topsoil had been hauled in, lately too, because no weeds had yet got to it. Her lawn bed leading to a grazing pasture, though nothing grazing, that pasture backing up to a split-rail fence some hundred yards off. Then the tree line.

He went on further. The land here was rolly, running off into steep mountain some distance behind the house, with another mountain behind it lost in scurmudgeonous cloud. If he looked at it from her rooftop, he'd see his own Goose Neck habitat, see Goose Neck range and the valley hooking up with hers, some little dips and divides in between. A spring was nearby, he could hear it trickling. A stand of apple trees over there, maybe at one time a working orchard, and on down there, large as a house, the verdant thickness of scuppernong, the vines so thick you could climb up and walk on them. You could see wind there in the treetops, a soft breeze. Over on the rise were two graves, the one attended, the other left to whatever weeds would claim it. But he didn't want to look at graves. Here beside him now, a plow beat the color of weather, same as everything was. Two sheds in fair condition. No, make that three, for another was nestled away yonder in the woods. Now who would want a shed that far off? Maybe the smokehouse. Yes, a smokehouse, you could see how its logs were chinkered. See the smoke pipes, see there won't no windows. Over yonder, braced up against the steep, a two-story barn, not sagging any, the hayloft door open. A fence leading off to the unsloped side, and what was that behind it?

He tread on down, but before reaching the fence heard the neighing.

Well, I'll be doggone. Do tell. There was her Bathroby horse. Well, I'll be spanked. Not a workhorse either, with earth-slung belly, but a riding horse, white she was with a spotted rump, and pretty smartly groomed. A mane you could fill a mattress with.

The mare reached the fence the same moment he did, and plonked her head haughtily over the railing. Swishing that tail. A real Roby-type horse. Stroke me, she said, but feed me first. Toker yanked up a spangle of grass and patted her up between the ears as she munched. She nuzzled his palm, asking, Is that all? She stood, he estimated, about sixteen hands high, a sturdy, muscular beast who rippled her flanks as he admired her, saying, as Roby herself would, Buster, you've not seen nothin yet. Buster, hold onto your hat.

He crossed on back up by the side of the house and on around it. To end up pretty near the same place he'd started. By this tree stump. Now what was it she'd said about this stump? Somethin about a—

You'll be wantin cream with it, I reckon, he heard her say.

And saw she was hiked up there on the porch side with a

white porcelain pot aloft in one hand. The other hand down on the slung hip.

How long watching? Seeing him prowl her property like a tax collector.

Cream? he said. Well now, cream is the vision I see afore me.

He smiled, but she didn't move or smile back. Her gaze blank and steady.

You'd think that hip would git tired, he thought, it always slung. If not slung one way, then on its way to being slung the other. That foot beating out its boogie-woogie. Her hair looking even more disarranged. But hardly what you'd call your snake-pit hair. Her feet were still naked and she still had on that robe, it, as usual, sloshing up and down her flesh like water in a tipsy bucket.

Answer, goddamn you, she said. You want cream?

She made to throw the pot at him.

The baby had rolled over to its crawling and sliding mode. She had come about five feet across the yard, squirming and dragging her pillow sack. Now she had her head peeking from the sack, taking gauge on hardwon territory.

Roby had brought out to the porch a low round table and two low white chairs so delicate of structure they looked like they'd crumble the minute you so much as breathed on them.

You can stop lookin, she said. They's Danish and they don't bite.

She'd brought out a white round tablecloth with lace edging and whipped that up over the table.

She had a silver vase built like a wingless bird in the table center and out of the bird curved a plump, yellow zinnia.

Now where in high hell had she found bloomin flower?

You don't speak, damn you, she said, I'm goin to rake out your eyes. Cream?

Nome, he at last said. I don't want cream. It can't git too black for me.

Can't?

I like it strong enough to walk.

She relaxed a smidgen. He even saw the threat of a smile.

You'd like sugar though, I expect.

Sugar?

Yes. You spoon or pour it or dump the whole goddamn bowl into your beverage and somehow it sweetens that beverage.

Not me, he said. I like Nescafé sour enough to skin shellac off a table.

Her eyes swirled.

This here is coffee made from the goddamn bean, she said. She plopped the pot down on the table and whirled away again inside.

Toker hopped onto the porch and raised the lid of the pot, as if looking to find beans. He sat down gingerly in one of the white chairs. He crossed his legs and uncrossed them, suddenly made nervous by all this fanciful elegance.

When a minute ago she'd of bin pleased to run a pitchfork thue his belly.

She was a woman had a sleeveful of surprises.

This chair was a heap smartern he'd thought it to be. You could sit in it, you could squirm, and it let out not the whitest rattle. Yes, a pretty smart chair. That tablecloth a soft, honest thing.

He lifted up and smelt the flower.

She appeared now, conveying white cups and saucers the match of the coffeepot, and a white dish ringed with cookies of a wide variety, the steam still rising from some few of them. She thudded the plate down.

So she had bin cookin all mornin. She'd knowed he'd come.

You can eat'um or don't, she said. I don't care a sweet goddamn.

Toker got up. He wasn't any too sure about what he was doing, but he circled behind her and drew back her chair from the table and stood waiting behind it.

Both hands smacked up to her cheeks. Her eyes went thunk. Her face turned scarlet. In a rush she sat down.

Thank you, she said, her voice of such faintness the sound was all but lost.

For the next little minute she appeared smote by chagrin, unable to look his way.

This Don Wan business, it had its rewards he reckoned. It was worth gittin the hang of, it paid off this well.

The baby caught Toker's attention; it seemed to him to have done some sharp head-over-heels flip.

That baby, he said, can near walk already. Pretty soon she'll be struttin like John Philip Sousa. Next week she'll be sittin at the table.

Not at mine, Roby said.

Didn't you never want no baby of your own?

She looked at him, then away.

Didn't you?

She fidgeted with her white cloth napkin and slung disapproving eyes at his still unfolded by his plate. She had a flour smudge up on one cheek.

Never agin, she said.

What? He near raised up out of his seat. Had she had one, then? He leaned over the table, better to hear her, her voice that quiet.

My ears didn't quite catch you.

She picked up a cookie, nibbled, crumbled that cookie, then drew lines through the crumbs on the plate.

Do I want one? Not lessern it came up inside me thue God on High and no man didn't have a hand in it.

That's one way, he said.

Even then I'd likely drown it.

You and men don't git along, then?

A hummingbird had zipped through the yard, was now hanging a few feet above the baby. She solemnly watched that. Then the bird switted away.

The act itself I can recommend, she said. No, of the act itself it's the peaches and I'm the cream. She swirled coffee in her cup, sipped. That little finger pointed. Her eyes lowered over the cup rim.

He could see the half of one breast. A patch of scarlet on her chest came and went.

It's not every day I get the itch, she said. And it's not every day I git the chance to scratch, once itch sets in. There's few around here worth my time or trouble. I said boo, they'd blow away.

Toker said he could see that.

I don't mind confessin I had that itch yesterday. I was so far-gone you could of stirred me with a spoon.

What about now?

She didn't reply. She clutched the robe up to her neck, her shoulders scrunching, a worried look on her face. As if ravaged some little bit in heart and mind. In the strong light he could see dark circles under her eyes. She maybe rode a white horse, he thought, but he could see she'd known torment in her time.

I'm not sayin what I've had and not had, she said. No morn I'm sayin I could separate what I want from what I dream, or even from what I've only dreamt I wanted.

Unhuh, he said, thinking about that. And when you have these dreams, where do they take you?

Smack-dab into paradise, she said. Her head did a small, happy dance above her shoulders. Then she grimaced.

I don't make no apology for it. You can't have it in your dreams, at least there, you might as well be content snugglin up with nightmare.

The baby threw up a yell.

Whyn't you never married? asked Toker.

I've spared myself that agony.

She fell silent then, and that silence stretched out. She went on drawing pictures on her plate. Faces. She'd give a face hair and then scratch it away. Ears, the same. She'd draw in a smile, then erase it. Then put in a frown.

She left the one face frowning. She gave that one hair.

This was how she ate cookies, Toker supposed.

He reached over and wiped the flour smudge from her cheek. She ignited then, jumping at his touch.

Don't do that, she snapped out. Don't touch me.

She drew up her knees, encircled them. He watched her toes execute a brief dance on the seat edge. She twisted about under his gaze.

What you think you're lookin at? she said. She flung the gown over her feet. Stop studyin me. The feet stomped down. She lunged forward, reached out, and with both hands whipped his head about. She tilted up his face, her fingers digging. Her face hove up and her mouth locked tight as a walnut against his. Her nails gouged. She squared about, the mouth opened, and her tongue slid hard as a smooth stone against his. Then it unhinged and wrapped all around his.

She came loose with a plopping sound, shoving his face back.

There, she said. That was to show you I can be hot-blooded as the next one. Now will you go cryin the news? Will you say how I moaned and groaned and couldn't keep my hands off you?

Toker rubbed his lips. He felt a mule had kicked him in the mouth.

She was some number.

Don't ast me about children, she went on, striding the porch. I've had to raise a houseful and me not much morn one myself. Not that it didn't have its high spots. Two or three brats chawin on your ankles each second goes by, at least you know you're breathin. Then when I could, I went away from here. God knows why I ever come back.

She strode down the steps and out into the yard, where she picked up and turned the baby about, smacked two fistfuls of dirt from its hands, and set it back down.

All in about one second.

Now she strode back, her eyes flaring.

The day comes I have to offer explanation to a sonofabitch says he's goin to do somethin, says he's goin to come and then don't, and him haulin a grungy homelessass baby, is the day I'm laid out six foot under, my cheeks packed with dirt. Goddamn you.

No, she won't never going to forgive him. You committed a crime against this woman, you weren't never going to walk upright again, or your eyes see glory.

You walked upright with her, though, you might be arm-in-arm with glory every minute.

She hung by the porch post, switching her weight from one leg to the other, staring off through her valley where nothing stirred except the sway of trees, each inch of that vista baleful, her look said, and not worth spit.

That kiss a minute ago didn't do nothin for me either, she said. I'd sooner stand knee-deep in swampwater as do it again.

Toker laughed, but cut it short when she sent a scalding glance his way.

I might say I had me a baby one time and it died, what would you say?

I believed you, I'd say I was sorry.

You can save your pity. I never had one.

Then why say it?

If I had one, or so much as thought of havin one, you'd be the last one I'd say it to. You'd have a thousand questions.

I might ast who the daddy was. I might ast when. I might ast what she died of or how you loster and what happened to the daddy and where's it buried. I might ast how she figured in that paradise you mentioned. I might ast why you can't make up your mind whether you've had one, and why if you've had all those others chawin at your ankles how come those ankles today are so all-fired pretty.

Well, I never had one, so ast what you please. But you can leave my ankles out of it.

She sighted down at the baby, who made a crowing sound and lifted its arms to her. Roby skittered back.

Was it all bloody? she asked. When you found this baby?

She was smeared a good token. Though not as much as the mama.

Roby's head shot up.

Her mama? What do you know about the mama?

Toker squirmed. He could tell her right now.

But an hour later would be a noose around his neck. Two, and he'd be in jail.

He didn't answer.

She looked at him a minute and saw there wouldn't be one.

I can see you findin the baby, she said, her voice fading wan. The bright mornin, you traipsin thue the woods. I can see you washin and carryin her, carin for her, and comin here to see could you foister off on me, but I can't see what happens next.

Me either, he said. I could see it, I'd maybe skip to high heaven. You'd see me a bleedin bullet on the horizon.

He could see hisself running, hear a passel of bloodhounds on his tail, hear a sheriff's posse, the men calling: Let's git that murderer! Let's mow'm down!

The two of them pondered their separate roads, her pouty for a moment. Her look bleak.

He could see here was a woman had secrets would stifle a chimney. Moods would fill a well.

But she won't by her lonesome, it come to that.

I can see the baby growed up, he said, after a minute. I can git that far. But what she's doin, and what her life's like, I can't see.

You can, huh? See that much?

She's a world-beater, I can see that.

And her mama? she asked. What do you see there?

He didn't reply.

His eyes veered off her, down to the baby.

The baby was pitched over on her stomach, only her belly button touching the ground. So it seemed. The arms were pointed wide, the legs straight to the rear. That head straight up.

Flying.

Toker held his breath.

He saw Roby move a cautious step nearer the baby, her mouth open, her eyes popping.

They watched the baby fly.

After a minute it went crumbly and puddly again.

I be damned! Roby said. Her voice hushed.

She descended the stairs, circled the baby with acute distrust, then stooped and picked the baby up. She slid her hands under its arms and held it aloft, the baby dangling, its head a goofy tilt on its shoulders. She shook her and the ba-

by's limbs jumped about like a puppet's. The baby laughing.
She splayed the baby down over one arm and with the other
poked and prodded.

Then she returned it to the grass and stood watching it out
of uneasy, puzzled demeanor.

She poked the baby with her foot.

I don't believe it, she said. Make her do it again.

Toker laughed. Cripes! he said. She's only a baby!

Toker shied up from the white chair and went down to stand
beside Roby, with nothing to say, but holding himself there as
if he imagined someone might any second be coming up from
the road to take a Kodak shot of them, one he could pull out
years from now and say to friends, say to a grown daughter
maybe, Here's the one lifted me from my hole in the ground.
Here was the day Toker's life took a turn for the better. Here's
how we looked in them days, at that junction. There's me on
the left, needin a haircut and smellin of dogs, and there's
Roby beside me in that green robe I wouldn't swap for a thousand virgin acres.

For a brief space he held her hand, and she allowed it. He
squeezed her hand and she squeezed back. She even swayed
against him. He put his arm around her waist and she didn't
shudder, she didn't fling him back. But she didn't seem to
much notice either. He placed his hand up behind her neck
and caressed there, without response. He could swing around
and press against her and it would be the same to her as
that swamp she'd mentioned. She was off in some coma, it
seemed. Off in some deep reverie.

He maneuvered, embracing her. Her head swayed back
onto his shoulder, her breath on his neck. Some little jigger of
action in the pelvic region, either her own or his'n.

There it was again, that hip-nudge.

Her hand up behind his neck. Her lips at his ear now.

He had that Kodak man out in the yard, he'd say to him, Hold it a minute. Hold it. Step back a mite and git a snapshot with the baby in it. Git us all three. Then come in close and git one with me here my arms around Roby. Git one of her with her face dreamy as you can make it.

And then you stand by, because that baby will fly again.

But Roby pulled away from him and drove up by the side of the house, stopping at that stump.

Just standing there, to look at it. To look a long time, shivering. Her face troubled.

You take too many liberties, she said, low of voice. I feel I'm lost in some swirlpool.

She sounded it. He had that Kodak man, he'd say, Snap a shot of that swirlpool, for we are both aswirl in it.

He had a feeling, in that second, that he could cross to her, slide the robe from her shoulders, and the two satisfy whatever was this unspoken thing between them. She would join right in. But he had the feeling too that if he did so, did so now, she wouldn't never forgive him.

A short space later she summoned him back to the table.

The coffee will get cold, she said. I'm sorry. Sometimes my moods go crumbly as these cookies. I've not slept a wink all night. I been jumpy as a bedstead in the Garden of Eden since the minute I saw you climbin my road. Though it won't work. We won't. You're down in a hole, and I'm still climbin that tree over there.

The coffee was good. Better than good. It won't coffee anyone could secure around here. It was coffee come from another kingdom, the same as that baby. The same as that green robe, that spotty horse, these white dishes, Roby's blossomy skin, and her fits of temper. If he went out and probed in her load of new topsoil he'd no doubt find that won't from around here either. Maybe it was Danish.

A breeze drifted over the porch. In the silence he could hear the flow of the spring.

He wondered the old duffers at the store giving their blessings to this romantic expedition: Be true, you want to avoid heartache, son.

He wondered Sarah's taking to bed. How she'd wanted his baby: A hundred dollars and you git visitin privileges day or night, Toker. But we won't tell Cal yit a while. Let me keeper the day, the next few days, till he gets used to havin her underfoot. He'll come round and bein a daddy will make a man of him. All right, two hundred dollars. I can add on a bitty nursery with a sunny window lookin over the dog pen.

So the baby's fortunes were on the mend.

He wondered, could she speak, what the dead mother would say he ought to do. What advisement she'd render.

Wondered would she condemn him too.

Or maybe she'd say, I'm past heppin, so you jist go on takin care of that baby.

He had to do something about her. It made him shudder to think of her inside that car.

You walked long enough, you'd think a remedy would come.

Could he tell Roby? He itched to spit his tale out.

The thing was, you hugged the good and the bad both to you, the bad swamped the good and you had not enough left over to invite another party to enter your orbit. You got penned-up and panic-eyed the same would a lone hog, or a wild one, for that matter.

He studied Roby's face, it serene for the moment. Now there was a lesson in beauty, that face. There was a face would

go up inside you and turn on razzle-dazzle lights. It would
wean a wizard away from his wand, that face.

Not to mention the goodness residing in that creamy, green-
drenched body. A gold necklace, slim as a thread, up at her
throat. That hadn't been there yesterday. It hadn't been there
an hour ago either.

He took a cookie out to the baby, Roby observing this,
though she didn't say no. Plain to see that flying trick had got
to her. Her chair placed so she couldn't miss it, it happened
again.

The baby took the sweet in both hands and jammed it full
into her mouth. Gums set to work, the baby jiggling, changing
color like a lizard, it was that pleased.

He'd eaten about ten of her cookies hisself. He'd eat more,
he won't ashamed to show his greed.

They'd drained the pot. It was the best breakfast, if breakfast it was, ever he'd had.

He'd make her a meal would supercharge her too, one of
these days. If ever he got out of this jam and had a place he
could invite her to. Make her one of his cayenne stews. Thow
in a wildcat or two, she'd lap it up. Remember to set by a
stack of these cloth napkins, haul in a couple of Danish
chairs. Don't forget fresh zinnia. He could move up out of that
hole. Sell off some of his timber, get a grubstake that would
see him thue winter. They'd bin after him, those strip-and-
drag people. Leave him sittin pretty, so they said. His daddy
never would let'um. His daddy would of sold his children before he let a tree come down. But his back up against wall
now, maybe it was time. Get a grubstake. Get a foundation in
on a new abode. Them old codgers down at the store, they
could hep'm.

Find his mama wherever she'd got to and money-order her

a spot of cash. She'd done wrong, but there was another side of the story. His daddy had beater. That was one side you could look at. She'd never had nothing, that was another side.

Them old kneebenders down at the store no doubt had a hand in building half the houses around here. They could handle hammer and saw.

He could put in a roof window. A roof window—you could lay in bed and witness the stars, the deep night—had always made sense to him. The window might leak, rain pour in, but still that view on the world would be worth it. Jist lay by plenty of tar.

Roby was standing now, backing away to the door. Her brow damp, her flesh spotty. Suddenly nervous as a pony.

Now what was she up to?

I want you to see my house, she said. Her voice breathy, the words fumbly. Fumbling at that door too. To see inside, she said. To see how pretty it is, I mean. Her hands flew to her face; she hid herself there behind her fingers, all trembly of body. Crimson to her toes. Flustered head to foot. He scraped back in his chair and saw her look up in panic. No! she said. I've changed my mind. It's too messy. It's too—I'm ashamed of myself for—

Her hands flying. Her words spurting out. *Don't move!* she cried now. Stay where you are! *Stay!*

She might have been scolding a dog, her voice that arch.

He sat back down.

No, *don't!* she said. *Don't sit!* I want you to go now. Her eyes shot from right to left. She sucked in a chestful of air. She plopped back down herself, hiding her face.

You must think me crazy, she said.

Toker, amused, didn't think to deny it.

I am, she said. I don't have the brains I was—she stuck a

cookie into her mouth and chewed on it ravenously—born with, she said. Yes, you best trot on off now. You and your baby. My visitin hours are over.

She arose and floated toward him, her hand outstretched for him to shake it.

Rise, Toker, to meet her.

Was she under a spell? Her face swoony. Her arms rode up his chest and on up to encircle his neck. Her one hand roved back and forth through his hair and she seemed not to know it. That other around his waist now, holding on tight, and she seemed not to know that either. Her cheek up against his. That bathrobe sliding. No, slinky bathrobe didn't have a chance on her. Her hips wedging in. Or was it hisn?

Kisser, Toker.

The loop on that robe-tie slipping loose. One little breeze, one little move, and she'd be naked. The same as yesterday, behind that door. But there won't nothing deliberate about it. She was unaware. Maybe there hadn't bin none of it deliberate from the start; it was the way she came. Or the way that robe came. You wore it, you were obliged to do as that robe commanded.

The truth is, him loath to admit this, he hadn't never seen a naked woman. Not one proper. Not in a full daylight hour.

His brow was hot, his heart clanking.

He felt any more amorous, he'd wilt.

Holder, Toker.

Why don't you kisser?

He thought, Hey now, Toker, will ye take this woman as your wedded wife? Will ye lover and keeper? Will ye cherish and honor thue thick and thin? Say I do, Toker. Say ye will.

Or maybe for now you jist holder and kisser.

He wondered love hadn't clamped eternal arm around him.

He did so, or they did, and later on he squinted open one eye, to find the baby looking at them.

Keep lookin, he thought. Tomorry I'll buy you a sweet green robe, and little bow-tie shoes you can wear. Later on, you'll be growed up, yankin our toes to tell us breakfast is ready. We'll rise from sleep to look from the window and see you ridin that horse.

He thought this, the two clamped against each other. Holding and pressing and kissing.

It started on the porch and was brought to swift conclusion there.

Then they steered for her bedroom, getting no further than the front door. The two together down on her porch, wallowing and rolling, with no thought to skinned knees, to skinned elbows, to blistered flesh. Flesh was blistery all over but heavenly inside where matters were of more consequence.

What's them bites? she at one point said, her eyes alarmed. You got bites all over. I wonder your little hammer ain't got bit off as well.

Not yit, he said. Is it that little?

They slid as one over the floor, groping and kissing the while. Through the front door, down a hall. *Wait! Can't you wait?* No, the neither one of them could wait. A carpet twisted and slid in lumps along with them. Something clattered down, a lamp, and next, the table. Sonofabitch, she said. Oh Toker! And kicked the table spinning. A chair snagged his foot, to leap like a wild thing in between them.

In here, she gasped, climbing the bed, but he pulled her down, and at the foot of the bed, oily with sweat, they joined again. Afterwards, he slid free of her body and tried wriggling up onto the bed, hassling for breath, but she yanked at his ankles and slithered him and half the bed down upon her. They rolled midst the bedclothes and the scatter rugs, midst assorted chairs, oddments of figurines, books, candle holders, and vases of crumpled dry flowers, weeds from the fields, to find each other's flesh and reclaim it again, the moans and yelps of one indistinguishable from the other's, a length of siding board cracking loose from the outside wall, interior plaster rumbling, a bed slat smacking to the floor.

Later, eyes closed, the deed over, her hand in his, her to say:
I'm pole-axed. You?
Him to spin his eyes open, to leap up.
Damn! Where'd I leave the baby?

Afterwards, all three dozed, the baby between them.
Then he awakened, only pretended sleep. First, to find her propped up on her elbows playing with the baby. Second, to find her seated on the floor, the baby swinging in her arms. Singing to the baby as she flipped pages in a book. What kind of book? A stamp album, he saw, old and inches thick. He squinted, saw her come to a page and stop. Saw her extract from a yellowed envelope a tattered scrap of print cloth.
What's that? he asked.
She pressed the cloth to her chest with both hands and didn't answer.
It was private, whatever it was.
Then he saw her fold the tatter and tuck it back inside the envelope and return the envelope to the stamp album. Her eyes blinked up at him.
Who? she asked. What did you say?
Her eyes cloudy with some old pain.

. . .

Later, her limbs again looped within his, he asked about the stamps.

What's that called? he asked.

They's called stamps, she said. If you sell'um, you're called a post office. If you deliver'um, you're called a postman. If you lick'um you're called a stamplicker.

She struggled free of the pillow he smushed over her face.

My daddy collected'um, she said. It's the only thing about him I have kept, or can bear. You don't know what happened here, do ye? When I was a little girl.

She told him about her brother being hung from the front-yard tree and how her daddy had gone crazy, the boy hanging there and her daddy not letting anyone near, all of it jist the most terrible thing a person could imagine.

We can pull that stump up, he said, her tale done. We can send it to fiery hell. But listen. Now you listen to me. I've got a story to tell you about this baby. About her mama.

He told her about the woman out on his land, in his daddy's old junked car, her throat slit.

Before he reached his story's end, she jumped from the bed, whapped hair from her face. She sprang out into the hall and looked off through the door at her front porch.

I know who done it, she said. Sonofabitch. That slinkhog was at my door this past evenin.

She told him about that.

 For some long while after his visit with Hindmarch, Truman
had sat in his car down on the road. The day waned, yet still
he sat on, hunched low and as if wizened under the wheel.
Periodically, a match flared and he lit another cigarette. Periodically, he attempted ignition of his engine, but the car
only shuddered vehemently, Truman clenching his jaw to the
raucous grind.

From time to time a car or truck rumbled by, or mule and
wagon, and he'd see the riders with stretched necks gawking
at him. Earlier in the day a lone driver had zipped by, catching his eye with a sidelong stare, then a few minutes later the
bird had popped along again, slung in, and parked his heap
by the opposite side.

They'd spent a minute in low watch of each other.

When the bird slammed his door and crossed over, Truman
wedged his knife from his pocket and stashed it, open and
hidden, in his hands between his legs.

Trouble? the man asked.

Truman saw him darting looks into the backseat; he reckoned he knew the man's car anyhow.

No trouble, he said. You got any?

The man went around to the back of his car and kicked up a shoe against the bumper and studied the plate. Truman watched him out of the rear window, their eyes catching again.

The man came back and stood a few feet away from his window. Somewhat burly of chest, a tie knotted dime-hard up against his gizzard.

Passin thue, are ye?

Truman didn't speak.

How long passin thue?

Truman cleared his throat and parked his glob down by the man's shoes.

I'm huntin a thief. You seen one?

Truman shook his head.

Was that a yes or a no?

Truman grinned up at him.

The man stepped nearer and made no bones this time about his interest in Truman's goods stowed in the backseat.

I'm lookin a thief done siphoned my gas, the man said.

That so? Truman said.

He done stole my jack too, and a case of oil. You carryin them things?

Nope, Truman said. Jist carryin what's got my own name on it.

You wouldn't want to show me the inside of your trunk, would ye?

Nawp. Nawsir, I wouldn't. I wouldn't ask a second time either, I was you.

Their eyes hung together for a spell, Truman rubbing the knife blade against his thumb, waiting would the man sink face into his window.

When the man did nothing, Truman smirked and said, What makes ye think I stolen your goods?

The man considered this.

Then said, Because I can spot a sonofabitch. Can't you?

Truman nodded.

I'm lookin at one, he said.

They studied each other a spell longer, neither moving. Then the man snatched at his collar, cursed him, and sauntered on back to his car. His car kicked up dust in the turnaround, he shook a fist at Truman, and him and the car careened on away.

Truman got from the car, wet a rag in ditch water, and sat on again in his car, the rag up against his cheek. He tried his starter, and swore a string of oaths as the motor refused to catch.

He cursed as a dead sonofabitch the man he'd got this car from.

A car whirred up with a toothy-faced driver behind the wheel, two oddball smilers shoulder against shoulder in the rear, and he fingered his pocketknife, but they whirred on by.

Singin, goddamn'um.

He spent a time wriggled up under the car, wrenching at the fuel line, aiming to find some corruption there, though knowing the while that such fixing would be to no avail. He spent still more time under the raised hood, unhitching the spark plugs, wiping their sludge on his sleeve and shoving them home again. He unhinged the distributor cap, wiped it, and banged it back into place with a rock.

That'll do ye, he said. You sonofabitch.

He got back into the seat and tried the starter again. It screeched at him but he kept at it, feeling the key bend between his fingers.

Later, the battery went dead, and the car would not chooger even a token.

Later still, he flagged down a man driving a black Studebaker, and he ran to open the door to ask did the man know where a man could buy something a body could drink, but turned out the driver was a Sunday preacher. He listened a minute to the man's rank preaching, and was ready to haul him out, when the preacher stomped the gas and hurtled away.

It November, an alien month anyhow.

He'd bin born, so it was told, in November.

He kerfloogled up under his wheel again, and for a duration slept.

In the afternoon he slung his mink trap about his neck, locked the car doors, and disappeared into the woods.

Some hours later he emerged out at that same forest point he'd entered, talking to himself a ragged whisper, stopping when he saw the car, to settle upon it and the road which held it, a new bevy of oaths, comminations, and invocations. He was wet to the waist, and shivery. He took off and drained his shoes and climbed with haggard breath into the backseat, where he quickly found and slipped on dry clothes. He eyed the trap suspiciously, but said nothing against it.

It was the goddamn black pooled water was at fault.

He tried the starter, which would not turn over.

It was black November, and what could you expect?

He alighted and leaned against the door, fumbling with his cigarette pack. He had but two left, and his pockets empty. He lit one, and eyed the highway, and smoked the cigarette down to the nub before moving again.

Then he altered the wheels and began pushing.

Move, damn ye! he said.

Tongue between his teeth, his feet aslip beneath him, he got the car onto the road.

He left the car there and returned to where he'd started,

picked up his tossed nub, and got two more sucks from it, then went back to the car.

Abandon ship, he said, snickering. He raised his trunk lid and flung his heavier belongings into the weeds. He crawled into the backseat and flung away without examination sundry more of his possessions.

Leave only wife and children, he said, and laughed heartily to his environs.

His brow was sweaty, tooth and gum raging.

He hadn't ought to of waded into that black pond. He hadn't ought to of come here. It won't a road that bespoke a worthy mission.

He looked at the sky, pleased to note some drift in the hour.

Now let's bust-gut this rascal.

He pushed the droning vehicle along the grade to what he perceived to be the crest of a hill, and once there he gave a last heave and ran abreast of his driver's door until he at last succeeded in yanking it open and flinging himself onto the gearshift and floorboard. He turned the ignition key and stomped the clutch down, and slammed his gearshift into third, happy to see the woods flowing by at a quickening pace. It was a good downhill run and she was a sweet chariot and would do it. The speedometer hit thirty and there he gripped the wheel, freed the clutch. The tires skidded, lifting him upright into the windshield. The engine wheezed and coughed, throwing up a volley of smoke in that second before it died and the car again rolled on.

You rank bastard, he said. I'll git ye this time.

He had another try before reaching the bottom of the hill, and this time the engine caught and purred and held.

Tole ye, damn ye, he said.

He motored tranquilly on over the next hill, and the next one, and with gathering speed around a long curve into an

inviting straightaway; he was reaching to put fire to last cigarette, gloating at this proof of his automotive genius at the
expense of those arrayed, faceless barons and magnates of
steel who would have had it otherwise, when the engine began
to shriek and clang, to give earsplitting whine and swoosh
black gaseous cloud about his windshield, then the car to
heave up off its axles as flames blazed plume-like from the
hood's crevices, all in that second before the hood exploded
powerfully from its hinges, cracked like a gunshot against his
vision, and sailed with smoking tail off into the bushes where
it would be seen no more. Truman snatched up the mink trap
beside him. He wrenched the wheel to the near wooded side
as he leapt stark-eyed from the car, and as his left knee struck
pavement and his right ankle folded beneath him, and his
body thunked and rolled and slid its guideless way, his trap in
one fist and a whirling, clanging disk beside him, he had
sense of his car leaping the road gully and soaring in a fiery
loop of ornamental wizardry and crashing on, as he did himself, into such flimsy or solid obstruction as the wilderness
boasted.

Catgut music was awash in the air, awash in wind, rutting
obscure symphony by and over his head, causing his mind to
loft up visions of ancient furred or horned ruminants in heat
through the acquiescent brambles in which he lay. Odorous
caterwauling as they cleaved unto each other their weird and
potluck secretions, a pyorrhea without end, and yet more
ghoulish the ballooning to follow. He opened his eyes and for
a while felt terror, for he could see nothing, nor could he feel
of his body much of anything either. He did not move, except
to lift his head, and with that lifting forest mulch adhered to
his face, and he dropped his head back to its rest there. His
mouth drooled saliva or blood and only when the gathering

pool threatened defilement of his very breath did he whimper and forlornly shift his head, and give timid test to his limbs. Pain romped through him from foot to head and he gave aching wail of lament to this. His brain swirled and the wind's catgut music died away and for a time, then, though he stared with open eye into his darkness, he did not know he did.

Sometime later he whimpered anew, seeing God's visage at bivouac within a range of teaming clouds. *Yea, do I speak. I speak to ye of the bones of your father and of his father's bones. From my house of bones do I speak.*

Truman listened with unblinking eye.

Would ye know my secret? Would ye? Oh, I think ye would not, but I will tell ye.

I'm not innerstid, Truman said. Tell it to somebody else.

I have coupled with troglodyte and millipede. With dinosaur and gnat and mud tortoise in the deep.

I'm done with couplin myself, Truman said. You can git on now.

I have commingled with moth and cockroach, no less than with winged pterosaur. I have burrowed thue rankest slime to invent earliest mollusk stewin in my brain.

You're a swarmy bastard then, ain't ye? Truman said.

He saw God had gargoyled face and spake with a quaking fury.

In my olden days, God said, *when my brain was festerin with purpose and my every void was to be filled.*

You'd best of rested, Truman said. You'd best not of riz from bed thue your seven century-long days.

With mine own juices have I secreted larvae and salamander, newt and toad, conifer and seaweed and lowest bedbug. From moldy lichen to rarest cockatoo, so has it bin. Breath of my breath and body of my body.

You can jist shut your mouth up, Truman said. I ain't listenin no more.

He closed his eyes and summoned his hands up over them.

Now would ye know more? Then listen. I am done with mud rat as with soarin bird. I will commingle no more.

That's good, said Truman. Amen to that.

Would ye know more?

I'm done with knowin, Truman said. I've knowed out.

You will know yit more. Are ye listenin? For all my seedin, I did not seed thee.

Truman sat up. God's gargoyle face was fading away into the stewing clouds.

Ye are no longer my servant, God said. *From my left side do I release thee and from my right side do I release thee. From my very ribs do I release thee. How are ye, how are ye? How are ye?*

His flesh seemed to peel and slip free of his bones, to vanish and be as lost, here in the immensity of these odorous surroundings.

He moaned, and clapped hands up to his head, wanting to issue ragged and destitute cry of protest, for the world had partaken of some rare hue not in accord with his liking.

Truman could stand. He could stand, though his kneecaps felt rubbery. His ankles folded. His skin blistery, shredded. Open wounds stinging, biting in the cold air. A cut in his brow that near shut one eye.

But one was enough. Did a man need more?

His breath sloogered thin and raspy, like a straw you'd suck the last dregs through. A numbness coiled up from his heels.

Swelly, all over, he thought. A real swellbelly.

No, I won't win no beauty prize. Not this week. But I ain't crow bait yit. I'm still alive to lick the kingdom's butter.

Cream rises.

He hunted about in the woods, limping, stumbling, from minute to minute stooping over in wild clutch of his head— but bound he would find his trap.

And determined too, to stroll upright out of this quaghole he'd been pitched into.

He hadn't known God for his propagation had to couple with his nasty, sludgehole creations.

You ought to of tole me afore, he said. You ought to of have, like that sorry old uncle guardian of mine ought to of have with my mink trap. He wouldn't of perished, grabbin up over that sill to shag me, he'd bin a better man and had tole me what I ask.

Won't nothin wrong with me askin what made the proper mink bait. Won't nobody of never did tell me nothin.

Ere the night turns, Truman thought, so shall one of ye betray me.

Amen, he said aloud. Amen. You got what ye deserved. You with your woman's hair.

God the pig suckler, and Jesus the piggly-tail boy.

He was done with touching. God had coupled in sludge, in dredgewater, in watery crypt with mollusk and slimebug; he'd had at it with all deformity of creatures. From eye to wing to tailbone down thue the ages, and it had depleted his loins and marked as a proper wage God's ogreish features.

No, he'd not touch women again. He'd done that and propagated his seed as the Book commanded and that ugliness was behind him now. There won't no need anyhow to climb up over a woman's flesh and pound foot into floorboard and pretend your exhalations of wonder or yelp madness with your pretended flooding. Best ye dribbled your wad into copious snowbank. Thaterd be a better way than touching. Ye dribble your wad into snowbank jar, and freeze it inside that jar till the desired occasion. Then ye haul in jar and bedpan and roll up your sleeves and flick your knife and cut the woman's belly and slide in your freezer unit. You'd be sunny-faced scientist rolled in on skatewheels to insinuate your cold-pack seed into the willing body. Thaterd be the better way. And no, you'd never, never, have to toucher.

Thatern the other night, in her green bathrobe was the very picture of vile perfection. He'd of touched her, he got the chance. He could see her now, there behind her window, snooty, her nose in the air. The fancy, high-thighed, loose-hipped type woman he'd never had no luck with. Though all the same in his mind now she was calling to him. *Truman, Truman, now don't ye leave me, Truman. Truman, Truman, do ye have gum? My mouth is somethin else.* He closed his eyes, he could hear her calling. *Are ye scaredy-cat? That ye won't come in?* He could see her dancing. Shedding that gown. He clenched his eyes, he could. *Holy-moly, Jesus is Christ, Patty-cake, patty-cake, kill your lice.* Only it weren't her now, it was the youngan with the skimpy flaring skirt, the black shiny shoes, the black play purse, the bow in her hair. His life's dream, till ye saw the flipside. *One, two, buckle my shoe.* She had a scrubbed face, and thin white socks came up to her knees. *Three, four, ye can't see no more.* She had puckerish lips and curly ringlets about her face. *Five, six, git your kicks.* Oh long ago that one was, but near enough to him now he could reach out and toucher. *Seven, eight, don't be late.* The very house she'd lived in, and the droppy-leaf grounds upon which it stood, seemed to rise and flow before him in wavery stream of welcoming beauty. *Nine, ten, I'll do you in.* Oh another world, thatern where Flary Skirt lived. A paradise, or so he'd thought, and all inside that paradise unattainable to him.

But he'd found out better. He'd come eye to eye with the flipside. *Eeniemeenieminey, kiss my hiney.* She'd say that, hiking her bloomers at him. He'd catch sight of her in the woods and she'd whirl her play pocketbook. She'd hide from him. She'd say, *Oh, trash, that's what you are. You're oldern me. Ye best not touch me. Ye touch me, I'll scream my tonsils out. They'll string you up.* She'd say that, scrunched down in the bushes, and never he could finder. He finder he'd whipper with sticks, but never he could.

Each evening back then, and some days too, he'd throw down his hoe or pitchfork, finish whatever backbreaking labor was his chore, and run over the hill from his orphan's hellhole. He'd slink about in the bushes. He'd snake hisself up on his belly, and part the limbs, and spy on that little girl. *Patty-cake, patty-cake, now if ye have salt, spin baby in your batter and call it a halt. Scaredy-cat, scaredy-cat, have ye no tongue? My pie's in the oven and will ye not come?*

She had new dress and a play-clothes doll and a bow matching her own, for the doll's hair, but she hadn't never let him play with it. *You're too big. You'll break it. Play with ye own self. Ye can't play with nothin of mine.* She'd cry that out, and spit out her tongue. *Your feet stink, your feet are rotten, your nose is full of stinkin cotton. Dinky-dinky Danny, kiss my fanny.* She had a milk bottle no biggern a thumb, and he'd see her holding that bottle to the doll's mouth, singing the while: *Drink, lil baby, and don't ye cry. Or Mummy will spank ye and you will die.* She had a teensy white rockabye crib the dollbaby slept in, and she'd rock the baby and sing it her ugly cradle song. *Rockybye baby in the treetop, when the breeze blow your breath will stop. Jiggly-piggly, count your sheep; the Boogerman gits you, Mummy won't weep.*

Patience. Patience, that was the girl's name. Peculiar, it to come to him after lo these years.

Lo, lo, the bridge has broke down; Baby's cracked her skull and can't git to town.

He'd watch her play with that doll. She'd wring off the doll-baby's limbs, snatch off its head, whap that baby against rock and ground.

Now you'll behave, she'd say. *Scaredy-cat, scaredy-cat, what do ye say? You bin a bad baby, now ye will pay.*

She lived in paradise but she was baddern him.

Oh, heaps worse.

A mean, prissy, selfish thing.

That last time he'd seen her, she was in the front yard, spinning on a tire rope swing. Dusk, it was, and him on his belly spying from a rocky mud bank.

I see you in there, she said. Ye can't hide. Whun't ye come up and play?

He'd crawled out.

Ugg, she'd said. You.

He'd sat in her tire swing and she'd told him to git away from there. She'd huddled up in it her own self and told him he could push.

It's my swing, she said. Ye won't push, I'll turn you into maggot's broth.

Can't.

Can.

I got a jump-rope, she said. I'm the best jump-roper in creation.

Ain't.

Is.

Ain't.

She tied one end of her jump-rope to a tree. She put the other end in his hand. She showed him where she wanted him to stand.

Now ye jist whirl it, she said. You let the rope thump the

ground and ye whisk it over my head and ye keep whiskin that rope and I bet I can jump fastern you can whisk that rope. What you bet?

He wrung out his pockets, but he hadn't nothing to bet.

You got to bet me, she said. Or I won't play.

I bet you a kiss, he said. I bet you a kiss on your shut mouth.

Ugg, she said, and wiped her face. Ugg. I'd sooner be dead. But all right, then. You bet me a kiss and I bet you the nose on your face.

Jumpy-rope, jumpy-rope, jump the rope high. If I can't jumpy-rope, I surely will die.

She'd swung on her tire swing, but she hadn't let him swing.

She'd jumped, but she hadn't let him jump.

He'd whirled that rope with both hands, hard as he could, his teeth clamped, his arms achy, but she'd kept up.

She'd crowed every minute, crying *Faster, faster!* her feet flying, not missing a skip, her skirt flary, her jist laughing at him the whole time, *Faster faster, can't ye go no faster!* her feet scarcely touching the ground, that rope no morn a blur and her feet a blur as well, and he knew then it won't fair, that she was cheating, that this won't how the game was played and he hadn't never had no chance, so he whapped that rope straight out and caught her neck, tumbling her over, the both of them in that second hollering and her scrambling afoot to shoot straight at him, crying *Gimmie that nose, I've done won it,* and raking her hands at his face, the both of them rolling in the dirt then, pulling at each other's hair, gouging the eyes, spitting and kicking and flailing and biting each other, that rope tangly between them and he saw itterd got looped between her legs so he kicked at her face and scrambled loose of her and the second he was on two feet he whooped up that

rope and chunked it over the first limb and caught the dangly
end, gave the rope a big yank, and in a jiffy she was strung
there, hanging, no morn one foot touching the ground, all hog-
tied and every inch beat. But would she say she was sorry?
Would she say now she'd play fair or give him a turn on that
tire swing or say he could jump or even let him look at that
doll? Her who had everything? No, she was hollering how
she'd kill'm, how she hoped he'd perish from this earth, as
she twisted each which way and got that rope swinging, tugging back on that rope with both hands as she huffed to reach
that tree trunk, the both of them screaming at each other as
her legs split wide and forked that tree trunk, her feet scam-
pering around that tree trunk quick as a monkey's, her hanging belly-up in the air but straddling that tree trunk with her
legs and holding on with crossed ankles, that high limb sagging and creaking, the rope chewing the bark, but she had the
leverage now with that tree trunk and it won't fair, she won't
never would play fair, she was winning again, she was plain
lifting him off the ground, lifting him high into the branches,
now crowing her laughter again and he ought to of knowed it,
to of expected it, because there won't never no way you could
beat them who had everything and won't never they'd share
one breath of they's bounty or part with one token of they's
blessings and itterd bin better he'd never bin born, him who
would never have nothing while she herself had everything.

Someone ought to of seen to it. They ought to of seen itterd
be different.

Because won't he innocent? Won't he the injured party?

God ought to of had, way back at the beginning, or when he
had his beasts of the earth and his birds of the air entering his
ark two by two. He ought to of had, Truman now thought, as
he scrabbled about over the forest floor in search of his trap.
God would of seen to it, might of arighted the matter, he

hadn't been from day one so scorchy-eyed busy with his demented coupling.

Faint the chance now.

There won't but one caretaker you could rely on, and that one's your old buddyrole Truman.

I'm sheep-dip in the cripple's bucket, he thought. Bejeweled with mine own blood and beseeded with thine own pestilence, but I'm the single square-shooter to be found in these parts.

What's mine is mine.

That trap is mine, and that baby is mine.

I'll go and gitter.

In the next little while he found his trap, and it not broke, though the pan and spike bent and the teeth snaggly.

His good star was still looking after him.

Mine the glory.

He tied the trap to his belt loops, with swollen eye gauged, and took aim on the skewered heavens, and scabfooted onwards.

Hindmarch hadn't seen any need to go directly to Toker's lodging. He didn't want to embarrass the boy with his thoughts, or to kindle in Toker any notion that he was at fault for not coming up with the obvious. It gladdened him to think that the boy was not apt to be around anyhow, this hour of the day, and he could go about his look-see without a boy's interventions. In his day he'd searched this land up and down, for one thing or another, and he reckoned he knew it well as he did his own hand. He'd hunted up here, one time or another, and fished along the streams, and cleared some of it, and plowed it, and once he was in a party looking for a lost girl her parents thought must of wandered away by herself into these woods.

One of the Hodson girls, as he recollected, not any of the Hodsons strong in the forward region. Three or four years that girl had been lost, then to find she'd been sealed up in a icebox thrown out to their front porch the whole time. You couldn't fancy what a child would think to crawl into, or where parents dim as the Hodsons would not for so long think to look. But you had no morn what you come blessed with, or so some said, and maybe that was that, and you couldn't blame the Hodsons. He seemed to recall he'd gone out with a Hodson girl, way yonder him no morn a bean sprout. He wondered now if he'd had any luck with her. He hoped he had, and hoped her memory was better than hisn.

So he knew the land and knew the spots most likely the body'd be found. He hoped the sight, when he did finder, wouldn't be too frightful.

The thing that was so distracting to his mind was how come when Toker'd found one he hadn't at the same place found the othern.

Why that Truman fella hadn't hid away both baby and woman in the same bower appeared to his mind as a mystery.

But you couldn't hardly unravel a mind would do such nastiness in the first place.

From time to time over the afternoon he crossed Toker's tracks, and fresh dog tracks, and he stopped and dwelled on these, liking the notion that Toker seemed to spend a good podge of time out here in these woods. Toker's daddy hadn't. His daddy had talked woods, had talked country, but he hadn't much liked trekking about in them, or working the earth to git something good from it. He'd mostly liked putting his feet up on a table and drinking hisself under it. Thankfully the boy seemed to have been spared that calling. He was a nice boy, and a good deal more pleasant-faced since he'd found that baby. Jist proud of it as a rooster, you could see that. He hoped his and the otherns' rash talk down at the store hadn't riled the boy, though it seemed not to of had.

And that there baby was sharp as a safecracker.

On into the afternoon, Hindmarch took to scratching his head, and taking the longer pause in his deliberations. It surprised him the body hadn't long ago hove up. He wondered if that Truman fella won't a shade more practiced than he'd reckoned.

Maybe thue here.

He was a good deal winded now. He wondered if all his recent troubles with this feather-duster ticker of hisn didn't go back to that last cigarette pack he'd had when the price shot up to twenty cent. Or maybe ye stock jist run out, and there won't nothing more ye could draw from. No, it was no fun getting so old, or getting so old so fast every day was like waking to a thicket so deep and so black good sunlight could hardly reach it. He wanted to git this over with. He had his grave back there to finish. Some might find that pitiful, and some fathom it a mite eccentric, but such won't how he saw it. Another man ought not to be made to have the trouble of digging your own grave when you were yourself able. Able, and near enough to the time you'd crawl into it. When they found him, found his body on his bed in the trailer the way he hoped they'd find it—his dishes washed and the floor swept—at least they'd be able to say that when Hindmarch went he went without making nobody no trouble. He'd made it, made trouble, and plenty of it, he reckoned, in his time, but he hoped if you put the good Hindmarch up on the scales with the sorry one, the two would at least jiggle out about even. Ye helt your thumb to the one, it might. Let'um jist thow the dirt over his face. Let'um say, This here rascal come into the world a green sprig, and leaves it a dry stick. Ashes to ashes. Dust to dustmote. Let'um say that.

What worried him most was how ol' Wallace and Trout would make it up that steep climb. Yes, that worried him. It would near kill'um. They'd gripe and bellyache and call it a burden to good shoe-leather. But he reckoned they'd manage.

Itterd bin worrying his mind lately who he'd leave his good

whittling knife to. Wallace or Trout, they'd fume and fuss, whichever was the other one got it. They'd be no peace, and he'd hear no end of it.

Maybe leave it to the boy.

It was owed your race, he reckoned, that ye pass on something, however trifling the value.

You got as old and useless, as plain no-account, as he was, ittered be pure criminality to linger.

You wanted proof of how senile and useless he'd become, all you had to do was remark now on how all afternoon he'd traversed this land and hadn't once remembered that old junked car.

Thaterd be the place.

Thaterd be where that varmint had put her.

A Hudson, as he remembered.

First he saw the foot, and that stopped him, stopped him short, but when he saw movement inside the car, seeming to come from something that was a part of that foot, his heart near tilted over and for a second he went swoony of head. For a second the shock near squatted him down.

And when it spoke, whatever it was had moved in there, he felt shivers over all his flesh.

Who're you? the voice said.

For a minute, peering at the car, at the foot, and at the figure, or two figures, inside the car, his legs felt locked to the earth, just as his heart was clamped up at his throat, and he couldn't budge an inch forward. He stood blinking his eyes, wishing good sight hadn't long ago left him, the same as a good deal else had.

Ye can come on closer, ye don't mean us no harm.

A little girl's voice this was.

And yes, he could see her now, the girl in the backseat, or

what had been the backseat, her arms around a grown woman with her head slung back, slung so that her slit throat was, now he looked hard at it, all he could see.

Won't nobody hurt you, the girl said. Come on closer.

Hindmarch took a deep breath and did that.

She's cold and stiff, the girl said. I can't hardly mover. Not nothin. She's been perished a good while.

What brung you? she asked. Was it the blind man?

She's my sister, she said. I've known she was dead. I've known I would finder.

Ye can't hide, she said. Ye can't nothin hide.

But I've not seen the bad man. I've not seen hide nor hair, nor his car neither. I don't know where the bad man is. You didn't, did ye? See'm? He's the one done it.

I've seen'm, Hindmarch said. He looked away from the woman's slung head to her naked foot, and back again to the speaker-girl's scalding eyes.

She's had a baby, the girl said. But I've not seen a baby. Do you think the bad man has the baby? I don't know if I can find'm. The bad man. Somehow I'd figured I'd find both of 'um together, my sister and the bad man. I hadn't properly give my mind to considerin the baby. I hadn't seener. Not in none of my visions had I seener. Well, there was one, a man walkin a road, carryin a baby, not the bad man though, so I couldn't see how that picture was ahitch to my sister's journey. I still can't.

I bin walking the roads myself, she said. For a duration. But I ain't seen this place. It's all burnt out, or was burnt, and maybe this here place is the bad man's place. You don't think so, do ye? Do ye reckon? It was a blind man brung me up to this here lane and the blind man says his horse won't take the same road twice, 'cept it's a return journey. I ain't ast him what he meant. Do ye know the blind man?

Hindmarch stared about at the gutted car, and nodded. He looked to the space where a driver of old might have sat, and blinked his eyes to whatever departed figure or figures it was his mind hoved up.

I've heard tell of his existence, he said. Though I've not never set eyes on'm myself, to my certain knowledge.

The little girl's head bobbed up and down as he spoke. One hand grabbed at the air as if to hold it. She was half-bolted up now, poised like a jackrabbit you'd come across in stilled forest.

It was him give me this coat, she said. The blind man. He peeled it off his own backside and spread it over mine and now I done spread it over my sister. Did you ever knowed her? You'd liker, you had. But it's a heap of a surprise to my head, findin there's bin a baby. I known there'd be one, was one, I mean, in her belly, but I hadn't known itterd be born. I hadn't hardly suspected. But she's had it. You can see where she's done had it. We'd be kin to each other. I don't have no other strong kin. Now my sister Lena's gone I don't have a single kin, or none I'm crazy about. I ought not say it, because I've got folks, but they's not dear to me. The baby is. Iffin I can find it. I'd have claim on it, wouldn't I? On the baby? Mine would be the firmer claim, wouldn't it? Bettern hisn? The bad man's? You don't, do ye, know where is the baby? Where I can find it?

The girl said some of this inside the car, clinging and huddled up against the sister, and some of this outside the car clinging and huddled up against Hindmarch.

She said more, a string of words that would not stop pouring, Hindmarch answering to some, finding no answer to others—Hindmarch holding her.

To get to his place through bypass of the store road, which they both reckoned was quicker, and together on horseback, which was quicker yet, Toker and Roby had to follow the base of this mountain down from her lane, weave in and track along the basin of several others, then hike up the wing of the high Goose Neck range and come at his place from the backside gorge.

In the first basin, they had to ford a river called High Creek, where there was a plank bridge and a little car turn-around alongside a good swimming hole. What he'd done as a boy, he told Roby as they approached that spot, was to jump in the water up by High Creek, shoot the rapids, tumbling and turning and scraping rock the mile or so of snake-turns until he reached the more placid depths of Low Creek, there where the ruins of Frog Eye's Fish Camp once was, and in a manner of speaking was still. You either somehow learned to swim over that distance or you drowned or got your neck broke.

I never learnt, Roby said. I'd sometimes take the youngans down to my creek, and let them wallow, but I never could find time enough by myself.

We'll fix that, come summer, he said.

The first time he'd done it, he told her, the first time he'd jumped in . . . the first sunny day after a run of hard rain, the current had carried him tumbling and spitting along all the way from High to Low Creek, some ten miles as the raven flew, there in the Low Creek marshes finally to grab hold of an overhanging limb and drag himself up soggy and half-dead to shore. He was maybe eight years old then, and it was an old man on a mule clearing tree stumps from the lane to the Fish camp had tried to find out how come he to be in that fix, and where was home. Toker hadn't known. It was up one way or another, up one of them mountains, somewhere up there. Unhuh, the old man said. Well then, young fella, you jist hold on. He had watched the old man unhitch his stump from the mule's traces, then to go over and palaver a while with the man called Frog, who argued his road won't never going to be cleared, them stumps to petrify afore it was, and hadn't he, the old man and his mule, give fair handshake to git the job done? Ain't we had us a contract? Or is a handshake goin the way my kidney is gone?

Yip, the old man said to Frog, the both spitting tobacco juice and eyeing the stumps. And though them stumps has my blessin and my word is my contract and a contract is my law, they's a boy over there in distress, and it comes a time a person has to forsake one duty to take up the other. Now wouldn't ye say that was so?

Frog said he would, though he clearly didn't like it. It's always the contract a man has with me, Frog said, is the first one to find wings.

So the old man had come back with his mule to where Toker was waiting, and had said to him, Now, boy, I got no elevator so you jist sling yourself on.

He dropped down a hand and hooked his fingers around Toker's wrist, and in a flash Toker was slung up onto the mule, him draping the mule's neck and clinging frantically to the mule's ears so as to hold on. Like that the old man had walked him a goodly distance back, not talking overmuch, only pointing out the random dwelling of this and that forest creature or some unnatural manifestation in the terrain, at last to sling him down, saying, Now young fella you jist follow the riverbank uphill a mite and after a day or two you'll wind up naturally where you started from and have your bearins then to find your way to nestin-home. Won't ye?

Yessir.

And young fella?

Yessir?

You git lost agin, ye do it on somebody else's time. Do I have your man's word on that?

Yessir.

That was the last time Toker'd jumped into the river after hard rains, that river or any other, and some time later it was before he'd try rapids-shooting at all; but by the time he'd screwed up his courage enough to go at it again, he found he could swim.

Over the years, Toker told Roby, he'd often thought of that old man and his mule, and how it was a stranger with a loose arm around his waist, and tobacky juice droolin down his chin, had directed him home. Afterwards, and thue many teenhood years, he'd wished morn once that old man had been his daddy.

Hindmarch was as much mine as anyone was, Roby confessed. After Daddy shot hisself. It was him got our crop in that year. He'd buy us treats down at Cal's store and leave them by the front door. He'd bring us vegetables from this patch he had, and if anything needed fixin he'd send up lumber by mule and wagon and on his weekends git it done.

The horse hooves reverberated on the planking on the High Creek bridge, and here they dismounted to let the horse drink.

Oh I'm feelin good, he told her and the baby. As though the sky has opened, has split wide open, and sung me a song, revealin to me my life's full spectaculars.

What kind of song? she asked.

A Roby song, he said, and they held each other and watched the horse drink.

What will you name that baby? she asked, the three of them going on again.

I don't know, he said. Is it mine to name?

Well, I believe so, she said, since you've taken ownership of it since practically her first breath.

I could caller Robyette, he said, in case she's got your taste for gowns.

They rode on, thinking about it, and before long she said, I'd liker to be named Josephine. I've always thought that a good strong name.

Toker stopped the horse and squirmed about in the saddle to look at Roby.

What's your name? he asked. I've never even knowed it.

She glanced away, shyly.

Josie, she said. That's short for—

I *know* what it's short for, Toker said. You mean you intend us to have two Josephines in the same family?

Roby didn't answer to that.

It was getting on toward dark. Neither of them able to figure how the day had careened by so fast.

This here tyke takes to horseflesh, Toker said. Looky here how she's holdin the reins.

I can tolerate the baby, Roby said. It's what's ahead of us—
what's out there—*him,* that slinkhog—that gives me goose-
flesh.

They went on then, the both of them silent with their
thoughts, the baby bright-eyed in Toker's arm.

Near sunset. The way alien. The air misty.

It won't becoming to a priest or father-figure of his scope to be limping slung-footed and stoop-shouldered through the cold nethers of forest. But something had busted in his leg when he rolled from Satan's weapon, the automobile, and he couldn't help that. So here he was, his tail dragging. A man had no dignity on foot anyhow, and he hated that. On foot, a man was akin to muskrat and hedgehog, to glairy beast in sorry quagmire. But he couldn't help that. He couldn't help his face either, the one side skinned and charred by highway, the other side still carrying, as though with a mission, the proof of his toothly condition. His good knee, if you could call it that, was ripe and sorely swollen. He carried his left arm up tight to his chest, it wanting a sling. But of sling he had not. One shoulder rode high and he dared not in any way rehinge it or malign the general disorder. He was broke or chawed and fried all over. His very innards were scoured. His head pounded. His trap, spliced by two hooks to his belt loops, jounced habitual impertinence against his leg, the chain muttering as though at a demons' conference.

Yes, it would take some getting used to, this return to raw
nature. He hadn't mapped his road to have it strewn with this
misfortune. But could a man mount a just grievance? Who to?
Who'd listen? You cursed your luck, poured rebuke on the
world, and it was only your own voice come rumbling back.
To harry you with the disruption or harpoon you with its vengeance. To spear you where you stood. Where you hobbled
with your baggage of rancor. The heavens were hung jury,
mute witness to a man's dishevelment, no less than these
mountains. Soon the sky'd be hoary with blackness, and
awink with derisive glitter. Jist hog-swill, all in all. He'd wondered in the beginning what malevolent configuration he'd
find up here, his tarry proved sufficiently lengthy. Now he
knowed: You shed one burden, you only picked up another
one greater—that's what he'd found.

My starch, he thought, done quit my sails.

But I ain't finished.

I still got me my healthy outlook on life's knotty intangi-
bles.

But it won't all bad, being ruint citizen: folks took heed
of a cripple's needs so long as the needs won't askew of
their own.

Up there, they'd said. And they'd lifted they's arms and
pointed.

Why, sure. Up thataways. Ain't them consarn Tokers always lived up there?

A shovel? Nawsir, we can't give you no shovel, much as
we'd like to. Nawsir, nor money, sure as it would be to our
blessin.

But up there you'll find'm, sure as daylight has matches.
Thatern with the baby.

So trudge on. Git there. He had claim to the baby; she was
hisn.

He'd gitter.

He dragged his leg along, communing with its ache and diverse other essences that flagged their damaged rhythm. His flesh was under infidel attack now. Mere fang-ache of old seemed now to of been a tender mercy.

He'd trudged a good many miles these last hours, over and around mountains, and he won't used to it. It had been a steady climb, and he won't accustomed to the footwork. He felt bedraggled and weary. Bereft to his very shoe-leather.

But soon night would fall and night was his natural element. Daytime was alien, the month was, no argument there. But night would revive him. Him and night got along with each other, like tick inside a dog's ear. He'd manage. Could a man forsake his flock? Could he surrender his sworn objectives or alter by a decibel his avowed intentions?

He felt stronger, now he knew God hadn't had nothing to do with *his* making.

Was he not the caretaker?

He came to a glade violaceous of hue and in it were wheeled stones harnessing what remained of fires of old. A buttress of high, naked rock on the one side leered out at him its funereal impeachments and the very air bespoke tidings as though in the reign of a perverse and malign antiquity. Here troglodyte and bewinged serpent might dwell, though he saw none. At his approach a low creature motley of fur sniggered its teeth at him, then swirled away with glaring eyes into the encroaching wilderness.

Here was a vicinal trail of sorts, and a cliff, and tire and wagon tracks up to that cliff. Over the cliff, under misty divinings, was a darkened valley festooned with humanity's garbage, and more glaring eyes apace within it.

He studied this space for a moment, then scrabbled on.

He could hear gurgling river.

It came to him a picture he'd carried of old, of a woman seated on a front-porch chair, her legs flung wide, holy bejesus Bible flapped open on her lap. She was eating saltine crackers from a red box. Stuffing these in, finger to fist. With each chomp, cracker dust burst from her mouth and floated before her face like a cloud of churning gnats.

His uncle's old woman, he reckoned, with her claw-track skin and a hickory stick beside her to slash him the minute he pondered up on the step to ast could he have one. Jist one nibble?

I'se hungry, Elder.

Scat! It churns my insides jist to look at rubbish of your disposition.

But he won't going to lacerate his brow repoking the embers of that hellhole.

Them two had set hunched over the kitchen table and now and again his old uncle would throw a scrap out into the backyard at him. They'd had attic room he could of bedded in. But no, it was off to stable pallet for the orphan-likes of him.

He reached the river on toward twilight. It was roiling, foamy against the swollen banks. A mist steamed up above the rapids and he stood a minute in abject scrutiny of the gargoyle shapes.

He rounded up twigs and dead sticks and got a blaze going.

He won't far from his destination now. He'd gitter. He'd scootfoot in.

A knot in his temple pulsed its brew of intermittent colors. He felt swoony, but gritted his teeth and hardened his brow and drove the swoon back.

He warmed up to the crackling fire, only then aware of the deep shivers that had been his company the past hours.

He leaned to the fire and put his hands palm-face to the licking flames. He could see bone on the backside of the one hand, and strands of loose flesh heaped with grit, and he wondered this aberration didn't pain him more.

He'd warm a while his flesh, and forage among his vicissitudes, and nurse hisself a while in the arms of his affliction; then he'd go and gitter.

He steered both hands between his legs and rocked, again come over with dizziness for the minute. It hove up from nowhere, and spun his eyes as vomity fluids pumped at his throat, and he let out a meek cry of rage and burrowed his head.

A man on a wagon earlier that day had dug under hay bales and handed down a near-full pint mason jar. The man hadn't offered no ride, going as he was the wrong way, but he'd done that much.

So he had his nurse with'm.

Here's lookin at ye, Truman said.

He pitched his head back and wet the liquor to his tongue, swished liquor about in his mouth, and guzzled it down.

They's a good fella, he said.

Oh yes, folks were kind and upright to a fault, they passed on the road a battered cripple orderly in his needs. They could nod fairly to ruination, it stayed arm's-length away from their own doorstep.

He unhitched his trap and clamped the trap between his knees, and by degrees got the jaws open and the trigger set. The exertion left him panting for breath, but all required now was bait, and he wished to goodness he had bait. He'd neglected to inquire of anyone whether mink resided in these parts. But here was a good mountain river, engorged with feast aplenty, and he'd be surprised mink didn't know it.

He studied again the shredded rags of flesh on his hand. He flapped aside his rent trousers and investigated the miserable condition of his legs.

Yes'm, he was charred and fried all over, and here was mink bait aplenty, he had the nerve.

He looked for his knife, turning his pockets, but knife seemed to of had found wings.

He gnawed flesh loose from his hand.

He bit flapping hide away from his knee.

Whammyjig surgeon, he thought, couldn't of done it better.

He speared the flesh up about the bait spike and took up his set trap and hobbled with it to the riverbank. He dropped to his knees and dipped in his arm, probing for the bottom. Water slooshed up over his shoulder and purled over his ear. He settled the trap down.

There, he told the trap. Git that sucker. You got ten minutes.

He was wheeling about to return to his fire when he felt a chill sweep along his backside and crouch down behind the hairs of his neck. He won't alone. That was the feeling come to him.

He scrunched down into the wild, and scouted his eyes along the mist-swimming river and up and down the far shore.

In a minute he descried through the rising vapor a man on horseback halted on the shore directly opposite him. The man was looking his way.

A haint, Truman's first thought was.

Then he saw the man dismount, and a beast smaller than the horse drifted up, and he saw the man sling his arm up over the beast's head, maybe to tether it there. A common mule, it looked like.

The smoky mist, in and out this while, thickened now, hiding this sight away.

Truman glued his eyes upon the spot. Now why would a man want to tether a mule at such a fool place? He waited, and when the space thinned once more there won't nothing there.

He clambered back to his fire, shaky of limb, and killed the last of his drink.

Then he sat down again to his fire, his back to whatever it was he'd seen or not seen.

You come far as I have, he thought, stirring the flames, there ain't no allowin for what might hove up.

The day was sinking. Darkness getting on toward the steep side now.

Soon now he'd git what was hisn, and flit on out of here.

He'd give that mink a minute or two more to fathom its bait.

His head was tumbly, the thoughts floaty. Now and then he felt himself nodding off, and snatched his head alert.

He wondered he couldn't hardly keep hisself awake.

He wondered that little girl hadn't let him skip.

He wondered him to moon over such a sorry piece, near the whole of his life.

A bat swooped low over his cranium and lodged enviable claw into the bark of an adjacent tree.

A dog whimpered up out of the woods, lame in the leg, and halted a fit distance off, beseeching him with sorrowful eyes. He thought it a dog. But he stared a while at where it stood, and decided he won't sure.

He pitched flaming stick where the thing lingered, and shouted onwards whatever thing it was.

He won't the merry kind to up and leave a youngan orphan in this world, was what it come down to.

He'd do better than his own musty-mole folks had done him.

He'd gitter.

He was the last solitary caretaker on this planet, he reckoned, and he'd raiser.

God could go on curling up to whatever freehold monstrosity his mind hatched up, but he'd have his newborn to stand always as his noble companion. It was fitting that infant child should be his one worthy confederate.

God could say to his face, I didn't seed thee, but he hisself won't that depraved.

He'd do the rightful thing.

He dozed.

A rodent with glinting eyes consumed the encysted corpse it had been devouring nearby, then to rasp and egest the summary, and gnaw its minute foot-tracks along Truman's napping body.

In his doze Truman moaned. Once in a while his sound arm lashed up, and he flung it helplessly about, as though he wished to discard it, or as a signal, or verdict, or appeal ever-elementally rooted to a darker mystery.

Roby and Toker and the baby came out about a half-mile below the old Dealer place and from there they began their descent, traversing the banks of the river for a brief spell. Timber and deadfall and the odd uprooted tree were awash in the current, islands of foam swirling by like small refugee boats in migration from another world. The roar was mighty and they had to bend mouth to ear to hear each other above the din.

River's high, Toker said. It's swift. They's bin a pot of rain somewhere today. Used to be there was a swingin bridge up here. Stretchin from gorge to gorge. I don't know who it was built it, or why.

It's all new to me, Roby said. Us girls were made to stick close to home, and after our trouble my choices were no morn thimble size. I don't reckon I ever will forgit that day, or have a day goes by the memory won't once or twice flit thue.

No, Toker said. All a body can do is hope to pile better stuff on.

She smiled, the thought a comfort to both of them.

The horse was surefooted and no risktaker. It seemed to know it carried a baby.

Toker was of a mind to slow its gait. To slow it to a standstill. He hated to imagine what Roby would think of him once she caught sight of how he'd been living these past months.

She was craning her neck, already looking for his place.

I think it's best we bury the woman, Roby said out of the blue. The law is called in, there's no tellin what might happen.

That fella might git caught. That's one thing that might transpire.

Unhuh. And if they can't, and lay it all at your doorstep, then what?

Toker didn't reply to that. But he smiled somber appreciation, warmed by the notion that Roby had concern for his welfare.

On a lofty knoll near his abode he reined up the horse and they got off a minute to admire the snake-turns of river, the enfolded roads, the graceful, undulating mountains in variety of silhouette one against the other, their slopes now steeped in mist of a darkening shade. On a clear day, you had a vista, looking the one way, of maybe thirty miles. And if you found that saddle-gap in the range behind Cal's Place, which you could in hard winter, the view went on for thirty more.

Your place is some bit higher than mine, Roby said. I do like these mountains. That's likely the foremost reason I come back.

He squeezed her hand.

They looked for her house among the folds, but couldn't find it, it hidden by the upper hump of Hindmarch's ridge, which was itself cloaked in mist, but her place there in such a way, both reasoned, that one could measure the strides that would deliver one back and forth.

Daylight was all but played out anyhow.

He wondered aloud you couldn't build a house up here in these clouds, with roof windows that opened to the heavens, and windows that looked out at everything else.

Maybe, Roby said. It's a smart site, this knoll. I doubt I've ever seen smarter.

She twisted about, and studied his face. Who is it you're thinking would live here in your fancy house?

The damp air seemed to reach them with a fragrance.

Well, Toker said. This here baby, for one. And me, for another. I could tack on a back room a third might could hole up in, come a blue moon, and she brought blue cheese.

Roby laughed.

They remounted and he clucked to the horse and they cut back to the lane and rode on the final short stretch through weeds brushing their knees.

But when Toker reached the turn-in to his hovel he touched his heels to the horse's flanks and encouraged her on past. I'm nervous about that dead woman, he said. Ye best brace yourself.

They were under apprehensive mood, now, riding through a falling darkness, the horse hooves making light impact against the grassy earth while otherwise all about them seemed to endure in a stricken hush.

The woman's body was not in the car. They were studying the space, in a haze of tremulous speculation, when they heard footsteps in the darkness away from them, and a minute later beheld the old man Hindmarch materializing out of the growth. He carried a shovel slung up over his shoulder.

Behind him, approaching with caution, came a stick-limbed, ragged girl with swollen eyes.

She stopped where Hindmarch had and the two fitted their arms around each other's waists.

For a moment all appraised each other in silence.

Then Hindmarch spoke.

We bin busy, he said. I reckon you have as well.

He grimaced, and huffed in a deep breath, then turned and headed back the way he'd come.

The little girl inched her way up. She looked from one to the other of them, and did not disown the horse, though mostly she kept her sight riveted on the baby.

She held out her arms.

I'd like to holder, she said.

Roby looked at Toker, who was standing with his head down.

Even in the fallen light they could see the strong likeness.

I know it's a good baby, the girl said. Her voice was low, her eyes misty.

The baby wriggled about in Toker's arms, as if searching the night for all friendly or familiar faces.

No, said Toker. No, you can't holder.

He looked at the girl with suspect and hooded eyes, and continued to even as Roby cursed and gave him a shove toward her.

All right then, he said. But only for a minute.

They all three joined in tight formation around the baby.

She is, ain't she? the girl said. A good baby?

Toker was displeased and out of sorts, and in full disagreement with the others. Roby was for it, and Hindmarch argued
they had no choice, and the little sister said she wanted Lena
buried here. She wanted Lena given to earth here where she'd
had her baby and where she'd gone to such ends to see the
baby was in good hands, and she liked it her sister was now
bein laid to rest by people who would of liked her, they had
knowner.

She told them it was what the blind man expected, Lena to
be buried here, elsewise he would of said something. Elsewise, he'd be here now, this minute, to take her, and Lena's
body, on to another place. He'd already bin here, she said, up
this lane with his mule, and that was why he had that mule: to
carry away on the mule's back, to wherever it was the mule
ordinarily carried them, her sister's spirit. The blind man's
horse and mule didn't make the same trip twice, she said,
lessern it was the hind part of a journey. But he'd already
made that journey, and wouldn't like it he was told he'd done
it wrong and was ought to return now and do the job better. So
it was right Lena would be dropped to earth here, here among
her friends, among them who were her friends even if they'd
never knowner.

She talked on and on about the blind man, the little girl
did, and only Hindmarch seemed to know who the blind man
was or what a blind man had to do with any of these transac-
tions.

Hindmarch was down in the hole, throwing up spadefuls of
dirt, and would hardly let Toker relieve him. He was displeased himself with Toker's attitude and said now was no
time for the boy to go hardheaded and sorry of jaw and act the
damn fool. He knew about gravedigging, he said, and gravedigging was the thing called for. Handling a shovel took the

itch from between his shoulders and made his poor ticker take notice he won't yit done with it. He was more spiry than he looked, he said, and he said furthermore he resented Toker's suggesting that shouldering a shovel was something beyond his capacity. It's the right and decent thing to do, Hindmarch said. To bury her. She's become family, more or less, this luckless woman has, so you can quit arguin.

But Toker did argue, and continued to, even as he grappled the shovel from the old man's hands and flung up dirt himself.

They buried her, he said, Toker said, it was the same as letting that scoundrel killer go scot-free. It was the same as telling him, by not calling in the law, that he could skedaddle on to another county and any time he took a notion to he could up and kill some other woman. It's wrong, he said. Now my head is clear and I can see what I ought to of done in the first place. Dammit, it's my hide I'd be riskin by callin in the law, but I'd choose to risk it rathern take the chance on havin that bounder go scot-free.

The little girl told him she liked him, and liked he liked the baby, but that he ought to git on with it now, and be quiet about it out of respect for her sister.

Roby told him to hush-up. Jist to hush his mouth, and keep digging, and to quit arguing with everything anyone said, because it was already decided, and she'd seen noose around one innocent neck, and one, thank you, was sufficient for her lifetime.

They were out on a clear rise under the dark moon, with no end to these discussions, and Toker getting more peeved by the second, when a figure crotched up out of the tall scrap bushes nearby, they heard the clank of a chain, and the man's shallow curse, and his shadow the next minute was looming up over them.

Say. Ye don't none of ye have no cigarette, do ye?

It was that voice, whipping out of black night, that stilled them, turning their skins clammy cold.

Say. That there you're buryin, ye know, is my lawful-wedded wife.

Yessir, she's done had a spot of sour luck, thatern there has. But it's the doggonest thing. I done run myself ragged, seekin shovel, but come now to find ye had one the whole time. Now ain't that the doggonest thing?

He could have said a good deal more, they were that long recovering from his abrupt appearance. But he fell silent then, holding himself in unlikely repose against the night that had exhumed him, his figure tortile and bedraggled, bedaubed with injury, but his head brazenly cocked, as if in surmise of what might be their civil response to one who had presented himself so attractively, or as one who had arrived late to a meeting they ought not to have convened without his authority was given, or called to its deliberations before he himself was present.

A swampy blackness. Water won't there and then was. A brigade of infidel shriekers panting at his heels. And then he was in water. He was in up to his knees and still running, before water slowed him and he knew water was what it was. Oh there was a yowling bedlam full tilt around him and he didn't know what deranged urgency spurred them or why this horde of young and old should elect themselves his tormentors. It defied any explanation. He couldn't see how come them to not hearken to a man's pledge of innocence. But itterd always bin this way. He ought to of expected it.

He scrabbled to his knees and flayed the water, and skimmed it from his eyes, still running. His feet in the gummy mud bottom slid from beneath him, his trap looped the air, the water scooped him up and toppled him along on his rear end into faster current, whanging his flesh against floor-strewn, unseen rock, as he muttered and flung back at them and the corrupt world his stoup of curses. *Would ye not mind your caretaker? Would ye risk your caretaker his vengeance? Or will ye be as dappled mink shit in my Armageddon's water?*

He could see someone's floundering shape in splash behind

him, calling out his own threats and rank admonitions, and
behind him two others in steady, vile charge, long-haired grislyhags heaving up raucous defamation. The very mutterings
of these river rapids, the swirling foam, the black hang of
trees hugging the banks, were alive as like a spangle of midnight hooters. He could see the old man ashore running the
bank, the baby jouncy in his arms and wafting into the night
what his ears took to be a mewling cry.

He squawked out his fury, tumbling along, grabbing at
overhung branch or grappling at boulder, slapping at debris
whichever seemed to find and cling to him, in exasperated
ache now to upright himself and drive his caretaker's sword
into this relentless posse. Into these night-hipped, waterborne
tormentors. *Step aside now. Step aside. I done saved you on the
road, though I resent now my gamble. Git ye down now to my
fiery furnace. Git ye. Shrivel ye there, like pork rind in the pork
barrel.*

He hit shallowness, a sandy undertow aswirl at his ankles,
and scrabbled afoot.

The man behind him lunged, and struck, and rode astride
his back for prolonged minute, before the next two screamers
wrapped and wallowed clapperclaw one end to the other of his
face and body, him rising up to his full-size caretaker's heft
out of the water, in the chewing sand, to haul aloft these trinal
flesh-eaters. Meaning to sling away first woman and girl, these
soft-fleshed necromancers, and bring end to their odious jo-
bation. But he was one-armed, and bone-broke, weary of
breath, and now he snickered, he laughed—oh yes, he could
feel now the pleasure—as the grislyhag limbs coiled and
tightened about his neck, their legs intertwined with his, and
their wet cheeks for an instant smeared slick against his own,
much, he thought, as though coupling was now their calumi-
nious, womanly intention. He laughed a hoarse laugh, cough-

ing up water the while, and let them wiggle and pitch, oblivious to their mosquito swats, their slavernous cries, his sound arm circling the grislyhag waists to adhere their flesh to his own flesh, as he jiggered about to keep his footing in the swirling sand. One of them a little girl, alike as like a twin to that ancient jumpy-rope one, and where was her play pocket-book, why was nice bow not in her hair? Oh, pity no improvement in a little girl's outlook after lo these years. He raked his arm up this impostor's backside and pressed her face into his neck. Jumpy-rope, jumpy-rope high, let's all jumpy-rope into the sky. He sang this out, to their clamorous wailing, and pressed harder, heedless of their hell-sent claws, of their hair-yanks and fingers agouge at his eyes. Jumpy-rope, jumpy-rope, jumpy-rope high, hobble out from your hellhole and give it a try. They were screaming blue murder, ferocious intent to sear hair from his head, the skin from his bones, and won't he the innocent party? It won't fair, and never it had bin, but won't such sedition ever his portion? Never they'd play fair and he ought to of expected it.

The man's hands found hold upon his throat, and he felt the fingers tighten their squeeze—*Do ye give up?* they shouted. *Do ye give up now?*—and he laughed anew at this outrage. Would a caretaker give up? Would a caretaker abdicate his title, surrender his duty? Did they want utter calamity swamping the world? Down to fly baby, cradle and all? Oh, alien the month, alien the breath. Alien this gimpy-rat year.

The weight of the three catapulted him facewards over water, and he hung airborne, with fragile squawk, in that second before they all four plunged away from sandbar into deep, rocketing river.

Through to the bottom where his trap thumped and plowed and where for a time they trolled in combat among eel grass, churning the mud into thick pudding, him grubbing shrimp-

eyed in the muck for loose rock that he might lay it against his
assailant's head. The females slipped away from him in a
swoosh, but still the man's hand clamped and squoze at his
gizzard. He slammed his trap against this tormentor's arms
time and again, and ripped at the iron twist of fingers, as water
ziggered up his nose and shut off his breath and his head
swole up to bursting-size, the grainy muck lancing his eyeballs. He gobbled up water and tried to spew it back, and
more flowed in to harpoon his chest. Then the grislyhags were
back, aswim and aflutter in a tangle of legs, and he wished he
could uncork his chicken-wing arm so as to steer good damage
their way. He wished the man for one gibbet would let go of
his neck. He wished he could gulp deep air. He could feel the
one female wrenching at his shirt collar and the other in tug
of his belt. The grislyhags wanted him naked, then. They
were God's scurrilous instruments, wanting only his commin-
gling down here. He ought of had known. It was what he ought
to of expected. O brothers and sisters, is this not an alien
time? Alien hour in an alien month in a grislyhag year? They
was all every one God's pawns, his indentured hepmates. O
ye sons and daughters of the night, let's invent itch kelp of the
deep and give it frog eyes. Let's incubate split-hoof toads can
flit about in mud. Let's give birth to misshapen henchrat and
flyhead and scaly moxdyke here within the eel grass sludge of
a darkling world.

He flapped his sound arm and found what he fancied were
the skinny grislyhag legs of the girl, and shot his arm up to
her crotch. She had grainy buttocks would mold to the palm
of his hand, though it won't buttocks he felt for. He'd wed her,
and spread her, and let God take the rap for whatever eyesore
her loins hatched up. *I do*, he tried to say. *I do, and will, and
have.*

But the flesh he held floated free. His arm went slack, he

undulated with the river's flow along the bottom. Limp now from head to toe. Drinking in the mud water. Bone snapped in his throat, the pain striking him as though from afar, zigzag finger of pain fomenting no more wrath in him than would a twig snap in distant, sepulchral forest. The man still held him; he knew that much.

After a time he and his rider both were at float on the roof of the coursing water, his tormentor asprawl of his back, with limitless patience and no recognizable divestment of or alteration in his handhold.

He heard voices, shouting. A high, hollering voice, although it reached him soft, a faint whir down in his ear: *The sonofabitch won't quit! Ye can't kill the sonofabitch! I can't hold the bastard!* And with that the chokehold loosened. The hands slid from his throat and his tormentor withdrew.

Here was epitaph of some merit. It was bettern he'd ever hoped for.

But won't it right? Won't it fair? Without they had their caretaker, where'd they be?

He felt himself afloat high on the rapids, and did not think to lift his head or roll about in sniff of the air, or in disgorgement of all he'd consumed, for that seemed an indignity not worth his pursuance. It didn't seem a worthwhile task. He had his mink trap and he held on weakly to that. He wished he'd ever knowed what constituted proper mink bait and how he might better advance such a victory, now that his own flesh had proved to be bait that was unworkable. You'd think a man's own flesh would serve the purpose, though it seemed not to be so. It seemed not to be intended. That was spit in his face, mink spit, but he'd turned other cheek to man and beast's contempt before. Such contempt was a trifling thing, and would not stand in firm mark of his passage.

All he'd ever wanted was the certain, firsthand knowledge.

All needed in the world was something you could count on. Something reliable. Not God the mud-dauber. Not God the mollusk-cradler. Best he'd bin content to be a slow worker of fields, and gone out and got hisself a good bird dog. Stayed away from automobiles. From jump-rope and cracker dust and foxy mink. Bed hisself down, as would sunny-faced doctor. Ye have pebble in your shoe, then take that as your destined course.

Scaredy-cat, scaredy-cat, have ye no home? The bough has broke and you're falling alone.

He'd of done as well in life, he thought, had he walked right in and had sup with the lepers.

But he won't not a widget-bit sorry he'd done as he had. He'd jumped in with both feet and altered by his every breath that way they'd set down and said was hisn.

A good caretaker, he thought, wouldn't settle for less.

You couldn't do with ye life no better.

My baby, he thought, as on his backside he shot the rapids, will carry and heften my staunch name.

He hadn't never helt the baby. That did worry him. He liked babies.

A NOTE ABOUT THE AUTHOR

Leon Rooke is the author of many books but is best known for his
novels *Fat Woman* and *Shakespeare's Dog*, for which latter work he was
awarded Canada's coveted Governor-General's Fiction Award. He is a
native of North Carolina, and now lives in Eden Mills, Ontario.

A NOTE ON THE TYPE

This book was set in Bodoni Book, a type face named after Giambattista Bodoni (1740–1813), a celebrated printer and type designer of Rome and Parma. Bodoni Book as produced by the Linotype Company is not a copy of any one of Bodoni's fonts, but a composite, modern version of the Bodoni manner. Bodoni's innovations in type style included a greater degree of contrast in the thick and thin elements of the letters and a sharper and more angular finish of details.

Composed by Graphic Composition, Inc., Athens, Georgia

Printed and bound by The Haddon Craftsmen, Scranton, Pennsylvania

Illustrations by Miriam Schaer

Designed by Valarie J. Astor